Falling Stars
and
Trains at Night

Written by Carly Linn

Illustrated by Amanda Morris

DEDICATION

For Sue because she said I should.
For Christi and Amanda because they said I could.
For Ryan because he said I wouldn't
(while really knowing that I would.)
C.L.

For Carly, who invited and inspired
For Kathleen and Sandy, who encouraged
For Mom and Jessica, who understood
A.M.

Somewhere out in the world that we've all left behind is a tree. There's nothing spectacular about this tree, but it holds something special for us.

Our soles.

Hanging from this tree, we all left our shoes, tied together at the laces and dangling from various branches in the summer sun.

"Just leave them," Iphy said. "We'll come back for them."

We never did.

AUTUMN

This is a true story. The names have been changed, but not to protect the innocent. I don't think there are such things as innocents in this story. The names were changed because I still have nightmares about this and I thought it would be easier if I pretended that it happened to someone else. Calm asked me to write it all down; she says I have a way with words. I think it's more likely that she doesn't like thinking about that summer, either.

I remember that year so clearly; it was a year of magic, when ghosts haunted the blackened woods beyond our homes, darkness lurked in the shadows out of sight, waiting to creep into our eyes, and shining gods walked among mortal children. It was the year that we all grew up. How clichéd, huh? But it's true; thinking back, it was also the year that everything went to pieces. And I mean everything. Us, our families, even our country. We were at war both on a national scale and a personal one as well. But I won't tell you which war. Because then you could tell what year it was, and this story isn't something confined by time: it's not something that can be labeled by a year, by a blip in our nation's history. It could have happened a year ago, or ten, or fifty. It doesn't matter—we weren't concerned with time back then, not like we are now, and it isn't relevant to what happened.

There were six of us, almost enough to make a gang. A 'hang-out' gang, seeing as that's all we ever did. We hung out, trekked through the woods and explored every nook and cranny of our town eager to learn, to see, and to follow. Our view of what mattered was so narrow: it consisted of us, our parents, the few kids we knew from the neighborhood, and the town. That town and the woods surrounding it were our whole world. I won't say what town it was, or even what state it's in. If I do, you'll dismiss this story as something that happened *there* and it won't mean anything. This way, it could have happened *anywhere*; California, or New York, and this way, the town won't be defined by a single action—an event that took place on its soil. Because that's what happens. Laramie. Columbine. Places defined by actions and events that took place there. Our town—that place where we grew up—it's much more than just what happened there that year, and that wonderful, horrible summer. Our town was our first experience of the world outside of our houses; it's a huge chunk of who we are, just like that year was. But enough about our town for now. Iphy always told us that there was more in the world.

Iphy was the oldest, and as such he was the leader of our gang. He was thirteen, tall, but not overly so, trim and fit and extremely self-assured. He was the light in our lives that year; he was our leader and our savior. He thought he knew everything about the world because he was homeless. He'd run away from his own town several states away and had taken up residence in the woods behind my house. He liked to claim that Child Services never found him because his parents didn't care enough to report him missing. After having met them, I believe it.

All of this started with Iphy; if I hadn't seen him sneaking into our hen house that night, none of this would have happened. Sometimes I wonder if it would have been better that way, but if there's one thing I learned that year it's that you can't change what happens, no matter how much you plead with gods and stars. Iphy, Korvid, Eddie, Calm and even Jax. We all needed each other that summer; we wouldn't have made it otherwise. And Iphy started it all.

I remember it was hot out, which was surprising for October. Normally, this close to Halloween, it was colder and the wind was whipping. Not that night, though: it was hot and muggy and I had both of my windows open, but there was no breeze in the dead air. I was doing a report on the Moon for class, borrowing Calm's telescope to look up at the glowing orb. It wasn't a very good telescope; it was made more for looking across the street than at the heavens. I was leaning forward after having dropped my pencil, my eye still looking through the eyepiece as my free hand groped blindly at my feet. As I leaned one way, my shoulder pushed the end of the telescope up, which brought the front end down. It was then that I saw a blurry shadow cross our yard.

Startled, I shoved the telescope to one side and leaned out of my window, my eyes trained on our hen house where the shadow had gone. Sure enough, a few minutes later, the shadow re-emerged and darted back to the darkness of the woods.

I stayed up late—later than I should have—watching the spot where the shadow had disappeared, as if hoping that it would return under my watchful gaze. Sometime in the night, I thought I heard a faint, far-off whistle, but I couldn't be sure. I fell asleep at the window, waiting on a shadow that didn't return. My mother found me in the morning; boy, was she mad. I told her that I had fallen asleep while working on my report, but she didn't believe me. She never did. She sent me off to school without any breakfast. I didn't complain, though; her eyes were red and puffy and I had heard her crying that night, like she did every night back then.

I walked to school, like every kid in our town did. It was the general consensus of all the adults in our town that we children had been born with legs, and there was no godly reason that we shouldn't use them. Our school didn't even have a bus route. As such, I walked a mile and a half to school every morning, and walked that same mile and a half in reverse in the afternoons. To pass the time, I walked with my best friend, Calm, who lived two houses down from mine.

Calm was eleven, a year younger than me, but she had skipped a grade a few years earlier and now had most of the same classes that I did. She was almost a full head shorter than me, with large hazel eyes that always made her appear frightened. She was tiny, even frail, with a fawn-like innocence that was only further perpetuated by her meek manner and silent grace. She was the kind of girl that liked to watch ballet when her parents weren't home and practice the steps in the safety of the empty living room, but would never think herself strong enough to dance in front of her friends. That morning she shuffled over to me, her impossibly dark blue black hair hanging over her eyes as she stared down at the ground, watching where she put her feet, her small shoes hardly making a sound as they passed over pavement and asphalt.

I always liked her shoes. Her shoes were small and black, shined to an almost reflective surface. Even her laces were black. She told me once that she had picked her shoes because they were just normal and ordinary, but I thought they were wonderful—even if they did have laces. Calm often said that she hated her hair color (and, consequently, her shoe's color) because black was like Nothing—the absence of Anything. But I'd learned long ago, when messing around with finger paints and trying to paint a bad luck cat, that black could also be something else, something that reminded me much more of my best friend. Black could be the presence of Everything.

I was waiting on top of a manhole cover in the middle of the street, where I always waited in the mornings; she barely looked up at me as we started walking.

"You didn't sleep well did you?" she asked, her voice quiet, almost a whisper.

"How'd you guess?"

"You look like you got out of bed thirty seconds ago. What happened?"

"I fell asleep at my window, waiting for a shadow to come out of the woods."

"I think shadows like to stay in the woods," she said, still watching her feet. "I think they feel safe there."

"Yeah, but this wasn't a real shadow." My voice dropped to her level. I found that when anyone talked to Calm for any length of time, they mostly whispered, because she herself talked so softly. "It was this thing that went into our hen house. I think it's been stealing the eggs."

Calm nodded. "Then that's why it went into the woods: it didn't want to be found. Thieves are frowned upon in this day and age."

I shook my head, but these were the kind of things my friend said. She was what the adults called an 'old soul.'

"How are your parents?" I tentatively questioned.

"They're okay, so long as they don't talk. If they start talking, they can't stop until they yell."

By this time we had reached Main Street, where all the best shops in town where. There was the bicycle store with its jaw-dropping window displays of blazing red bikes with black leather seats and dazzling green bikes adorned with white seats, rotating under a bright light. This drew children like moths to a flame, and usually we were no exception. The dry cleaners, where older people with nice suits went to get them cleaned, and you could see their suits hanging next to evening gowns and fancy dresses by the hundreds if you peeked through the open door on your way by. And of course there was Smithy's Bakery, where Jax would sit on the curb every morning, waiting for Mr. Smithy to bring him some of the day olds that hadn't sold. We walked through the town, ignoring the details that never changed, knowing already what we would see with each step we took. We knew it so well, like a sibling that we had grown up with, still loved, but sometimes couldn't stand.

From the journal of Calm Sheldon

I told Eraliss to write about our Hang-out Gang and the year we spent together. She wanted me to add something to her scattered pages, but I don't know what more I can say about our town that she hasn't already said. She has a way with words; she can make them come alive, crawl inside the space behind your eyes and paint pictures.

Eraliss was everything in childhood that I wasn't. Where I was short, she was tall — one of the taller girls in our class, and still taller than quite a few of the boys. I was meek, but she was strong and hardy; she could run faster than the boys in our class, and she was always one of the first picked for kickball. Her hair was lighter than mine — light brown by normal standards, but golden honey in the sunlight — and it was almost always tied up in some fashion or another. Usually with hair ties, but rubber bands stolen from the teacher's desk would do in a pinch. Her eyes were brown as well, to match her hair, with a faint dusting of freckles spreading out beneath them. She was a boisterous tomboy, covered in scratches and scuffs of dirt, and I was a shy little deer that watched the world in silence.

I remember the first day we talked about Iphy; of course, we didn't call him Iphy back then: we didn't even know he was a he. For all we knew, he was a fox, a bobcat or some other small animal stealing eggs and scaring chickens. It never occurred to me that the shadow she had seen was an actual person who would change our lives and shake the foundations of all we believed possible until much later.

We made it to school with time to spare, as we always did. It was my idea to start heading to school early, mostly because without me, Eraliss was always late. We took our assigned seats, Eraliss near the front, me in the back corner. I always loved that back corner: mostly because it was near the window, where sunlight came through and I could see all the usually invisible particles that flew through the air, partly because it was right next to the science bookcase where our homeroom teacher, Mr. Neil, kept his collection of science knickknacks. He had a pearly white bird skull (I think it was a crow, because the beak was black as night), a giant shark tooth as big as my hand that stood point-up on a little stand, and a collection of jars that had preserved animals in them: a baby shark, a piglet, a lizard, and an octopus that he affectionately called Lawrence.

I would spend hours looking over at that collection of his while he stood at the front of the class, his back to all of us, writing things up on the board as he taught our core classes: social studies, physical education, language arts, science. P.E. was fun; he would take us all down to the gymnasium or out to the football field, if it was sunny, so we could get a good fifty minutes of exercise. In the seventh grade, our school still made us have a 'core' teacher that we spent most of the day with, but we had math and our elective class with different teachers. It wasn't until eighth grade that they started to prepare us for high school by giving us different teachers for all our different subjects.

Eraliss and I tossed notes back and forth, crumpled little balls of paper that we scribbled on, and talked about this and that until the other students started to shuffle into the room, in ones and twos. I've forgotten most of them now — their names, but not their faces. There was Tyler Whatsit, a strange boy who sat by himself and seemed intent on eating his school supplies. Eddie was in our class; he sat next to Eraliss, but they both ignored each other, at least until Iphy came along. There was the King boy, who always went by his last name because it made him feel powerful and important, and countless others who filled the seats between me and my friend.

I miss those carefree days. If I had known what was to happen that year, I would have paid less attention to the dead things on Mr. Neil's bookcase and more to the world around me. The dead can tell us many things, but not nearly as much as simple living has to teach us. I just never thought my world would ever change.

C.S

~*~

I kept thinking about the egg robber all through homeroom. I couldn't get the shadow out of my mind. It was like a nagging doubt that flitted in front of my eyes, distracting me endlessly while Mr. Neil was talking. He could have told me the answers to Friday's test and I wouldn't have paid him any attention. This was bad on my part, because not only could I have used the help, but it also proved that I was a lost cause that day. See, Mr. Neil was this big, tall man, with a barrel chest; he used to play some kind of sport professionally for a few years, but he gave it up to 'mold young minds'. And when he taught something, he'd always get so excited about whatever it was and his voice would boom out and the teachers across the hallway could hear him. With his short, cropped hair and his big ears sticking out, he made quite a comical figure, but he took his teaching very seriously, and if I couldn't hear him over my wonderings about the shadow, it proved that I was beyond help at that point.

I asked myself what on earth it could have been: some kind of animal, a fox or a raccoon? But it had looked like it was walking on two legs. Some kind of monkey or ape? Maybe a chimpanzee had escaped from the zoo or was it something more sinister? What if it was a murderer on the run from the cops, hiding out in the wilderness behind my house?

All during science, I doodled the shadow beast as well as I could at the top of the paper. With my first attempt it looked too beastly, like some black, misshapen animal, so I tried again. My second attempt? It looked like a dragon centaur. Again and again I drew the shadow, but it never seemed to look quite like what I had seen, even when I had a page full of shadow doodles.

"What's that?" I looked to my left to see Eddie McCloy looking at my page of shadows. At the time, I didn't know Eddie, didn't want to know him, and couldn't fathom why he was looking at my page of doodles so intently. Normally, he ignored me, and I ignored him.

"It's something I saw in my backyard last night." I said, hoping he'd just dismiss me as a crazy person.

He just stared at the drawings, nodding his head a bit, like my crappy drawings were the answer to everything.

Then, like nothing at all was unusual, he went back to copying the notes that Mr. Neil was writing.

I tried to pay attention—I really did—but the shadow just wouldn't go away. I was so wrapped up in the mystery that I was pegged in the head with a dodgeball before I even realized that we were playing.

"I think it was a human." I told Calm when core classes got out. I sounded a lot more confident than I felt, and she looked up at me, which was a big deal for Calm.

"The shadow in your backyard?"

"Yeah. I think it might have been some murdering fugitive of justice hiding out in the woods."

She considered this as we walked. That was the thing with Calm, she never laughed at you, or thought you were crazy; she always considered what you were saying, turning it over in her mind before she gave you a response. I liked that about her; her patience, her understanding.

"I suppose that makes sense. I don't think the woods like him very much though. I know I wouldn't want someone like that around."

"But think about it; some villainous lawbreaker living in the woods. How cool is that?"

Again, she considered. "I think it could just as easily have been something else; a wild animal of some kind. There are lots of foxes around here, maybe it was one of them getting some eggs to eat."

"Yeah, but foxes also eat chickens. Wouldn't the chickens *and* the eggs be missing if it was a fox?"

"Not if it was a vegetarian."

That was where our conversation died; we had reached room 215, where Mrs. Marks taught Advanced Mathematics to smart kids like Calm. Mrs. Marks had hawkish eyes that seemed to grab you and scrutinize you where you stood. She fixed her stony glare on me; she couldn't stand dumb students like me. Her nostrils flared a bit, reminding me of an angry bull spurred to wrath by the color red. "Calm, please take your seat; we have a class to start."

Calm muttered something affirmative and shuffled her way into the classroom, her eyes on her feet, leaving me to move eight doors down to room 223 where I had Art with Mr. Letham. Not that I relished the idea or anything; I hated art class. It was my elective, but I certainly didn't elect it. That was the thing with our school: we had electives; we just didn't get to choose them. It was all done randomly. Last year I had Health, while Calm got a class called Art of Geometry, which somehow blended art and math into one class. This year she lucked out; she got Music, while I got stuck with Art. Not for lack of trying to get out of it, though. I went up to our principal, Mrs. Nelson, who reminded me of a pear with glasses that made her eyes look huge, asking to be transferred to something I would be good at, like a library assistant. She calmly told me that the schedules were permanent and if I gave the class a try, I'd love it. She told me that Mr. Letham was a fabulous teacher.

Because he couldn't paint the walls of his classroom, Mr. Letham put up black and white butcher paper all over the walls, so his students could be creative with it and make the classroom sparkle. Most of the students just wrote profanity in tiny letters, as if hoping that because the writing was small it would go unnoticed, but nothing went unnoticed with Mr. Letham. He was short, balding, with glasses that sat on a nose that had been broken but hadn't healed quite right. He had a potbelly that stretched the fabric of the brightly colored Hawaiian shirts he so loved.

Our seats weren't assigned in that class, and I always sat in the middle. You had to be very careful with Mr. Letham. Everything you did meant that you wanted to share your artwork at the end of class. If you sat in the back, you wanted to share, if you sat in the front, you wanted to share. If you coughed, you wanted to share, if you scratched your elbow, you wanted to share; the man was a fanatic about sharing creative things.

That day was a free day, which basically meant that we had an hour to work on something creative, and as per usual, he'd call up four or five of the coughers and the elbow scratchers at the end of class to share what they had done. That whole hour I worked on doodling that shadow, filling several pages with different shadows, trying to find that right combination of hunched over and gangly that I had seen the night before. At the end of class I figured that I was home free, having been quiet all class while sitting in the middle of the room, just as inconspicuous as I could be. Then, I made a fatal error: I sneezed.

"Miss Cofler." He always used our last names; he said that he was preparing us for the real world, where we would be known by our surname and nothing else.

Knowing I couldn't get out of this—having already tried it once earlier in the year—I went up to the front of the class, papers in hand. I handed them to him, and he leafed through them with an amused look on his face.

"Miss Cofler, can you tell the class what these are?" He asked, tacking up my doodles on the wall for everyone to see.

"It's this shadow that I saw last night. It went into our hen house, and then crept back into the woods. I can't get it out of my head, and I can't draw it to save my life." I said lamely. Some of the kids snickered, but Mr. Letham cleared his throat to shut them up.

"On the contrary," Mr. Letham was always using phrases like that. "I think it's wonderful that you can't decide what it looked like; very mysterious. But, if you want the mystery to go away so badly, my advice would be to go looking for the culprit; once you know your subject, your work will soar."

For once, I didn't dismiss Mr. Letham's words as pure crazy at work. I took his words to heart.

The first thing I did when I got home, I went straight to the hen house. I didn't even go inside and drop off my school bag like I normally would have; I was way too excited to see what I would find. I saw nothing but chickens tracks and droplets of poop in the dirt around the coop, so I moved up towards the woods where I scoured the ground, moving back and forth over it like a dog sniffing for a scent. I went a few feet into the woods, my eyes still trained on the ground, and in a little patch of mud I found the print I was looking for. It wasn't a fox print or a bobcat print, or even the rare but still sometimes seen mountain lion print; it was a shoe print. It looked like a sneaker of some kind, a little bit larger than my own foot when I put it next to it for measuring. I was so excited: this was it! I raced home, eager to grab a flashlight and explore this new mystery further, but my mother had other plans entirely.

"Where have you been?" she shrieked when I came through the door. One look at the clock told me everything: I was twenty-five minutes late. My mother was a stickler for me being home on time; ever since my dad had left for the second time back when I was six, she seemed convinced that I was trying to leave her as well.

"I was just out back," I said, hoping that the fact that I was only outside would pacify her. Not so.

"You couldn't stick your head in the door and tell me that you were alive? I was this close to calling the cops. This close!" She put her fingers together to emphasis her point. "You could have been kidnapped, or murdered, or a dozen other things!" Not likely; the last time someone from our town was kidnapped was six years ago. The last murder was double that. Things like that just didn't happen in our town. There was the occasional bar fight, and a fire some years ago, but nothing really of note.

"Next time, I swear, I'll come right home." I said, still trying in vain to pacify her rage.

"There won't be a next time, young lady; you're grounded until Halloween."

"What?" I couldn't believe it; Halloween was still ten days away, and what if the murderer was gone by then? I couldn't believe that my mother was making such a big deal out of this, but back then it was really easy to set her off. She hadn't laid a hand on me since I was two (and that was because I was eating the rat poison from under the sink) but she would ground me over the tiniest thing. That was her big punishment for me: keeping me locked in my room without any access to the outside world other than school. Back then, it worked like a charm.

I stomped my way upstairs, letting her know how mad I was by how hard my feet hit the floor. Once in the prison of my room, I went straight to the window and watched the woods until nightfall, waiting for the shadow to appear. Whatever it was that was out there must have known that I was sniffing around, because the shadow didn't return that night, or the next night, or even the night after that. It wasn't until Halloween that I saw the shadow again, only he wasn't a shadow anymore, but a living presence that would change my life.

Extracted from an e-mail addressed to Eraliss Cofler from Korvid Fairington, dated ▮▮▮▮▮▮▮.

Hey, E. I got your e-mail; the kids are doing great, thanks for asking. And thanks for asking me for my input; I'm not sure how much help I'll be in unraveling the mystery, but I can tell you what I remember.

The night we first met Iphy. It was Halloween, and my dad had told me no trick-or-treating that year; apparently thirteen was too old for all the kiddy nonsense. And since my dad was working the night shift that year (like he did every year) I was left to my own lonesome devices. So instead of the usual monster movie fare, I figured I'd go exploring the woods. The last few nights I had seen some kind of shadow messing around near our shed. Of course, at the time, I figured it was some coyote or a bobcat—something like that—so I went prepared: I grabbed my old baseball bat from under my bed.

Everything was fine until I got the feeling that I was being followed. It was those woods; they would do that to you: make you think that a million things were out to get you, hiding in the dark treetops, waiting around every trunk and bush. Even after spending as many nights as I did out there, I never shook that feeling. I don't know how Iphy and Jax did it for so long, except that maybe the trees sensed their divinity, and welcomed them into their fold.

I started hearing footsteps behind me, leaves being brushed aside in the quiet, twigs snapping under careful feet. Finally, I got so freaked out that I darted behind this big tree, and I mean one of the big ones. Those woods were full of trees like that: trunks wider than your whole body. Anyway, I ducked behind one of them, listening, and sure enough I heard something moving closer. I waited until I could hear the footsteps right next to the tree, the soft breathing ringing like a rock concert in my ears. I jumped out, my jacket waving; I had been hoping to scare off whatever it was.

God, you were so scared. You were screaming so loudly; it's a wonder that your mother didn't call the cops or something. Then, you started yelling at me, calling me every name you could think of and a few I'm sure you made up on the spot. And there I was, totally dumbfounded; honestly, I didn't even recognize you at first. I hadn't really seen you in a couple of years, after all. I'm sorry about that, by the way. That's one thing that I'll always be thankful to Iphy for—bringing us all together that year.

"What are you doing out here?" you hissed, still mad as hell that I had scared you.

"Something's been sniffing around the shed—I wanna scare it off," I said, brandishing my baseball bat.

You rolled your eyes. "Put that away. It's a person."

25

I blinked. "What?" This was news to me.

"Yeah; someone's been stealing eggs from the hen house. I found a few footprints at the edge of the woods, and they were definitely human. I think it might be a killer or something cool like that." Your eyes shone in the moonlight, full of truth.

You seemed so sure of yourself and I was swept into your fantasy. "Then we should keep this out. You know, for protection. What if they attack us or something?"

You looked at me like I was a few burgers short of a combo meal; Lord knows what you were going to say next. Then, you saw the fire. Your eyes, which were locked with mine, suddenly slid sideways, and I remember looking behind me, thinking that the murderer was right there. When I saw the glow of the fire, I knew that this was it. I looked back at you, but you were already going for it, like it was some kind of race that I didn't know about. You know, if it had been a killer, or a criminal, or even the Wailing Woman we would have been toast. We were pretty stupid kids, weren't we?

When we first saw that place, I thought it was something out of an epic adventure novel. I don't know about you, but I was spellbound. It was like... nothing I had ever imagined could be in the woods behind my house. With the metal sheets leaning up against that huge tree, like a blind from the wind, and the fire pit, with the rusty cooking pot sitting next to the roaring fire, and all those spindly branches that he had woven together to make a roof that still let in starlight. I was amazed. I fell in love. I knew that I wanted to live there with all my might; with everything in me that I had.

And you; you started poking around everything, checking behind the metal sheets, the rocks around the fire pit and that big boulder that he used to sit on. What the hell were you looking for? A bloody knife, a gun, some proof that there was a killer, a fugitive, or a vigilante living there? Iphy might have had bits of all three, but you probably could have searched all year and never found anything more about him than what he told us. Our search for the Wailing Woman was less futile.

Then, Iphy came home. Boy, was he pissed when he saw us. He came around the tree, arms full of branches and wild vegetables, his pale hair full of twigs and leaves—he looked like a miniature wild man of the mountains. The only thing he was missing was a big scraggly beard that had small animals living in it. You screamed when you saw him—I bet you thought it was some mass murdering killer coming to carve us into pieces—and that really got him going. He raised a big branch, one that looked like a caveman's club, and started waving it in the air, threatening to beat our heads in. I totally forgot about my own baseball bat, and when you bolted I just followed you. Iphy chased us for a little while, screaming at us to never come back.

We didn't stop running until we were in your backyard, and as soon as my legs stopped moving, they protested so badly that I dropped to my butt and just sat for a few minutes, catching my breath. Despite the beauty of his haven, I fully intended to leave the crazy person alone. Then, you said it: "That was a kid."

I stared up at you like you had grown another head. "What?"

"That was a kid back there, living in the woods." You looked back over your shoulder and, hand to God, E, I thought you were gonna plunge right in there and go looking for him. If nothing else, I knew that you weren't going to let this thing go. "I wonder who he is."

"Whoever he is, he's crazy." I said, though I couldn't stop seeing his beautiful Eden in my head. I sat on your yard for a few more minutes, catching my breath; we didn't talk, but we didn't need to. It was as if the years of silence between us had melted into mere minutes. Then, you got up and said goodnight, and I said likewise, and you went home and I went home and I stared out my window, looking out at the woods, wondering the same thing that you were: who was that kid?

Hope this helps, Eraliss; I'm glad Calm put you up to this whole thing. Have you managed to get a hold of anyone else?

All my love,
Korvid.

From the journal of Calm Sheldon

I knew something big had happened on Halloween by what happened in the morning; Korvid was waiting with Eraliss at the sewer. The older boy lived in the almost empty two story house that separated Eraliss and I, and in the three years that I had lived on that cul-de-sac, I hadn't once seen him out playing or doing much of anything other than mowing the lawn. He was in eighth grade and, like most eight graders, he never walked with underclassmen — even his neighbors. And that wasn't all he never did; he'd never wave to us, or say hello or anything else pleasant like that, though admittedly we never really attempted to engage him in conversation. I tried once, the first day that I moved into the neighborhood. Eraliss had told me to just ignore him, and when he hadn't even nodded in my direction, I took her advice.

I didn't know anything about Korvid, and from what I could tell by the way Eraliss always stiffened and glared the few times we saw him, she didn't like the older boy any. But, there they were that chilly November morning, talking away like they had always been the best of friends as I shuffled up to them with my eyes on the ground.

"Calm, we saw him!" Eraliss said, so full of excitement; she looked like she could grow wings and fly away, she was so lighthearted.

"Who?" I asked. It never occurred to me to even think about the shadow from a few weeks ago. Eraliss had stopped talking about it after it was a no-show for a third night; I assumed that she had forgotten about the whole thing.

"The murderer!" she said, waving her arms as if to emphasize a point she was trying to make.

"It wasn't a murderer," Korvid said. He had a gentle sounding voice that I really liked; it was calming, almost musical in its own right. When he told me that things would be alright, I always believed him. Even more so than Iphy. "You said it yourself: it was a kid."

"Doesn't mean he can't be a murderer." Eraliss said, sticking out her chin. Korvid rolled his eyes but didn't say anything.

I looked back and forth between the two of them, and then looked down at my feet, following my shoelaces wherever they led me. "He must be lonely," I said after we had started walking to school, "living in the woods, all by himself."

Eraliss gave a snort. "He didn't seem too thrilled to have visitors."

"I think we just startled him, that's all." Korvid said with a thoughtful look in his eyes. Sometimes he would stare off into space, a blank look on his face, but he was always thinking. "I wanna go back there tonight and see if I can find him again."

Eraliss shot him a mild glare, as if he had wandered into the privacy of her own mind and stolen the idea with black gloves. "Yeah, but let's hope that he doesn't swing his club and ask questions later. What time should we meet?"

Korvid blinked at her while I looked up for the first time since the conversation had started. "What?" we asked in unison.

"What time should we meet to go into the woods?"

"Are we all going?" Korvid asked, looking at me skeptically. I was almost a whole head shorter than he was, and with my hair always in my eyes, and my habit of always looking down, I know I looked frail; he seemed worried I would get hurt.

"Of course we are." Eraliss said. She looked down at me, her hands on her hips. "You want to come, don't you, Calm? I mean, this is huge! A kid living in the woods — they make movies out of stuff like this."

I quickly looked down at my shoes again, trying to discern the answer from the knot my laces made. They didn't help me any, but then again they never did. "I bet he'd like some friends," I said my voice quiet. "And I don't think the woods are a very good place for a kid to grow up, unless he wants to live there his whole life."

"Right" Eraliss said with a nod of her head. I wasn't sure if she actually understood what I had said, but I couldn't blame her; sometimes I didn't understand me either.

We walked in silence after that, walking along Main Street, past the cycle shop and the dry cleaners; the same route we always took to school. The only difference today being Korvid's presence.

"Korvid?" The voice was so soft; if we had been talking to each other, we would have missed it entirely. The boy in question looked down, and Eraliss and I followed his gaze to the curb. Sitting there, in his usual spot in front of Smithy's Bakery, was Jax.

Everyone in town knew Jax; he was the town's only orphan. There were several homeless people that wandered the streets of our town, but they were all adults, whose dreams had been shattered and whose life had slipped quietly on by without them noticing. Jax was different; he didn't know what his dreams were yet, and his life had just started, and because of that, everyone in town loved him. The story goes that his parents had died in a terrible, terrible fire when he was only eight years old; it was a miracle that he survived it. He had no living relatives, so he became a ward of the state, but when the state came calling, Jax had disappeared.

He vanished for a few months, but he came back to our town and was seen sleeping in the church and looking for quarters and spare change in the hard-to-reach places of our small world. He was terribly afraid of foster homes, and since he slept in the church over on Guild Street every night, everyone figured it was none of their business, and that he was okay on his own. The townspeople would buy him sandwiches from Carver's Deli on Breakers Avenue and old Mr. Smithy made it a point to give Jax whatever hadn't sold from his bakery the previous day, so he was never hungry. And he never wanted for a friend, or for some kind of appreciation. Our town absolutely loved Jax. He was everyone's child or sibling: some long-lost family member that had finally shown up after years gone by. It was his sweet, beaming smile and the always-happy look in his blue eyes. He had that same smile that morning looking up at Korvid.

"Sorry, Jax; I had my head in the clouds," Korvid said, rubbing the back of his head like he would always do when he felt embarrassed or unsure.

"It's alright. I just wanted to return these." Jax tossed up a jingling pair of keys that Korvid caught with practiced skill. "Where were you last night? I got kind of worried."

"I was in the woods out back; we found a kid who's living out there."

Jax's eyes widened. "No kidding?"

"Hand to God," Korvid said, placing his right hand over his heart; that was one of his favorite sayings. "We're gonna go talk to him tonight; you should definitely come with us."

"Maybe." Jax murmured, his eyes sliding beyond us. He gave us a smile, rose and excused himself as Mr. Smithy began opening up the bakery; on the counter was a bag of bagels, biscuits and a few loaves of bread.

We started walking again. Eraliss gave Korvid a look that straddled the border between a pout and a glare. "You didn't tell me that you knew Jax," she said, failing to keep the twinge of irritation out of her voice.

Korvid shrugged. "You never asked."

C.S

~*~

Korvid was my best friend before Calm moved into the neighborhood three years ago. I moved in when I was five years old — right after my dad left my mom for the first time — and Korvid lived in the house next to mine; naturally, we became the best of friends extremely fast. Back then, we were the only kids in our neighborhood, so far as we knew.

We lived in a cul-de-sac, near the empty end of town, where small farms, wide yards and sprawling woods were common. Besides our families, there was crotchety old Ms. Edwards, who lived in the house that Calm's family later moved into, and on the other side of my house lived a couple that I hardly saw when they lived there. Their house is falling apart and abandoned now: the roof caved in and most of the second floor is totally gone. Next to that was a house that was probably larger than any of the other houses on our street. I didn't know who lived there, but I had seen two older boys playing basketball from time to time, so I knew the place was inhabited. Korvid and I left the older boys alone and they did the same.

Korvid and I would spend hours playing together, exploring the edge of the woods, walking down to Main Street to stare at the bikes on display. I used to stay the night at his house, and he would stay the night at mine; we would push all the chairs together and drape a blanket over them to make a fort, where we would pretend that we were rabbits, or foxes, or any other kind of animal that we'd seen in the latest animated movie. Korvid's dad worked nights and sometimes days, so we could always stay up as late as we wanted when we slept at his house, watching movies and eating cookies until we were sick. When we got a few years older, Korvid made us cake because he liked to show off the fact that he could use the oven on his own even though he was only seven; his dad had showed him how because his dad was never home and they couldn't afford to hire someone to take care of him. We stayed friends for a number of years, but then he went to Middle School and stayed after class, or hung out with his older friends, and we saw less and less of each other.

We grew apart as the year went on, then Calm moved in and I started to hang out with her. Soon Korvid was just another memory, a blip in time that had no real bearing on the here and now. It happens sometimes: friends you thought were your world suddenly disappear, leaving you empty and hurting until another friend comes along to fill the void the first one left behind. That's what Calm did: she filled the void that Korvid left when he vanished from my world.

Then he suddenly reappeared that Halloween night, two years later. His black hair was different: longer, wilder. He'd hit a growth spurt; he was almost half a head taller than me, which really burned me up because I used to be the tallest of us by a few inches. He was gangly and awkward in his adolescence; he never knew what to do with his hands and he was all knees and elbows when he moved. There were only two things that hadn't changed about him. The first was his eyes: they were still the same, brilliant green. Whenever Korvid got excited, those eyes would shine—literally *shine*—like green glass bottles in the sun. And, like when we were kids, his shoes were double knotted; I always imagined that he was afraid that his laces would come apart just from the daily activities of walking around and occasionally running. They weren't the canvas sneakers that so many kids liked, but they weren't boots, or worker's shoes. They were mature sneakers for older kids, made of leather, with tight stitches and thick laces. He tried to keep them clean, but there were some stains that would never leave, no matter how much he worked to rid his shoes of the slight blemish. His eyes and the knots of his shoes were the same, but everything else in between seemed to have changed. His shirts bore the names of bands I'd never heard of; his once cherished pants now had gaping holes in the knees; his double knotted shoes were streaked with the mud of adventures I hadn't been privy to. He'd traded me in for something else; for older friends, for more harrowing adventures than playing pretend animals, for a different school, a different life. And as irrational as it was, I blamed Jax.

Jax was the town orphan; he was only twelve, but he was tall for his age, only a few inches shorter than Korvid. He had light brown hair that always stuck out in every direction it could other than the direction it was supposed to. His messy head reminded me of a hedgehog, with its quills sticking every which way. He had cloudy blue eyes that seemed to shift to gray whenever he was upset, or feeling sad. His clothes were a bit too big, given to him by various townspeople, or found on the street. His shoes were a mismatched pair; one a rough and tumble blue sneaker, and the other a brown hi-top with thick patches of dark red fabric stitched helter-skelter. He said he'd lost the other hi-top in the year before we met Iphy, but that he wasn't ready to give up its counterpart just yet. So Jax wore a blue sneaker that Thomas Smith had found in the junkyard where he worked, along with his cherished brown hi-top.

He was long of limb, but unlike Korvid, he was graceful. Every single move he made seemed choreographed, and watching him was like watching a dance or a play where everyone knew their lines. Street life was not for the clumsy and uncoordinated, and Jax had adapted well. He had long, graceful fingers—he could have been a fabulous pianist if he wanted to, or a wonderful pickpocket.

That first day of November, I remember that I didn't like Jax. I thought he had stolen Korvid away from me and I resented it. After Jax went inside the bakery, I glared at Korvid. "You didn't tell me you knew Jax."

Korvid shrugged. "You never asked."

I frowned at his logic, still sore about being dumped by my once best and only friend. "So, what was that all about?"

He gave me a quizzical look. "What was what all about?"

"What was he doing with your keys?"

Again, Korvid shrugged; it seemed to be his answer to everything those days. "I let him come in and use the shower and dig through my closet for any clothes he might want. Usually I'm there to cook him up some soup, or make a sandwich; I hope he had the sense to take whatever he wanted from — "

"He's a total stranger!" I exploded, Anger and Hurt swelling in my chest. "You don't let someone like that into your house — especially when you're not there!"

"What's your problem, E?" The use of my old nickname sent another stab of hurt directly into my chest. "The kid doesn't have anywhere else to go; it's not like he's dangerous or anything."

Anger and Hurt propelled my actions; I gave a loud snort. "You don't know that."

"Sure I do. Jax is perfectly harmless."

"Whatever." I wanted to stop — to leave well enough alone — but Hurt and Anger goaded me even further, forcing another burst of poison past my lips. "I heard that he started that fire himself — killed his whole family." (Jax, wherever you are, if you ever read this, I'm so sorry for saying that.)

I knew it was a horrible thing to say, but I was so furious. How could Korvid have given up all our years of friendship? I hadn't realized until then how much I had missed hanging out with Korvid, how much it hurt that he'd replaced me, and how much I wished for his return.

Calm suddenly looked up at me with big appalled eyes, and Korvid stopped dead in his tracks; I knew at once that I had crossed a line.

"That's a terrible thing to say!"

"I can't believe you, E!"

I winced under their angry gazes and their onslaught of words, clutching my books like they were my only defense against their ire. "I'm sorry," I cried, and as soon as I said them, I knew that I meant the words from the bottom of my heart. It's been said that everyone in our town loved Jax; I was no exception, even before our little hang-out gang. He was the soul of our town or a lost puppy that needed looking after. I looked guiltily at Korvid, whose eyes were cold and bore into me like venom. If I wanted to regain his friendship, this certainly wasn't the way to do it. "I didn't mean it... I just... I just missed hanging out with you." I had spoken the truth, so I couldn't figure out why I suddenly wanted my words to disappear from everyone's memory.

Korvid stared at me, dumbstruck, his own anger quickly evaporating. I felt my cheeks go red. Then, Calm's watch went off, breaking the spell of silence.

"We're going to be late."

For once school seemed to breeze on by like I always wanted it to, as though Time knew what lay ahead in our day and it was just as eager to discover the joys along with us. We raced home, each of us with an assigned list that Calm and I had come up with at lunch of things we were going to bring. I had the food, which was going to be easy enough, Calm was going to bring her father's big floodlight in case we were out later than we planned, and Korvid was insistent on bringing his baseball bat with him—just in case. I thought he was being overdramatic, but there was always the possibility that my imagination wasn't running away with me, that the person out there in the woods really was a killer of some kind, and Korvid just wanted all of us to be safe.

I was excited. No, more than that: I was ecstatic. This was better than Christmas. Korvid was just as excited as I was, but Calm was just going along with it, entertaining our fancy. I didn't know it then, but she did a lot of that in those days. It was like she was in a play, following her lines, trying to keep the act together before it all fell to pieces.

It was Friday afternoon, and as such, most of our parents wouldn't mind if we were out late, so long as they didn't know that we were trampling around in the woods in search of a killer. Korvid's dad worked nights anyway, and Calm's parents would think it grand that their daughter was getting out of the house; it was my Mother that was the problem. She'd have a fit if she thought for one minute that I'd be out late, but we'd planned this out at lunch and I had the perfect solution.

I got home from school a whole ten minutes early, and I made a big show of dragging my feet and keeping hunched over as I came in through the front door. It took a moment for my Mother to notice that her only daughter was ailing; her favorite daytime television talk show host was on, promoting a new book by some long-time bestselling author. Scattered in Mother's lap were the remnants of the local paper, the classifieds spread open at her feet. I was glad that she was looking for work again. When she finally saw me, she raised a skeptical eyebrow. "Are you okay?"

"Not really," I moaned as I shuffled slowly into the kitchen. Once there, I began to frantically fill my bag with whatever I could; crackers, cookies, bottles of soda, a few boxes of raisins and a package of beef jerky stashed in the cupboards.

I stopped stashing as soon as my Mother came in, pretending instead that I was getting a glass of water.

Once I had finished drinking the water, I coughed, ever so weakly. "I think I'm gonna go lie down."

My Mother glanced at the cat clock that she had hanging on the wall, watching the eyes go back and forth. "Dinner's at seven."

I waved meekly at her. "Just leave me a plate; I'll come down for it when I'm hungry." Normally, this kind of answer would never do, but right then my Mother had a million thoughts on her mind; a new job, her T.V host, the dishes that had piled up during the week, her diminishing savings, and my Father. She had no room in her brain for a sick kid who just wanted to sleep. She nodded her head distractedly, waving me on upstairs. I grabbed my bag and all but limped out.

Once upstairs in the safe confines of my room, I got to work. I quickly locked the door, and then set about emptying my bag of everything that wasn't food related. I glanced around my room, and grabbed a few candy bars that I had been saving on top of my dresser. And last, but not least, from my pillowcase I grabbed a Swiss army knife that my Mother didn't know about, stashing it in my pocket before I opened the window.

I had one of those easily escapable windows: the ones that are upstairs with easy access to the roof, once opened. That window saved my sanity more than once that year, and I always swore to myself that when I had children I'd make sure they got the rooms with the easily escapable windows so they could have as much fun as I did. Sometimes I would use it just to get to the roof so I could watch the stars: sometimes I used it to sneak out of the house, like I was doing that night. Once on the roof, it was easy to climb down the terrace my mother had bolted to the side of the house so that her cherished purple flowers could have something to cling to as they grew. And once on the ground it was as easy as waiting for the right moment to sprint across the backyard and vanish into the woods.

I met Calm and Korvid a few feet into the woods behind Korvid's house; Calm was looking down at the ground, Korvid was sitting on a rotting stump that had been there for years. He looked up at me as I approached, his face a mask of worry, "Where were you? I was starting to think that your mom had botched the plan and we were gonna have to call it quits."

"Relax," I said with a shake of my head. "She thinks I'm snoozing away — we're fine."

I adjusted the straps on my backpack and started walking, hoping I was going in the right direction. Last night, in the dark, the woods had seemed so much clearer. With the moon shining down, there was either blackness all around us or the blue grey of the trees ahead of us, giving us a perfect path. Now, with the sun shining down in the last remnants of the afternoon, we saw everything around us: the brush, the ferns, the rotting stumps, the overturned logs, the twisted roots that broke free from the ground. In the darkness, we had only gone one way, straight ahead. Now, we kept seeing signs of the kid everywhere in broken twigs, disturbed leaves, edges of tracks left in drying mud. And we followed these could-be-him trails, like hunting dogs locked on a scent. We'd see snapped branches, or a disturbed bush, and we'd follow in that direction for ten or fifteen minutes, never once thinking that there were plenty of other things that lived in these woods that could just as easily make those trails. Then one of us would spot a new clue, a new trail to follow so doggedly. We went around in circles for hours, seeing the same twisted branch heavy with lichen, the same moss covered stump that housed a sprouting of toadstools, until we finally spilled out into a huge clearing. It seemed large enough to house a three ring circus to my young eyes: a little valley that dipped down, covered in soft green grass, surrounded on all sides by a gentle slope blanketed in clover. We all sat on one of the slopes, marveling in the wonderful panorama of the sky that it gave us.

"This is hopeless," Korvid said, letting out a little grunt as he plopped down. "We're totally lost."

"Impossible," I said, lying down next to him, stretching out in the clover. "No one can really get lost in the woods these days; there's not enough wood."

He snorted good-naturedly. "Bull. You know in our state alone there's still enough uncharted forest to hide a small herd of *dinosaurs*."

"Okay, but what makes you think that *we're* lost?" I glanced over at Calm, who was the only one of us to remain standing. Her eyes were focused on the darkening sky; she was a million miles away from us. She'd gone to that little place of hers where she pulled her strange logic and where she kept all of the emotions that she never showed.

"Do you remember a clearing last night?" Korvid asked, breaking me of my musing.

"Korvid, we could have passed an abandoned amusement park last night and never seen it. Don't worry, we'll find this kid."

With a shake of his head, Korvid gave me a chuckle. "That's you, E: always optimistic."

"Of course." I stood, dusting off the bits of dried and dead clover and grass that clung to the seat of my pants. "So let's quit moping around and find this axe murderer." I don't know when exactly my imagination had taken a hold of the image of the kid and his club and morphed it into the image of a child axe murderer, but it had, and now I was convinced. I had to see this young axe murderer again.

Korvid hesitated, probably doubting the stray bits of my sanity that he'd seen in the last twenty-four hours, and in that silence, we heard laughter. It was faint, but it carried over the quiet forest, like a ghostly sound that haunted the woods.

Calm looked up at the twinkling light that had just appeared in the failing evening. "Listen: the stars are laughing at us."

"That's not a star, Calm, that's the planet Venus. And Venus wasn't laughing: that came from right here on planet Earth." Korvid stood, looking regal for a second, until his foot slid on a rock and he nearly tumbled down the hill of clover. "It came from over there," he said, gesturing vaguely to the woods behind us: the very woods we had just emerged from. I opened my mouth to argue— to say that the laughter could have come from anywhere— but he shushed me and started back into the woods, moving quickly and silently, as though he intended on finding the axe murderer by sound alone. Calm followed on his heels, her small green backpack jostling on her shoulders as she climbed over a fallen log in pursuit of our friend. I followed, nursing a wounded ego.

Through sheer force of will, or plain dumb luck, Korvid managed to navigate through the dense woodland and find the axe murderer again. It took us a while; night had already started to darken the woods around us, and we had to move in almost total silence to hear. But the farther we went into the trees, the louder the faint laughter became, and soon we could discern other sounds beyond the almost continual laughter: the call of excited shouts, what could have been two different voices having a jovial conversation. At first, I thought that the axe murderer had an accomplice of some kind: some front man that went into town and got him supplies and brought him news of the outside world, word on where the police forces were moving, and maps of the local wilderness, marked with hiding spots. We emerged from the trees into the same small clearing that we had found last night, and we were greeted with not one, but two faces lit by firelight; one was calm and familiar, one was startled and not all that familiar.

"Hey!" This voice — loud and angry — belonged to the face that I didn't know very well: the axe murderer from last night. He quickly stood, grabbing another club of wood from a pile next to the roaring fire. "I thought I told you kids to get lost!"

"Whoa, chill out, man." Korvid dropped his bat and held his hands up high — reaching for the sky, as the old western movies used to say — showing the kid that we were unarmed.

"Yeah, sit down, Iphy." This voice belonged to the calm face that I recognized from earlier that morning. Jax was sitting next to the fire, like it was nothing out of the ordinary for him to be sitting in the middle of the woods at

night with an axe murderer. The fire made his eyes shimmer like amber, despite their being blue in color, and even then he seemed to be in total control of the situation. He stood up, reached out a hand and lowered the axe murderer's arms. The kid finally pulled his eyes away from us to look at Jax, obviously debating the sense in the orphan's words. "These are the kids that I was telling you about."

This finally seemed to pacify the axe murderer's rage and he looked back at us with piercing blue eyes, as though judging at us with these new eyes would forever determine our worth. Jax didn't bat an uncharacteristically bright eye as he gestured to Korvid, breaking the ice by making introductions. "Iphy, this is my friend Korvid: he's the one who gave me this shirt."

Iphy grinned as he dropped his makeshift club. "I told Jax that shirt was way too good for a streetmonger."

His smile was contagious; Korvid mirrored it as he glanced over at the orphan. "Nothing's too good for Jax," he said. With a dorky grin still plastered on his face, he motioned my way. "This is Eraliss and Calm."

Iphy turned his grinning face and his appraising blue eyes toward me; he seemed to like whatever he saw, because he nodded. "Yeah, I remember you from last night; you had eyes as big as saucers." His voice was special; that was the first thing I noticed about him. It had a bit of an accent to it, which made it instantly exotic to my homegrown ears. His hair seemed impossibly pale, bleached almost white with tell-tale brown roots. And his eyes; they were brilliant and bright, even in the low light. They weren't comparable to jewels, because there was so much light and happiness and Life dancing between the lines in his irises that to compare them to cold lifeless gems is a great offense. His clothes were worn, riddled with dirt and small threadbare tears. The next things I noticed were his shoes. His sneakers were scuffed and rugged, with rips and patches of color from old markers or paint. They were even stitched in some places — a quick fix with needle and thread so he could keep going, race ahead and continue moving without breaking stride. They were held together with brown laces that surely had been white at some point in the past, but had gone through too much to stay pristine. And there was something in the way he stood — even that night, so early in our friendship — the way he held himself: his confidence had a tendency to rub off on anyone who was in his vicinity. It was impossible to be self-conscious when Iphy was around; you were one hundred percent sure of yourself and everything that you did, and you had the booming power of some long forgotten god coursing through your veins. It was amazing. You could fly when Iphy was around.

"Your eyes would have been huge, too, if you had seen yourself," I shot back with a smile of my own, confidence spurring me on. He laughed, and his laughter took hold of all of us, dragging our own laughter up out of our hearts to join his.

Now that the ice had been broken and we had found common enough ground to stand on without toppling over, we all sat around the fire, like it was a big campout, with Jax telling us how once he'd gotten a few bagels and a loaf of rye bread from Mr. Smithy, he had traveled to Korvid's house and slipped unnoticed into the woods. It hadn't taken him nearly as long to find Iphy, mostly because he just went in one direction; he didn't follow every false trail that he laid his eyes on, looking for an invisible presence that wasn't, and never had been, lurking there. At first, Iphy had been just as confrontational with Jax as he had been with us, but the orphan had easily pacified him with offers of bagels roasted over the fire. Talking about food suddenly made my hunger a tangible thing, a presence that was reaching out of the darkness behind us to grab at my torso and twist it. I slid my backpack off my shoulder asking, "Speaking of food, who wants what?" as I opened the zipper and turned the bag upside down, letting the contents spill out onto the ground in front of me. The audible gasp from Iphy gave me a satisfied smile. Already I was thinking of him as a great friend, one I'd gratefully pilfer food from the pantry for.

"You're not a girl, you're a god!" he cried as he grabbed a candy bar. He stared at the chocolate for half a second before taking a huge bite.

I laughed as I opened up the package of beef jerky. "Glad you like."

"Like?" Iphy snorted. "More like love! These are my favorite. My brother and I—" And suddenly he stopped talking. There was no slowing down of his words, no easy coasting into this silence; it was sudden and absolute.

For a few seconds the quiet was suffocating, but then Jax seamlessly brought us back into the world of conversation by reaching for one of the bottles of soda. "Can I have one, Eraliss?"

I looked down and realized that I had only brought four bottles. I nodded to Jax and tossed one to Iphy, who was staring at the soda as though it was the Holy Grail itself. "Go ahead; I'll just have a few sips from Calm's." I looked over at her; she had been silent this entire time, staring into the reddish orange glow of the fire as if she'd come to see it—not Iphy. "Is that okay, Calm?" I gave her shoulder a prod in hopes of bringing her back into our world.

She nodded distractedly, her eyes never leaving the flames. They didn't even budge when Iphy leaned forward, as though to see her more clearly.

He smiled, looking shrewd and wise, like he'd seen this sort of thing a million times before. "You don't talk much, do you?" Calm answered him with a shake of her head and nothing else. "Words are no good unless someone gets a chance to hear them." He leaned back, stretching his arms out over his head. "Some famous author said that; or maybe I made it up." He shrugged; trivial things like that never seemed to matter much to Iphy, even back then. And, truthfully, it didn't matter much to us either. He was already sacred and above ridicule or questioning.

Calm raised her head and looked at him, her large hazel eyes suddenly grabbing Iphy's and holding him there. She didn't say anything, but he squirmed under her unwavering gaze, as though she was arguing with him in the silence.

"But, whatever; they're just words," he mumbled, still unable to look away from her strange hold, though obviously wanting to.

Calm continued to look at him for a few more long seconds. "Words are the most important thing; they're all we have to judge each other on, and we have to make sure we say the right things."

"Not necessarily," Korvid said; I couldn't tell if he really meant it, or if he was just trying to get Calm's attention off of Iphy. "You can always apologize for the things you say."

"No, you can't." Calm looked back at the fire, her eyes reflecting the light. "You can apologize for your actions, because they're from your brain, and your brain makes mistakes. But you can't apologize for your words; words come from the heart, and the heart can never lie."

A moment of silence passed amongst us; no one seemed sure of what to say next. Then Iphy grinned. "I like her; she's a smart one."

Calm smiled; I couldn't tell if the color on her cheeks was from the fire or from Iphy's words.

And then we were talking, about everything, about nothing. We talked about what was happening out in the world, what was going on in school. We talked about odd dreams we'd had, strange things we'd found while digging in the ground. We talked about movies, about games, about birds we'd seen in the sky, and animals we'd seen in the woods. We talked about flying, about monsters that had once hidden under our beds when we were younger; about the many places in our town that we had explored. We talked about everything except our families; it was a subject that was never breached. We talked for hours, the moon rising and peering at us through the skeletal fingers of the trees. I glanced at my watch and blanched at the time; the hour was late and getting later. I stood, stretching my arms until my shoulders let out a loud pop. "We should get going."

Calm nodded, glancing up at the moon. She hesitated for a few seconds, straddling the fence between going home through the black woodlands or staying beside the warm glow of the fire, surrounded by friends. She eventually stood, dusting off debris from the forest that doggedly clung to her.

I looked down at Korvid, the last of our group who had to trek the forest to return home; he showed no signs of moving an inch from where he sat. I prodded his back with my toe. "You coming?"

The question hung in the air, unanswered for several seconds. A look came across his face, and his feet stirred, and for a moment I thought he was going to stand, but his stirring stopped and he shook his head. "Nah; I'll chill out here for a while longer."

Calm and I shared a look, brief and fleeting; neither of us moved, instead looking at Korvid in hopes of him changing his mind. It wasn't that we needed him to lead us back—we had Calm's father's floodlight after all—but rather, we were worried about him staying. He looked back at us over his shoulder, all grins and confidence; I could already see Iphy rubbing off on him. "Don't worry, I'll get home before my dad—he'll never know."

It wasn't perfect, but it would have to do for now. I nodded, Calm and I said our goodbyes once more— ending with promises to visit again tomorrow—and then we plunged into the darkness. One click later, the woods were filled with a deep, white light that made getting home a breeze. Calm and I didn't talk as we made our way home; our words had been stolen by the fire, leaving us without voices as we walked through the night. We doused the light as we got near my backyard, the empty expanse of moon drenched grass easy to see through the sparse trees at the tree line. We stood on the border of two worlds—the world of houses and parents and school, and the world of fire and darkness and freedom. Far away, on the other side of town, a lonely sound carried faintly.

"What time tomorrow?" Calm asked, looking past my house to the dark smear that was her own across the cul-de-sac.

"I don't know; early if you can manage."

"I should be able to." Again we hesitated, neither of us wanting to move past the trees and re-enter the world of rules, school and life as we knew it. Not when we had been shown a life of freedom, firelight and a wonderful exciting unknown.

"Good night, Eraliss." Calm darted quickly across the yard, leaving a dark trail in the dew, and then she crossed the cul-de-sac, and I lost sight of her in the gloom.

I waited a few more minutes, looking up at my window, wondering if I could ever go back to where I'd been before. I'd only been gone a few hours—and truthfully not much more than walking and talking had happened—but I felt like a different person: a smarter, wiser person. Worldlier than I had been that afternoon, freer than I'd ever felt before. Maybe it was meeting Iphy, knowing that he had a freedom that I couldn't even begin to imagine; maybe it was Korvid not wanting to leave and being bolder then I could be; maybe it was Jax, with those eyes that had shone bright and amber in the firelight—eyes that I could not fathom then and still cannot fathom even now.

I stood on the edge of my lawn for a minute, or an hour, I didn't know and I didn't care. The constant ticking of my watch seemed to bring me haltingly back to reality; I moved back to the trellis, where my mother's purple flowers clung to the whitewashed wood for all they were worth, and I climbed upwards, maneuvering easily into my bedroom. I grabbed my doorknob, turning it ever so slowly so it couldn't make a lot of noise, and I crept downstairs to complete the ruse I'd started that afternoon.

Sitting out on our small dining room table was a plate of now cold meatloaf, surrounded by green beans and mashed potatoes. The entire plate was covered in plastic wrap, as though my mother was trying to keep the ten plagues of Egypt out. I tried a bite of the mashed potatoes, but they tasted like chalk. I didn't bother with the rest of the meal; I scooped it off the plate onto the plastic wrap and threw the whole bundle in the trashcan. I moved some of the trash around to cover up the untouched dinner, hoping my mother wouldn't notice it later. I ran the plate under some water and hastily put it in the sink. I took the stairs two at a time, a prickly sensation making itself known on the nape of my neck; I was worried my mother would step out of her dark room any second and ground me for another few weeks.

My fear was unjustified; my mother didn't emerge to ground me, and I made it to my room without incident. Once there, I closed the door and flopped down onto my bed, sudden exhaustion creeping through me; it was all I could do to kick my shoes off before I crawled under the covers.

I reached for my bedside lamp—one that I usually left on to combat the darkness that I was still so childishly afraid of—but this time I didn't. Instead, I let my hand fall and hang over the edge of my bed; I wasn't scared of the dark that night. I didn't believe that some drooling Hell Beast was going to crawl out from under my bed. When I thought about the absurd possibility, I just remembered Iphy's booming laughter; it scared away my monsters, leaving me free to sleep.

From the journal of Calm Sheldon

After that first night, it became a regular thing for us to spend every spare minute that we could with Iphy. There was something so distractingly charming about him and the little niche that he had carved out in the forest. Not to say that he didn't have any bad habits; he would spit great goobers of things off to one side; he often interrupted when we were talking—so sure was he that what he had to say was more important; and he would make it a point to swear when we were all together, as if it made him cooler. He had worse habits, but we didn't know them until later.

We'd always bring food whenever we could, and soon Iphy had a cache of crackers, cookies, candy bars, soda bottles, beef jerky and anything else we could get our hands on. We went to Iphy's place everyday—soon we all started calling it Our Place. We spent more time there with Iphy than we did at home. Jax had even taken to staying with Iphy, going back into town in the morning for the bagels and bread from Mr. Smithy and checking his usual haunts for anything of interest before going back to the woods to spend the day exploring the surrounding woodland where he and Iphy talked the hours away.

Today we couldn't have gotten away with it, trekking through the woods on our own for God knows how long; parents these days are so much stricter with their children. But, back then, in that town, with our parents, we could easily get away with it. Korvid's father worked nights, and sometimes days, so Korvid could spend hours at night with Iphy and Jax, staying up until the wee hours, then go home before his dad even got off work, and his father was none the wiser. Eraliss had the most trouble, I think; she often had to sneak out, but she was good at that. Her mother was unemployed back then, always out and about looking for work or drowning away her problems with soap operas and daytime talk show hosts; her father was out of the picture—had been since I had known her. Eraliss always mentioned that if her mother ever caught her she'd be grounded until she started collecting her retirement, but she luckily never got caught. As for me, I had turned invisible at my house, so I could move wherever I liked; my parents never seemed to speak to me, but then again they never spoke to each other either. Ours was a house of silence and fog and all the things that you can never forget, no matter how much you want to. I guess it rubbed off on me; I'll never forget that first conversation I had with Iphy.

Every night, I always tried to speak up more, and every time that I did, he would beam at me. It's funny to me now, how much we all wanted to impress Iphy; we thought he was so exotic, so far away from our own dull lives, and we would do anything for his favor. Back then, we didn't know that he was doing the same thing. We spent every night with Iphy for three weeks—it wasn't until the middle of November that something came along to change what was rapidly becoming our routine.

It was a Saturday, surprisingly dry. The last week or so had been nothing but rain: some downpours, some drizzle, but water, nonetheless. We were in Eraliss' backyard, preparing our bags and getting ready to head back to Our Place. The ground wasn't really ground anymore, but rather a thick slopping of mud that grabbed at the soles of our shoes and tried to keep us from moving. Korvid was struggling to put a big book of animal tracks in his backpack without letting the bag touch the muck at our feet, Eraliss was sampling a cookie from the batch she had made earlier that morning, and I was looking down, watching as a worm snaked its way through the dense growth of grass.

"You ready?" Eraliss asked.

"Almost," Korvid said through a mouthful of backpack. He somehow managed, and with a flick of his hand his bag was hanging from its natural place on his shoulders and he grinned. "Good to go."

"Go where?" It was a voice that I vaguely recognized, but certainly didn't expect to hear, especially not on a Saturday.

We all turned, varying degrees of confusion on our faces, and we saw Eddie McCloy standing a few feet from us. Eddie was a kid from school, and not one who we knew very well. We certainly didn't know why he was standing in Eraliss' backyard.

"W-where did you come from?" Eraliss asked.

Eddie looked a bit taken aback. "From my house."

"What?" She looked over at me her eyes asking for help. "Where the heck do you live?"

"Over there." Eddie gestured behind him, past the abandoned house, towards the largest house on the cul-de-sac; a dark trail led through the grass, marking his progress through the dew. It must have been a simple matter for him to cross behind the abandoned house and walk right up to us; none of the houses in our neighborhood had fences—we were allowed to roam and wander as we saw fit, provided that we didn't trample anyone's flowers. It was an odd freedom, one that I don't see anymore as I look around at the neighborhoods I pass through. I still don't know if it was good or bad for us to be so free.

The house Eddie pointed to was the biggest house on our street, but we knew nothing about the people who lived there. I'd seen older boys playing basketball in the driveway on occasion, and I'd seen several large, expensive-looking cars come and go, replaced every other year by newer ones, but I had no idea that Eddie McCloy lived there. I could tell from the look on Eraliss' face that she hadn't known either.

"Who is this kid?" Korvid asked, looking down at the newly arrived.

"He's in our class," Eraliss said, "and apparently he's our neighbor. How long have you lived here, Eddie?"

His confusion mirrored our own. "I've always lived there."

This was startling news to us. "Why do we never see you?" I asked.

"Usually I'm upstairs, or out in the shed. Sometimes I go out to the woods…" He was obviously uncomfortable talking so much about himself because he quickly changed the subject. "So, where have you guys been going?"

Instantly Korvid stiffened a bit, squaring his shoulders. "What do you mean?"

Eraliss followed suit, looking around us as if to catch spies beyond the hedge. "Yeah, what are you talking about?"

Eddie gave the both of them a pouty look. "Don't play dumb. You guys have been going into the woods every day for weeks. What's out there?"

"Nothing!" Eraliss replied, probably a bit too quickly.

"As if," Eddie scoffed. "You have to have something out there; if you won't tell me, then I'll just follow you. Make it easy for all of us and just tell me what you're hiding out there."

"We're not hiding anything," Korvid said, which was true enough. We weren't actively hiding Iphy; he was doing that on his own.

Eddie still looked dubious so I spoke up. "There's a boy living out in those woods; he's our friend, and we like to keep him company and bring him food when we can."

There was a long moment of silence. We all waited for Eddie to say something, to laugh at us, to freak out, but he didn't. Instead, he got a thoughtful look on his face, "We just got a bunch of doughnuts; think he'd want any?"

Before Eraliss or Korvid could say anything, I nodded. "I bet he'd love some; we all would."

Eddie got an I-thought-so look on his face. "I'll go grab a bunch; be right back!" And he turned and raced back to his house, his short squat frame running with a new sense of urgency. We waited for a few minutes and soon Eddie came running back, a large rectangle box under his arm.

"There's a bunch: some glazed, some bear claws, a cream filled—I don't know the rest." His round face was red, his breath coming in small gulps.

Korvid grinned. "That's great, thanks, Eddie." He started towards the woods. "We don't keep the place marked, but there are a few landmarks you can't miss."

Eddie followed on his heels, and Eraliss went after; I brought up the rear.

Eddie McCloy wasn't like most other kids his age. He didn't find solace in friends (until Iphy and the rest of us), but rather, he liked to share his company with dead things. He was the middle child of six, and his parents owned a bookstore on 7th Avenue, so there was a deep disconnection. Eddie was twelve and he had three older brothers, a younger brother and a younger sister. His oldest brother, Carl, was away at college, playing football and getting evaluated by the professional recruiters; his second-oldest brother, Richard, was just starting school at Harvard on a full ride scholarship; his third-oldest brother, Dan, was a senior in high school who had the looks and the talent to make it as an actor; his two younger siblings, Travis and Sherry, were seven-year-old twin prodigies who were already reading college level books that even Dan had trouble with. Eddie was in the middle, not a bad student by far, but not exceptionally good at anything that he did. Except for his bones.

Even as a small child, Eddie had a fascination for bones, and as soon as he was big enough to go into the woods without supervision, he began looking for dead animals. He'd bring along a pair of bright yellow rubber gloves, and a big five gallon bucket, and he'd pick up any small critter that he could find in the hours that he scoured the ground. He'd then take the bucket full of corpses to the long-abandoned shed that his father had built but then forgotten about as his bookstore took flight. Eddie had transformed it into the perfect place for making skeletons. He'd bury the animals along the shed and wait for several months until nature had taken care of everything except the bones, which he would then start to treat.

He'd boil them in a kettle, carve off any knobs of cartilage that he found with a carving knife he kept hidden under a never used badminton set, soak them in kerosene to kill any remaining germs, scrub them with soap and water, and finally bleach them until they were a shining white.

His room was full of small mounted skeletons and the skulls of larger animals that he'd found but couldn't drag out of the woods, but that collection — probably ten skeletons and fifteen skulls — was nothing compared to the Bone Room that he had constructed in the second story of the shed. He'd found that the shed had a second floor when he was setting a half-rotted bobcat head on the roof, out of view of the house. He often put the larger animals up there so the dogs couldn't get them, but the crows could still pick away the remaining meat. Seeing a window on the side of the shed — one that he'd never seen from the inside — he investigated further and found a pull-down ladder that led to the second floor. He concealed the entrance with various stacks of boxes, but he really didn't need to: if his parents weren't at their bookstore, or gushing about their sports star, their brilliant student, their famous actor, or their tiny geniuses, then they were sleeping. No one else gave the shed a second glance, but it wouldn't be long before the Bone Room became as familiar to us as Our Place was.

I can only imagine what Iphy thought when he first saw Eddie. Here was a short, squat boy with a bright red face, buzzed ginger hair, ears that seemed to stick out too far, a chin that seemed too small, short thick fingers and muddy brown eyes standing before him and brandishing a box of doughnuts. Clothes that looked like they had been worn for years before, brandishing a mishmash of ideas and images that had nothing to do with Eddie's own likes. Like everything else he wore, Eddie's shoes were hand-me-downs, worn first by his brother Richard, and then by Dan (and several members of the High School Drama Department) before being passed down to him. As such, they were half a size too big and they looked like they were just about falling apart. Still, he treated them with care, revering that he even had shoes, and that they hadn't just crumbled off his feet. His shoes were literally tokens of his family's disinterest in his life, and he'd only get new shoes when Dan decided that his didn't fit anymore, and bestowed upon Eddie his old pair.

"Who the heck is this?" Iphy asked Korvid. Because he and Korvid were the same age, Iphy always seemed to have a bit more of a connection with him.

"This is our neighbor, Eddie. He brought us all some doughnuts."

"He's in," Iphy said, grabbing a bear claw and eating it in three massive bites. "Oh yeah," he said through his last mouthful. "He's definitely in."

Jax frowned a bit. "This isn't a club, Iphy; Eddie can hang out with us if he wants to."

"Yeah, yeah," Iphy said, brandishing a maple bar with a huge bite taken out of it. "So, Eddie, what do you do?" he asked, taking a long drag of the soda we'd brought.

Eddie tilted his head to one side. "What do you mean?"

"I mean what do you do? You know, for fun."

Eddie suddenly got shy; his eyes darted to the fire, as if the flames held the correct answer to this unexpected test. "Nothing, really. I tool around in my shed and go exploring in the woods mostly."

"Your shed? Sounds like a real blast," Iphy said with an exaggerated eye roll. "What's so cool about your shed anyway? Is it some kind of super cool hangout place your folks don't know about?"

I could see the swell of confidence that came over Eddie at the thought of impressing Iphy; he was always trying to do that, impress the older boys. He was like the little brother of the group, always looking for some kind of acceptance that he never got at home. "Actually, it is; it's my Bone Room."

This got everyone's attention. "What the heck's a Bone Room?" Eraliss asked, leaning forward on her boulder.

Self-consciousness was beginning to creep back on Eddie's face. "It's... it's where I keep my skeletons. That's why I wanted to follow you guys today. I thought you'd found some kind of giant dead animal, like a moose or a bear and I wanted to see if I could get its bones," he babbled, the rush of words leaving his mouth in a flood.

"Wait, you collect bones?" Korvid asked, his eyes shining with morbid curiosity.

Eddie gave a short, miserable nod, red painting his already flushed complexion.

"And you keep them in a Bone Room in your parents' shed?" Jax asked, his voice placid and neutral.

Another brief nod with still more red.

"That's so effing cool!" Iphy yelled, leaping off his boulder. "Where's your shed? I wanna see them!"

Eddie blinked his muddy eyes. "R-really?"

Iphy nodded. "Hell yeah! It sounds like a blast."

Eddie's eyes roamed around everyone else — stopping on each of us for a fleeting second — but we were all interested. After seeing our interest, he seemed to gain a bit more confidence. "Okay, it's this way."

With a wave of his hand, he started the procession: Iphy walked next to him, talking excitedly about what kind of bones Eddie had; Eraliss came next, excited despite her early indifference of Eddie; I walked next to Eraliss, Korvid behind us, and Jax took up the rear. It was a longer walk through the woods than usual, mostly because we were moving parallel to the tree line, heading for the woods behind Eddie's house. He grew more and more confident every step we took. Soon, he was in woodland that he easily recognized from his corpse hunting days; he led us through a small batch of large oak trees, and we were in his spacious backyard. And in the middle of the backyard loomed our destination.

The shed was huge, larger than any shed I had seen, and I was more tempted to call it a workroom than a shed. It was two stories, easily fifteen by twenty feet, and it had electricity, as proven when Eddie hit the light switch and two bulbs flickered into life, bathing the large shed in warm light.

"Pardon the mess," Eddie said as he made his way around jugs of kerosene, buckets of dirty water, giant moving boxes labeled with the names of various holidays, a riding lawn mower that was covered in several years' worth of dust and cobwebs, and a massive spider who sat on a beautiful web that Eraliss blundered into. She screamed bloody murder, flailing her arms around her head, effectively smacking Korvid in the jaw, and stirring up clouds of dust. Later, she would claim that the beast was the size of a tarantula, but I'm pretty sure it was just a really big orb-weaver spider.

"Careful," Eddie said as he and Iphy moved aside some boxes, exposing the drop down ladder. He bent down and scooped up the scurrying spider, who settled in his palm like it had done the action many times. "You'll scare Theodore."

"That thing has a name?" Eraliss cried; she'd been afraid of spiders for as long as I'd known her.

"Yeah," Eddie said, jumping up and grabbing the twine that released the ladder with his free hand. "He's great; sometimes I feed him little bugs that I find in here."

Eraliss shivered. "That's so gross... I've still got the heebie jeebies."

Personally, I thought Theodore was a beautiful spider. He wasn't the usual kind of garden spider that I would see living between my mother's flowers. Theodore was a deep golden orange with a splotchy white back and little flecks of green. His legs were long and they gently moved him about Eddie's hand like he was drifting lazily on water. "I think he's very pretty," I told Eddie as he gently set Theodore down on an old crate in the corner of the shed.

"He's been my friend for almost a year and half."

"I didn't think spiders lived that long," Korvid mused.

"If they have a warm, safe place for the winter, they usually live longer than they would normally," said Eddie with a fond smile as the spider scurried up into a corner of the ceiling.

Further talk of Theodore was suspended as Iphy's voice came down from the second story; he'd gone ahead of us, eager to see what there was to be seen. "Holy shit! You guys gotta see this!"

At Iphy's command, we all made a mad scramble up the ladder and entered a world wholly different than the one we had just left. This room was exceptionally bright; a wide picture window on one end filled the space with dazzling light. That same light then sparkled off all the bones in the room. And there were a lot of bones. Close to twenty completed skeletons and a great number of skulls, were all arranged on shelves made of wood planks and cinder blocks, and were all meticulously put together with thin jewelry wire and tiny globs of super glue. There were a great number of rodents, but even some larger ones: wildcats and even a fox and a coyote.

Each skeleton and every skull was labeled with a little note card, and on the walls of the room there were several posters of bones, and even a map of our town and the woods behind our houses. Gray lines marked the roads and a dashed outline marked the city limits, cutting through the green of the forest and even nipping the thick black train tracks. Here and there were hand scribbled notes, marking the kinds of skeletons, and when he'd found them.

"This is incredible," Eraliss said, gaping at the spectacle of gleaming white around her.

Again we could see the pride swelling up in Eddie's face; it seemed he never got this kind of attention at his house. "Thanks. It's not much right now, but it'll be great one day. I'll have all kinds of skeletons, even dinosaurs."

"How'd you get them so... perfect?" Eraliss asked, hefting a large bobcat skull and examining the teeth.

"It's easy. It takes a while, but it's not exactly hard." He explained the process of cleaning and bleaching the bones. When he was done, Iphy gave a low whistle.

"So how long did all of this take you?"

"A few years," Eddie mumbled.

Iphy shook his head, either in disbelief or amazement. "Is this all you've done? I mean, don't you have any friends?"

The self-conscious look came over Eddie's face again and he busied himself with pretending to study a squirrel skull. "Well, there's Theo, but beyond him...not really."

"No way," Eraliss said with a shake of her head.

"Yeah, we're your friends now," Jax said, peering into the eye sockets of the fox.

Iphy jumped in, eager to take charge. "That's right, Eddie. You're one of us now."

He said it so casually that it took the rest of us by surprise; we certainly didn't deny the statement, we were just surprised at the suddenness.

"Yeah," Korvid nodded of his head. "We're your friends, Eddie, and don't let anyone tell you otherwise."

Eddie's round little face was as red as a tomato, but he nodded his head vigorously. "I think this calls for a celebration! Wait right here." Quick as Thought, he had left the Bone Room, returning a few minutes later with chips, soda, a box of chocolates, and a bag of kettle corn. We sat up there, amidst the dead, enjoying the food, laughing, talking, and having a good time. As per usual, we didn't really talk about each other, but I think we all knew that we didn't have to. We spent the entire afternoon up in the Bone Room; it would soon become another sacred place for us to escape our lives, and over the year we'd add several skeletons to Eddie's growing collection.

With the addition of Eddie, our group was complete. We all shared something special; we wouldn't figure out what it was until later, but it all started with shadows in the night, and it ended with kettle corn in the Bone Room. The six of us had found our place in the world; I can't speak for the others, but I will always treasure the friends I had that year, the wonderful places that we explored (both real and imaginary), the seasons and their transitory nature, and the pure awe of a life lived with gods.

C.S.

WINTER

Like it always did, winter came hard and fast to our town. For only a week or two, the leaves rained down on the streets, lawns and buildings, creating storms of red, orange and yellow that looked like flurries of flat fire. Then, the trees were bare, the temperature dropped and Jack Frost visited our lawns in the early morning hours. Thanksgiving was cold that year and it was spent first with family. Then—when tryptophan and overeating took its toll—we all snuck out after midnight, bringing backpacks full of leftovers that wouldn't be missed, and we ate again with Iphy and Jax and talked about the upcoming winter.

This year looked like it was going to be a bad one; sometimes our winters were mild—we wouldn't even see snow until the end of January—but sometimes the winters could be brutal. It was mid December when the first snowstorm struck. We had been keeping careful tabs on Iphy and Jax, giving them old jackets and blankets, sweaters and big puffy overcoats we had stolen from the back of our parents' closets, sleeping bags that we hadn't used in months, or even years. Jax had told Iphy of the chill that often gripped our town during winter, and they had stockpiled a great mass of firewood accordingly. They insisted that they would be fine.

The snow storm buried them. It came without warning, blanketing the world in white. When I woke up and glanced out my window, looking back into the woods that I had grown to love, and saw nothing but dazzling white I panicked. I rushed downstairs, wrapping a black and blue striped scarf around my neck and darting into my denim jacket. I slipped my shoes on; they didn't have laces. They weren't Velcro (which I always played with in class, much to Mr. Neil's distaste), they were just slip-ons. I hated laces; I didn't have time for them. I was always going way too quick to have time to worry about tying and untying things. Even in the snow, I wore my slip-ons instead of boots so I wouldn't waste time.

"Whoa, whoa, whoa," my Mother said from the couch. The morning news was squawking on the television, a bowl of oatmeal sat in her lap and the newspaper was spread out around her. "Where are you off to in such a rush? Have you taken a look outside? School's closed—probably all week, they said."

I startled at the doorway; in my sudden panic I had completely forgotten about school and my need to attend it. "O-oh," I said. "Cool, well, since I'm already all done up, I'm gonna go out and play in the snow."

My Mother gave me a strange look. "You haven't played in the snow for years" she pointed out.

"Sudden change of heart," I called as I bolted out the door, hoping she wouldn't question my sudden lapse back into childhood fancies.

I could see Calm crossing the cul-de-sac at a trot, making a beeline for my house. Korvid was just now stumbling out of his house, half dressed in a tee shirt, scarf, snow pants, sneakers, and a dorky hand-knitted hat his father had gotten him a few years ago from the Saturday market. I didn't bother to wait for them; I turned on my heel and started around the back of my house, but I stopped at Calm's sudden yell.

"Eraliss, wait!" She stood on the sidewalk in front of my house, decked out in green and looking incredibly small in her puffy coat.

"Yeah," Korvid said, racing up to us. "We can't go to Our Place the usual way."

"Why not? It's the fastest." As soon as I asked, I knew the answer; it was the snow itself. Already I could see Calm's footprints crossing the road, Korvid's running across the lawn, and mine leading back to my front porch. We were already paranoid about our parents finding out about Iphy; we didn't need to leave them a trail to his doorstep. And even if our parents were too wrapped up in their own lives, other adults would notice. Most probably wouldn't care, but what if they did? Or what if a kid saw? Then Johnny Everykid would wander in the woods, find Iphy, and blab about it to his parents during dinner. Now, Mr. and Mrs. Everykid are good citizens so they would call Social Services and both Iphy and Jax would get hauled off to some foster home somewhere. It was a risk we couldn't take.

"We'll go through the orchard," Korvid said. "Kids are always messing around there; no one will notice."

We all agreed that it was the best course of action, and a quick glance over towards Eddie's house showed that he must have had the same idea; a trail of footprints lead from his door down the street. We took off at a run, ignoring the various adult comments of "Slow down" or "Watch out for ice".

The orchard was only a few blocks away, sitting on land that belonged to a man named Mr. Wisener. Apparently, many years ago, Mr. Wisener had a farm there, where he grew apple trees, had a barn filled with animals, and had a very good life. However, his wife had died some ten years before, and slowly the place fell into disarray. He sold the animals one by one and one year a great fire burned the barn almost completely to the ground. He never bothered to replace it. The orchard was the only thing that remained of Mr. Wisener's farm — that and his small white farmhouse at the corner of his property. The vegetable field had long since died, grass and weeds quickly conquering it. For years kids used it as a baseball or kickball field; running a trail in the grass, and putting out rocks and cinder blocks to serve as bases.

By the time we got to the orchard, kids were already playing in the vegetable-turned-kickball field; we paid them no mind and hardly stopped to catch our breath before plunging into the trees of the orchard. Kids normally didn't hang out in the orchard because it always had a sickly sweet smell, from mushy, rotten apples that littered the ground and stuck to shoes like a natural paste.

We zigzagged through the trees, Korvid almost slipping in the slushy rotten apple mess at our feet in our hurry to get to the denser tree line of the woods. Once we were in the quiet of the forest, we finally stopped; Calm and I sat on a fallen log while Korvid planted his hands on his knees, all of us gulping in great quantities of air and trying to calm our racing hearts.

It still amazes me how those woods could swallow up noise. We knew that fifteen or so kids were out there in that field — laughing, making snowmen, having snowball fights — but all we could hear was the occasional faint echo of their shouts and laughter. Those woods could have hidden anything that they wanted to and despite all the time that we spent there we still felt like strangers invading land that didn't want us.

After a minute or two of heavy breathing being the only noise, Korvid straightened. "Let's go."

Neither Calm nor I argued — we were just as anxious to check up on Iphy and Jax as Korvid was. We followed the tree line, keeping the backsides of the houses in sight through the trees as we moved as fast as we dared. It took us far longer to get back to my backyard than it had taken us to get to the orchard, but racing along sidewalk and running through snow-covered woodland are two very different things. Calm tripped over a hidden tree root, Korvid slid over slush and wet leaves, and I nearly tumbled into a well-concealed ditch.

The more we moved through the woods, the more it seemed that the woods were mocking us, trying their hardest to keep us from seeing our friends. The trees, with their massive trunks, huddled closer and closer together, making it harder and harder to see the houses that lay beyond their reach. The naked tree branches rattled together, laughing in the odd, choppy way that all trees do, and the precious few leaves that hadn't fallen with autumn clung to their branches and rattled about pitifully, calling out in vain to be spared from winter's wrath. The symphony of woodland sounds continued loudly around us, before dropping into unexpected silence. Then, the howling came.

It was a wail that came from deep in the woods, starting softly, but then rising into a fever pitch, until we were sure that the whole world could hear this horrendous screaming. It sounded like nothing we had ever heard before—like a frenzied woman howling in rage and anguish. The sound wrapped tightly around us, chilling us more than winter, or even the far away thought of Death, ever could. We were frozen in fear, our eyes wide and wild, darting around inside our unblinking eyelids as we tried to fathom what the noise could possibly be, and where on earth it was coming from. After what seemed like hours the wail died down slowly, until soon we just heard the wind's low whistle and the trees' mocking laughter.

We didn't move; our feet had been rooted to the spot by the Wailing Woman and her cries. Korvid finally turned his head back to us. "What on earth was that?" he whispered; the silence left by the howl made it sound like a shout.

"I don't know," Calm squeaked

"It was a ghost." I was surprised by the crack in my own voice. I had long thought myself past the fear of ghosts and goblins thanks to Iphy.

Korvid looked at me like I was crazy. "What?"

I felt myself nod. "Yeah, the ghost of a woman who was murdered out here."

"Don't be silly," Calm's voice was muffled a bit now thanks to her scarf, which she had hunkered down into as if that would shield her from the Wailing Woman. "It was just the wind."

"I've never heard wind that sounded like that." I looked squarely at Korvid. "Have you?"

He didn't answer; instead, he started moving forward. "Let's keep going. Iphy and Jax are still waiting for us."

I was about to protest — because there was no way that what we heard was just wind — but we heard it again. The lady screamed a second time; louder, angrier if it were possible, until the sound filled the entire world and we all screamed like we were three-year-olds scared of Halloween. We ran heedless of the snow, the trees, and the twisted roots that lay hidden waiting to trip us and send us flying. We ran until the sound died away, and Korvid stumbled blindly into a ravine, dropping head over heels to tumble down and rest in the mixture of snow, moss and dead leaves at the bottom. Calm and I slid down most of the way; I tripped near the bottom and landed sprawled out on my face, and Calm's feet went too far out in front of her and she fell on her butt. We stayed down there, silent, unmoving, until Korvid finally pushed his aching body up from the ground.

His snow pants had saved his legs, but his shoes were soaked through and they made a squishy sound when he stood. His shirt was no better, soaked clean through and sticking to his chest and arms like tape. Calm was fine, her snow pants and her boots saved her, but I wasn't quite so lucky: my denim jacket was soaked, as were my jeans, and when the wind whistled down into the ravine, Korvid and I shivered.

Wordlessly, Korvid began climbing up the other side, which was hard enough without the snow to make the path slick. Calm and I followed, cold and silent in the quiet wake of the Wailing Woman's call. We slipped back down only twice, and the last time was only a few feet, so it didn't even really count. Then we were on the other side of the ravine, and I felt a weight lift off my shoulders. Somehow I knew that the Wailing Woman couldn't get us over here; the ravine marked the edge of her territory.

"Look," Calm said, pointing through the trees. We could see the edges of houses once again. The farther we walked, the more the trees thinned, letting us see more and more of the civilization that was so close. When we came up on the back of Calm's house, we felt a wave of relief. This ground was familiar to us and the trees here were different. Not exactly friendly; it was more that we were a familiar factor in their world and they tolerated our presence. Soon, we heard the sounds of quiet talking, and we knew we had finally left the Wailing Woman behind.

Extracted from an e-mail addressed to Eraliss Cofler from Korvid Fairington, dated ██████████.

Hey, E.

It's a real shame that you couldn't get a hold of him—get his perspective on things—though I can see why he wouldn't answer. When you brought this whole mess back up, it was like a punch to the gut: I couldn't understand why you wanted to go through this again. He's probably still hurting after everything that happened; it's natural that he wouldn't want to think about it.

It's funny that you should bring up the Wailing Woman; I was thinking about her just the other week. I was having Father-Daughter day with Trevor and I told her that the Wailing Woman would swoop down and steal her away if she didn't mind her father. God, I'm such a bad dad. :)

The first day we heard her—that was the day the snow hit, right? Or was it the ice? Lord knows my memory for dates has always been sporadic. No, it must have been the snow; the ice didn't come until later. But, back on topic, of course I remember her; she scared the crap out of me back then. Even now she still does. I think it was all the stories you wrote about her: all that violence, murder, and blood... You were a very morbid child come to think of it. I'll blame that on your dad.

Anyway, you asked me about the night we spent at my house.

We left the ravine behind us, and finally came upon the woods around our houses; after that it wasn't far to Our Place. Eddie was there, looking almost like a ball, he was so bundled up. Iphy and Jax both had scarves, hats, mittens, and jackets (presents from the back of our closets), and all were huddled around an almost nonexistent fire.

"Are you guys okay?" you asked.

"Fine and dandy," Iphy said with his grin.

Jax, however, snorted. "If you mean soaking wet, freezing, and unable to make a fire."

"Why can't you make a fire?" Calm asked.

Eddie hefted a small log; it was covered in snow and dripping water. "These got drenched in the snow last night."

"Nice going," I said, more angry at the snow than anything else. "All that work wasted."

"It's not totally wasted," Iphy pointed out. "We just have to dry it out a bit before the fire catches."

"That could take forever," Eddie muttered, holding out a chunk of firewood over the tiny fire, watching as trails of vapor rose from the drying wood.

"We don't really have a choice," Jax said, drying his own piece of firewood.

"We might have a problem anyway, guys," you said, sitting in front of the fire, your own piece of firewood in hand. "My mom said that the schools could be closed for a week."

"That's not a problem," I scoffed. "That's a Godsend."

"No it's not," Calm shook her head. "Why would the school be closed for more than a day or two if this was all the snow that was going to hit? The plows could clear the roads before the afternoon. Unless more snow falls tonight."

Eddie nodded, his chin disappearing into his scarf. "I heard it on the radio this morning; we could be in for a blizzard if the clouds don't change course."

Iphy made a face. "That *is* a problem," he said. He glanced over his shoulder to the little shelter he'd made with sheets of metal and a giant tree; the space beneath it certainly looked dry, but not warm, and definitely not as cozy as it had looked a few months ago in the autumn sunshine.

"You guys can stay in the Bone Room," Eddie offered, throwing his now mostly dry wood into the fire. The wood popped and sizzled, and soon caught a little blaze of its own. "You can keep Theo company; Travis and Sherry tried to catch him last night so they could dissect him." Eddie gave a little shudder, and I had a feeling it had little to do with the cold.

You were horrified. "What? Why would they do that? Don't they know Theo's special?"

Eddie shook his head. "They don't care. If it's in the name of learning something new, then it's okay. I had to move him to my room for the night while they were looking in the shed." A shadow crossed his face and he buried his chin in his scarf, as if nestling away from whatever was on his mind. "I don't think he liked the cold; it's not good for him."

"Anyway, that plan's too risky," Iphy said, bringing the conversation back to the original topic. "With you four trampling to and from the shed all day, Eddie's folks are bound to get suspicious, and if not them, then his siblings. The last thing we need are adults sniffing around and sticking their nose in other people's business."

"We could sleep at the church," Jax pointed out. "Reverend Josh Potter will let us sleep on some cots downstairs, or in the pews."

Iphy shook his head again. "That's fine for you, because he knows you're an orphan. What if he starts digging around, looking for me? Then I'll be screwed — sent back home faster than you can blink."

I still find it odd that at that point we'd known Iphy for so long, but we still didn't know why he had run away. We were silent for a moment and I could tell that everyone was looking for some kind of solution to our current crisis. I came up with the only logical solution. "What if you two stay with me tonight? It's not a permanent solution, but the weather report might be bogus."

Jax raised an eyebrow. "And if it's not?"

"Then we'll cross that road when we get to it and *if* we get to it. Tomorrow could be bright and sunny and sixty degrees. I trust Weatherman Warren about as far as I could sling a couch."

Calm looked up at the sky, looming above us through the small roof of twisted, tangled branches that couldn't keep out snow or stars. "I don't think so," she murmured.

"Well, like Korvid said, we'll burn that bridge when we get to it," Iphy said, standing with a stretch. "Let's go."

Eddie also got to his feet. "We'll have to cross through the orchard. Our backyards are covered in snow; we'd basically be leaving the adults a trail."

Iphy snorted. "That's if the adults are smart enough to follow the trail."

You shook your head. "Well if our folks aren't, there are plenty of nosy people in town. Someone's bound to find out about you and Jax if we leave them a trail."

Jax nodded with you. "We shouldn't risk it." He dropped an armful of snow over the fire, extinguishing it with a small hiss. "How far is it to the orchard?"

Eddie considered, probably trying to convert it into miles or feet. "It's not far," he started. "It's just that..." he fell silent, turning red in the face.

"What?" Iphy demanded, suddenly sure that we were keeping some important secret from him.

Eddie shook his head, and because he wasn't going to speak up, I saw the light burst in your eyes and you took the lead. "There's a ghost in the woods."

"It's not a ghost," I said, but Iphy was already hooked.

"What? Are you serious? Where?"

"Past the ravine," you said, building up a head of steam. "She was murdered, and now she haunts the woods, screaming her head off like she's being murdered again."

I sighed again. "It wasn't a ghost; it was just the wind."

Eddie shook his head. "I heard it; that didn't sound like any wind I've ever heard."

You nodded solemnly. "That's because it wasn't the wind; it was her ghost."

Iphy had already started walking. "Well, I wanna see this ghost," he proclaimed, glancing back at the rest of us with his eyebrow raised. "You sissies coming?" There was no arguing with Iphy (not back then, or at all come to think of it) so we all filed in behind him. Then you took the lead so as to show him the way, Eddie on your heels, Calm next, while Jax and I brought up the rear.

We found the ravine with no problems, and as we crossed it we could feel the oppressive chill in the air as the trees seemed to close in on us to drive us away. You and Iphy would not be deterred, and we pressed further and further into the Wailing Woman's territory. But, thankfully, she didn't repeat her performance. I could tell you were disappointed, but Iphy still believed you. He was just that kind of person.

We made it to the orchard without incident, and once Iphy saw the great mass of apple trees just ripe for climbing, he challenged Jax to a tree climbing race. Eddie tried to join in, but he fell out of the tree from the second branch and he thought better of trying to make it to the top. We all laughed and cheered them both on, but the race was over almost as quickly as it started: Jax was far nimbler than Iphy ever could be. Jax was at the top of the tree before Iphy was even halfway up.

Jax was a good sport about the whole thing, cheering Iphy on, telling him which branches to grab, and which ones were still slick with snow. With Jax's help, Iphy made it up the rest of the tree quickly. The two of them stood up there, sharing a branch and looking out at the world. You hollered up at the two of them to come down, but they ignored you with a wave of their hands.

"Leave them be," Calm said in her small voice, her head tilted back, gazing up at the two of them.

"They're gonna get hurt," you huffed, still motioning for them to come back down to earth.

"No, they won't," Calm said, her eyes never leaving the two of them up in that tree. "The world doesn't want to hurt them; they are immune to the darkness that rages through the rest of us. They're special; the world would rather crumble into a thousand pieces than hurt them. Even the Wailing Woman shied away from them, and the woods let them live within their borders. They'll be fine; they've had enough pain." She said it with such conviction; like she had heard these very words from the core of the earth itself. I wanted to believe her. We all wanted to believe her.

You looked back up at them, this time with awe in your eyes, like you were seeing gods in the bodies of boys. Eddie looked up at them, seeing everything that he had ever wanted to be, seeing the very embodiment of freedom and happiness. I looked up at them, and in that instant, when all of our eyes were on them, the heavy clouds parted just a bit, letting a single beam of sunlight break free of the cloud cover and bathe those two in its warm glow. It was only for an instant, but in that instant everything in my mind changed.

They were no longer just homeless boys living in the woods to be helped and (dare I admit?) even pitied. Up in that tree, with that briefest instant of light, they looked regal; noble; yes, even godly. I knew then that they were not just homeless boys living behind our houses; they were something far greater in disguise, and they understood all of the complex things that the rest of us could not possibly fathom, like life and even the deepest reaches of death. They understood why the Wailing Woman screamed, why the trees of the forest hated us so, and I suddenly knew that we were just there to entertain them, to create noise and life and action around them. And in that shining moment, I believed Calm with all of my heart.

They came down after that, Jax showing Iphy the easiest way down. When they had rejoined the rest of us on the ground, Jax was all smiles and good cheer; to him, the tiny beam of sun, however small and short, was proof that the winter wouldn't be nearly as bad as the weatherman had predicted. It was strange—even though Jax was all smiles, there was something about Iphy. He smiled, but there was something hidden behind his eyes, a darkness that didn't belong there.

I dismissed it as a trick of faulty light, a shadow of a passing cloud. There was no way it could have been anger.

Iphy and Jax were immortal deities of freedom and happiness and nothing could ever darken their smiles.

You know, Eraliss, I really wish Calm had been right.

We spent the afternoon in the Bone Room; it was the best place for us to go, what with Eddie's promise of piping hot chocolate. Iphy was happy to see Theodore at his usual post in the upper corner, sitting on a beautiful web; Eddie must have deemed it safe enough to return the Bone Room's mascot to his rightful place. Our leader even went so far as to salute the large spider. When we were all settled upstairs, Eddie went and got the drinks: dark, rich cocoa, made with milk rather than water. Eddie even brought out a bag of mini marshmallows that melted and made the cocoa even creamier. For a few moments, we all sat in silence, sipping our cocoa, not talking for fear of ruining the moment. I can't speak for the others, but I just couldn't get that image out of my mind: Iphy and Jax, at the top of the tree, bathed in the momentary glow of sunlight when all the rest of the world was cold and dark. They were gods in children's bodies. They had to be.

Then, Iphy burped. Jax laughed, clapping Iphy on the back like they were brothers, and the rest of us cracked smiles. Suddenly it was okay to talk.

We talked for a few hours, telling Iphy of the winters that had gone past: the ice storm from before we were born, the big snowstorm we had when we were all still in kindergarten; the year that we didn't get any snow until March. Iphy listened to it all, (only interrupting a few times) then told us about his own winters, which seemed to be a bit more mild than ours were. He talked about how once there had been a great horned owl living through the winter in an elm tree in his front yard. Our conversation ended only when the snow began to fall.

At first it was small flakes that swirled and danced, but within the hour the flakes had evolved into big, fat things that slammed down in a flurry. We watched the evolution of the flakes until you tore your eyes away from the spectacle and stood. "I have to go now — my mom will have a coronary if I'm out in this."

Calm nodded. "Yeah, we should all be getting home." She fixed me with a look that straddled the fence between pleading and demanding. "Take care of those two."

We all stood to leave, stretching cramped joints; we said our goodbyes to Eddie and to Theodore and proceeded outside into the rapidly growing storm. Calm said her farewells and began crossing the street, while the rest of us took the sidewalk. As we passed the abandoned house between your house and Eddie's, Iphy stopped and peered at it through the storm.

"What's that?"

"It's an abandoned house," you explained.

"Can we stay there?"

"Of course not," Jax said quickly. "The roof's caved in and the whole place is falling apart."

"How did you know?" you asked.

Jax gave a small shrug, becoming uncharacteristically withdrawn. "You can see it from here."

"Even so, the bottom floor should still be fine."

"We'll check it out tomorrow," I said, "if this weather lets up a bit."

We passed your house; you gave us a final wave before we continued. Once on my front porch, I told them to keep quiet because my dad was sleeping. He'd be up and about in an hour or so, and then off to work; then we'd have free reign. We crept downstairs to my basement room, where I promptly wrote "napping" on a sticky note and taped it to my door before closing it and locking it, assuring that my dad wouldn't come blundering downstairs to find me harboring a couple of runaways. My room was a mess of blankets kicked off the bed in a night of restless sleep, piles of clothes, and stacks upon stacks of comic books, novels, and magazines. Stashed in the corner were other mementos of childhood; rollerblades, my baseball bat and a real baseball, rubber Halloween masks from years previous, and an old bag of marbles that I hadn't used since I was eight.

Iphy shivered a bit. "It's as cold down here as it is outside."

I laughed. "That's because it's the basement; hardly any heating."

"So you freeze every night?"

I threw a blanket at him. "No, I wrap up like a caterpillar in a cocoon."

"Why don't you have a room upstairs?" Jax asked, idly flipping through a travel magazine.

"Because, there's only two rooms up there; one of them is my dad's and the other one we don't use anymore."

This caught Iphy's interest; he smelled a scandal, or a ghost, or some other kind of outlandish thing that he didn't know about and suddenly desperately needed to. "Why? It haunted? Did someone die in there?"

"Yeah. My mother."

Iphy's face fell several miles, and Jax dropped the magazine in surprise. I tried to smile — to show them that it was no big deal—but it didn't work too well. Silence descended for several minutes, the ticking of my clock and our quiet breathing the only noise. Iphy's eyes drifted to the ceiling, and to the darkened, unused room somewhere above our heads. When his gaze returned to me, he looked ready to cry, or scream, or hide under the bed.

"Jesus, Korvid, I'm so sorry... I didn't mean to say that."

I thought back to the first night that we had met Iphy, and what Calm had said about words and how they came from the heart. Iphy had meant to say it; he just hadn't meant it to actually mean anything. "It's fine," I assured him with a pat on the shoulder, since my smiles didn't seem to be up to snuff.

"So, what happened?" Iphy asked, sitting on the bed with a plop. His eyes seemed to be searching mine, looking for some kind of emotion that he could not find, probably because I didn't know what to feel myself. It had been years since my mother's death, but I still hadn't come to terms with it. I still felt that one day she might walk through the door as though nothing had been wrong; she'd only been away for a while. I took a deep breath, trying to force those thoughts from my mind as I started my tale.

"She died when I was six. One day she got sick; it looked like just a regular cold, but she didn't want anyone else to get sick, so my dad slept in my room, and I slept on the couch. She was sick for a few days, and then one morning she didn't come downstairs to have breakfast like she usually did. Dad went up to check on her, and the next thing I know he's screaming and crying and telling me to call 911."

"The ambulance came and took my mom away; my dad went with them, and I just hid under the couch, waiting for everything to calm down. Dad came back from the hospital late. I asked him if Mom was coming back, and he just cried and went upstairs, to my room, where he shut the door and didn't come out. He stayed home from work for a week, and he wouldn't let me go to preschool, or even leave the house to play outside. Then, he started going back to work, taking the double night shift so he was only home to sleep, and that was that."

"I never got my room back. A few weeks after she had died, he just moved everything down to the basement, saying it would work out just fine because it was the biggest room in the house, and we moved on. He never told me what happened to her; every time that I asked, he'd get pale and go silent, moving from wherever he was into the living room where he would watch television with the volume at full blast. It wasn't until a few years ago when I finally looked it up in the newspaper archives at the library. It turns out that she had a brain aneurism in the middle of the night; she went to sleep, and she just never woke up."

By this time, Jax had joined Iphy on the bed, and he shook his head a bit. "Your dad never told you?"

"Nope. He still hasn't. I don't think he'll ever get over her."

Iphy was incredulous. "So... so what did you do? I mean, you were six! You just came down to the basement and waited for your mom to come back?"

I tried in vain to chuckle but the sound died in my throat. "Yeah, pretty much. I couldn't talk to my dad about it; he just shut his mouth and watched television.

Whenever I asked for my room back, he'd just tell me that it was his room now, and that my room was in the basement."

"What about..." Jax hesitated, obviously looking for the right words. "What about your mom's room? Have you ever seen it?"

I shook my head. "Dad keeps it locked up. I don't think he's ever been back there either; not even to get his clothes out of there. He bought a new dresser, new clothes, a new bed, even a new watch."

Iphy looked disgusted. "What a jackass." He glared up at the ceiling. "Sure he had a tough time, but what about you? You lost your mom *and* your dad." His face turned into an ugly sneer and he shook his head slowly. "Adults just don't give a damn."

I couldn't really agree. "It's not that adults don't give a damn; they just don't think that *we* do."

Further conversation was cut short as my dad started to mill about upstairs. We all kept quiet, our eyes trained upwards, listening as he shuffled from room to room and eventually left the house. There was a sputtering noise as the car started, and soon we were left in silence. I continued to stare up at my ceiling, looking for a rabbit, or some other icon that I could contribute to the childhood that I hadn't had. Finally, as the quiet became unbearable, I jerked my head towards the door.

"Shall we get something to eat?"

We spent the evening watching fuzzy cable channels that didn't come in very well, listening to soap operas in another language and feasting on popcorn and hastily-made vegetable stew. When we moved back to the basement, we talked in the darkness; I forget most of what we talked about, but it wasn't important to us anyway. We were talking just to talk at that point; we weren't comfortable enough with silence yet. Iphy talked about the abandoned house for a while, imagining out loud how wonderful it would be to explore there, and discover a place to shelter him and Jax through the winter. Jax tried to talk him out of it, but Iphy wouldn't hear of it. I told him we'd check it out in the morning but for now we had to get some sleep. So we slept, plagued by dreams and nightmares that we didn't recall the next day.

And there you go, E; the night we spent over at my place. Just let me know if you need more.

All my love,

Korvid.

~*~

Before that winter I'd never thought much about the abandoned house. As kids, Korvid and I had made up ghost stories about the house, and we'd dare each other to run up to the porch and ring the doorbell. I don't know how long it was abandoned, but I never saw any cars in the driveway, children playing, or even shadows passing through the windows at night. Then, a few years ago, some kids tried their hand at arson (so the story goes) and set the place on fire. The second floor had burned to cinders and most of the ground floor followed it to charcoal. The town never did anything with the house; it was never rebuilt, never torn down. It just sat on the grass of our cul-de-sac, gathering dust and stories, until it was completely forgotten. It was rooted in our neighborhood, standing still as the rest of the world moved on and left it behind.

Iphy expressed great interest in the abandoned house that first night of snow, when he and Jax spent the night with Korvid. When he first saw the house, he had the notion that he and Jax could stay there. Jax had immediately shot the idea down, insisting that the snow might not last. But, lo and behold, that very night the snow came down in droves again, covering the world with an even thicker blanket. Because school was again cancelled (and would likely remain that way for several days if the weather kept up) we met in the Bone Room to discuss where Iphy and Jax would stay the night.

"The abandoned house! It'll be perfect; no one even sees it as a house anymore." Iphy was adamant. "It's like the crimson letter."

"That's 'scarlet' letter," Jax corrected. "And it's a terrible idea: that place should be condemned."

Iphy scoffed. "It's perfectly fine!"

But Jax wasn't so quick to give in. "Most of the place was turned to ash in a fire!"

Iphy snorted, as though that settled everything. "And what isn't ash will be the perfect hiding place."

Jax shook his head and looked to the rest of us for help. "Someone talk some sense into him, please."

Eddie tried his hand at calming Iphy. "That place is probably full of holes and covered with snow anyway; you might as well be back at Our Place."

Iphy suddenly stood. "Yeah, you're right. That's why we should go check it out right now!" Without waiting for any of us to say anything, Iphy was out the door and racing down the ladder, hastily giving Theodore his now customary salute before he shot out of the shed.

"Iphy!" Korvid was on his feet, already going after our leader, muttering a curse as he descended the ladder with all of us close behind him.

We saw Iphy's tracks in the snow, making a beeline for the abandoned house, and as we neared it, I felt a chill crawl its way across my back. The house was pitch black, burned to charcoal or just painted with ash that had long since stained the wood beneath. The broken and charred bits of wood stood up against the grey sky, like the scraggly teeth of some angry beast. Gaping holes were burned into the sides of the walls that were still standing, and debris was littered around what still stood. A thick head of moss had grown over the few places that weren't blackened by fire, making them spongy and soft to the touch. Great long weeds that had been growing for years stuck out of the snow, making the soft white blanket appear hairy, and as the wind blew they tapped against the house, making a strange, hollow sound.

Iphy plunged into the house, heedless of everything but his burning desire to see the gutted building. The rest of us hesitated; there was something about the place, the way it stood stark and still and utterly naked before us. It was a hallowed place. I could tell just by standing near it: Death had visited this house. I didn't know how, and I didn't know when, but I could feel Death's presence at the house, and it scared me. The house looked hungry and lost, waiting for people who wouldn't return to do just that; to reclaim what nature had stolen. The house couldn't feel Death's presence, and it couldn't sense the spirits that seemed to linger around it, wallowing and wailing for what once was. The house couldn't feel these things, but I could, and it frightened me. It still frightens me.

Korvid followed Iphy in, Eddie and Calm after that, leaving Jax and I on the threshold, standing where we were, afraid to go forward, afraid to stay.

"We shouldn't be here," Jax muttered.

"But what choice do we have?" I asked of him, meaning it to be a playful jest, but as the words left my mouth I realized the truth in them. We had only known him for a few weeks now, but already Iphy had too much influence over our lives. Before Iphy there was no way that I'd ever be caught dead near that house, but there I was, standing at the threshold, trying to urge myself inside. With a wink and a smile he could make any of us do anything that he wanted, including snooping around abandoned and supposedly haunted houses. Eddie followed Iphy like a lost puppy, Jax and Korvid saw Iphy as the family they never had, Calm would follow him to the end of the earth, and I would do the same. Iphy had sway over our lives (how much I didn't know until later) but enough to get me to the abandoned house; enough to get us all there. He had the power of charm and the power of trust: dangerous things to give to a child, even if he was a god in disguise.

With one last glance at Jax I followed the others inside, still feeling Death's presence looming all around me and breathing down my neck. Surprisingly, the second floor above me was still mostly intact, creating a roof over what had once been the front room. Ahead, I could see sky and blackened tile floor; it looked like the kitchen was all but demolished. I heard Iphy and the others off to my right, so I edged around a pile of debris and moved down a mostly intact hallway until I got to what could have been a family room or a den at one time.

The walls were black with ash, but other than that the rest of the room looked untouched by the fire. There was still a couch, a loveseat and even a comfy looking chair, all upholstered with flowers and paisley. They were moth eaten and faded and covered with a layer of dust and ash, but they still stood, which is more than most of the rest of the house. Boarded windows kept out the light and the cold of the world outside. There was a rotten wooden mantel above an old fashioned stone fireplace, and a few end tables that looked like they would crumble to dust if so much as a feather landed on them. Iphy was near the fireplace, eyeing the roof above us with a grin.

"This is perfect! We could hole up here all winter; maybe even forever!"

"This place is awesome!" Eddie chimed in, poking around the stonework of the fireplace, getting caught up in Iphy's enthusiasm like usual.

Korvid was testing the walls, leaning up against them, listening to how much they creaked and groaned in protest. "I hate to admit it, but you might be right. The walls are fairly sound, and the roof isn't bowing or anything. Granted, you couldn't chuck a rock at anything in here without it crumbling to pieces, but it doesn't look like anything will collapse anytime soon."

Calm haltingly sat on the chair, dust billowing up around her. "Something feels strange about this place. I think this house is lonely."

Iphy gave a little snort. "How do you figure?"

"Think about it. This house used to have people living in it, right? And suddenly they left, and the house just sat here alone for years. Outside, the house felt angry, but now I think it wants us to stay. It wants to be used again; it wants to do its job and provide home and shelter to those who need it."

Korvid smiled, but Iphy just blinked. "You got all that just by sitting in a chair?"

"You need to learn to listen, Iphy."

Iphy shook his head, and in doing so he noticed me standing in the doorway. He gestured for me to join him, obviously glad to have found a convenient change of subject. "Eraliss, check this place out; it's perfect!"

I noticed that the floor didn't creak as much as I expected when I crossed it. There was a huge oriental rug that covered most of the floor; it could have been beautiful in days gone past, but now it was dark and ragged with age, and clouds of dust and ash blossomed where I stepped.

"What do you think? Jax and I can stay here all winter!"

I looked around the room, wondering if it really was as bad as I had thought outside. Calm was right: outside the house had been cold and aloof, but now that we were inside, it seemed to tolerate (even welcome) our presence. It was certainly warmer in the room than outside, and no one would notice a few kids poking around the ancient house, and no adult would ever investigate this wreck. Despite the still lingering feeling of Death, the place wasn't really that bad; better than any clubhouse I had seen in comics and movies. I suddenly saw the lot of us, bundled up in sleeping bags on a new rug smuggled from one of our parent's houses, sipping hot cocoa we'd made over a small smokeless fire, laughing loud enough to scare the shadows away. "Yeah, Iphy; this place could definitely work."

"I still don't like it." Jax stood in the doorway, looking around the room like a sulking child.

If the house had been lonely, or even angry with our presence there, it seemed to suddenly be brighter with Jax's appearance. The windows, broken and long since boarded up, seemed suddenly bursting with light that fought to slip in through cracks in the wood. The dust seemed to instantly settle, as though afraid to be in his presence and the house itself gave a small groan; of happiness or strife, I couldn't tell.

"It could work," Korvid repeated. "We'd just have to replace the rug, dust the place out a bit, and make sure you guys had firewood that didn't smoke too badly."

"My parents have a rug in the basement; they probably don't even remember that it's there." Eddie began measuring the length of the rug with his feet. "It's got to be as big as this rug, maybe even bigger! Sure, it's got flowers and stuff, but it beats this dusty old thing."

That seemed to settle it for Iphy; if he wasn't planning on spending the night before, he certainly was now. "Alright! Korvid, Calm, you two go with Eddie and grab the rug; Jax, E and I will head back to Our Place and grab some stuff. We're moving in tonight!"

No one argued; no one even batted an eye, not even Jax, who was so obstinate about not staying in the house. Iphy ordered and we followed, like the troops of some intrepid conqueror, following him past the known world and into places unfamiliar. We didn't question, we didn't doubt; if Iphy said it was so, then it was so. It was his confidence, his charm, his smile: we never believed that it would play us false. Iphy could make us do anything, be it silly, or stupid, or dangerous.

Because it was snowing faintly (but with the promise of another blizzard) we decided to take the usual route to Our Place, figuring that the snow would quickly cover up our tracks. Thanks to Iphy's lean-to, most of the stuff he and Jax had collected over the past few weeks was still relatively dry, albeit cold as ice. It took us two trips to bring everything, which included: sleeping bags, blankets, and pillows; jackets and clothes; a backpack full of dishes and two pillow-sacks full of non-perishable food. The firewood they'd gathered was useless until the snow thawed and the sun dried them back out, but Calm and Korvid both grabbed some from their respective houses and since most of the abandoned house was kindling anyway, we weren't all that concerned.

Eddie and Korvid pulled up the old rug and, after having rolled it into a floppy tube, they deposited it into the snowy remains of the kitchen. Calm had brought over some cloths and a bucket of cleaning solution and was dusting off the mantel and the fireplace, but she stopped to help the boys put down the new rug and then they all grabbed cloths and cleaning solution and went about dusting and cleaning the floor.

Iphy, Jax and I returned to a room that was much nicer than we had left it and had the faintest of lemony scents: we set about making the room a temporary home. Iphy and Eddie started a small fire and started to cook up some soup, while the rest of us made ourselves useful by cleaning or setting up what would become Iphy and Jax's winter retreat. Outside the wind and snow had started to pick up, but we were safe, even cozy, in our new place. We sat on the new rug, bundled in blankets and sleeping bags, centered around the fire, enjoying soup and cocoa as we talked about how nice this abandoned house really was. Calm was sure that the house was glad to have us, and as crazy as it sounds, I was starting to believe her. Since Jax's appearance, the house had really started to warm up, and with our little clean-up, the house was getting more and more like a home with every passing minute. We were not bothered by the wind wailing outside or by the snow falling in the torn open kitchen just a few rooms away or the thought of the Wailing Woman out in the woods; we were safe in our new place, God was in His Heaven, and all was right with the world.

We stayed with Iphy and Jax until the soup had run out and the cocoa was cold. Then we all slowly stood and prepared to go back to our houses and our other lives. I can't say what it was like for any of the others, but I knew that I always dreaded the return home: it felt like a worthless life, one that I got no joy from. It was merely the boring, annoying time between seeing Iphy, Jax and the others again. I had stopped asking my mother about her job search; I'd stopped asking her what was for dinner or if she wanted to watch a movie with me. I had stopped checking the mailbox, looking for my dad's letters and postcards. All I wanted to do was sleep, so the night would pass quickly and I could see my friends again. They were the only people that I had: my mother was almost a stranger to me, my dad even more so, and the only time that I ever felt remotely myself was when I was with my friends.

From the Journal of Calm Sheldon

Apathy is a dangerous thing: it attacks without warning and it can beat a person down until they can't do the simplest things anymore. After we fixed up the "New Place" (as we took to calling it) we all got bitten by apathy. I saw that Eraliss wasn't checking the mail like she used to. Ever since I had known her, she had been checking the mailbox at the end of the cul-de-sac religiously. Her father sent her postcards and letters, sometimes money, and she would always mark the places where he had written from on a large map in her room. Lately, she hadn't touched the mailbox, and her map remained un-updated. During the Fall she had complained about her mother not finding work; now, whenever she brought up her mother it was to complain about being grounded.

The same thing happened with Korvid, too. He used to tell Jax and Iphy about his father, and he sometimes wouldn't be able to hang out with us because he was busy doing chores around the house, keeping it in shape because his father couldn't. Now, he was with Jax and Iphy more than all of us, and his front yard was falling into disarray.

Eddie, too, was neglecting his life outside our circle; his Bone Room was dusty and the specimens that he'd buried near the shed were long past ready to be cured and worked. He didn't complain about his parents anymore; he never mentioned his siblings. Even Theodore became a rarely brought up subject, which was perhaps the most disturbing change of all. Before the New Place, Eddie had doted on Theodore, for the spider was his beloved pet, and his first friend before us. Every day before he had mentioned something about Theodore, from the new web the spider had designed, or the strange, wrapped up insects he'd find in the morning. Now, there was hardly any word on Theodore's antics.

And even I was hit by the string of melancholy; I felt myself slipping away from my parents, from the world I had known before Iphy and Jax and Eddie. I cared less and less about my parents' fights and I hardly noticed that they were becoming more and more of a constant thing, rather than fluctuating like they used to. When school started up again after three more days of snow, I paid less and less attention in class, and I didn't even notice when Mr. Neil's octopus, Lawrence, was replaced with a squid he named Bentley.

School just went on, and we all went along with it, waiting for those glorious afternoons when we would all sneak out and meet up in the New Place, where we would sit next to the fireplace and get lost with each other. It was a sanctuary, something that we all needed; there was nothing for us at home. It was all waiting there, in the abandoned house, or out in the woods surrounding Our Place. It was a secret that the Wailing Woman knew; it was what she had been trying to tell us that chilly day when winter was first upon us.

Then, one Saturday near Christmas, Eddie didn't show up at the New Place. Eraliss was the first to notice our friend's absence; the rest of us were discussing what we should do about the upcoming holiday.

"We should definitely do something," Iphy said with a nod. He stretched his arms above his head until his shoulders popped. "Have a gift exchange or something; hell, even just hang out."

Korvid was in agreement. "I know my dad has to work on Christmas Eve; I could probably hang out then."

I knew that my own father was going away on business and would be gone for Christmas again, which meant that my mother would desperately try to shower me with gifts and make me take her side; I definitely didn't want to go through all of that again. "I can sneak out."

"What about you, E?" Iphy asked, his winning grin flashing in the diffused light.

Eraliss didn't answer; she was looking over her shoulder at the door, as though expecting someone to waltz through.

Jax leaned forward a bit. "Eraliss?" he asked, his soft voice breaking the door's spell on our friend.

She turned back, her eyes questioning. "Where's Eddie?"

We paused, looking around at ourselves and taking stock; Eddie *was* missing. Iphy was the first to his feet, ever leading the expedition. He darted down the hall and glanced into the open air kitchen, as though expecting Eddie to be hiding in the piles of snow and ruined appliances, a great beaming smile on his face as he shouted "Surprise!" But Eddie wasn't there, and further inspection of the New Place proved that he hadn't come at all, which wasn't like Eddie in the least. Usually, he was one of the first ones over, always with a backpack full of food and a new deck of cards for Iphy and Jax to play poker or blackjack with.

We left the New Place and crossed the expanse of snow covered grass that separated the old abandoned building with Eddie's house, taking a cautious note of the driveway; lucky for us, both his parents' cars were gone. Still playing it safe, we moved around to the back of the house, checking the windows of the Bone Room while we were at it. They were dark, and almost foreboding, and I got the distinct impression that something terrible had happened there last night. Iphy, who by then had moved around past the shed and into Eddie's backyard, was looking up at the only light on in the house. It was the third window from the right: Eddie's bedroom.

"What the hell's he doing up there?" Iphy's look bordered on offended as he huffed. "He knew we had a meeting today."

Jax climbed up on the riding lawnmower parked under the patio. "We have a meeting *every* day." With a graceful swiftness he crawled up onto the roof.

Iphy immediately started forward. "H-hey, wait up Jax!" With a dogged determination he climbed up onto the lawnmower as well, but from there he paused, debating on how exactly he should go about getting onto the roof; it was too tall for him to just climb on, and he wasn't flexible or strong enough to haul himself up by his elbows. "How the hell did you get up there, anyway?"

With little acknowledgement of Iphy, Jax started further up the roof. "Hang on, Iph; I'll be right back."

Our de-facto leader bristled at being brushed off, and he tried even harder to get onto the roof. When his elbows gave out and he fell back onto the snow, Korvid shook his head. "Give it up, Iphy; Jax can take care of this."

Though Iphy nodded his consent, I noticed a darkness cross his face. It was only for a second, and even then I could have been mistaken, but in the seconds following Iphy's mysterious look, a knot of emotion twisted in my stomach, and I wondered why the winter was so terrible, and why the sun had gone and left us all alone.

We waited for a few minutes, standing out in the faintly falling snow, watching as Jax climbed to the window and disappeared into the lighted room. Snow continued to fall, getting in our hair and piling up on our shoulders and on the top of our heads. We waited, silent and still, as Iphy rocked on his heels and bounced on the tips of his toes, hunching his shoulders and exhaling with a huff. His impatience became infectious (like everything that he did) and soon Korvid was pacing about in a small circle, leaving a ring of grass that marked his progress in the snow. We watched the glowing square of light, expecting Jax to emerge from it at any minute, bringing news of our missing friend. I was surprised then, when he came around the side of the house from the front.

Iphy was on him in a minute. "Well? What's going on? Why wasn't he at the New Place?"

Jax gave Iphy a dark scowl; it was the first time I'd ever seen anyone look at Iphy with anything close to animosity. "Iphy, lay off." His words were simple, but in them there was a great conviction.

There was a pause, and the world held its breath and waited to see what was to come. I looked back and forth between the two—these two gods in the bodies of boys— and I couldn't fathom a darkness between them. But there was a kind of darkness; it was just a small, black trickle, but it was there.

"What'd you say?" Iphy asked; he had straightened, leaned forward. There was a tightness around him now — one crafted of anger and indignity — and he drew himself up, seemed to grow as though some great injustice had befallen him with Jax's words.

"Just... just lay off, Iphy; alright? Eddie's had a bad time."

This broke the spell of silence that gripped the rest of us. "What happened?" Eraliss asked, jostling Iphy aside. "What's wrong?"

As Jax led us around to the front of Eddie's house, he told us the story; it was simple and short. "Theodore's dead."

I stopped cold on the porch, right outside the warm square of light that was Eddie's front door. "What?"

Jax nodded, not looking at any of us. "Just this morning. Eddie found him curled up on the floor — "

"Stop!" Eraliss had her hands clamped tightly over her ears, her eyes already wet; despite her initial dislike of spiders, she had grown extremely fond of the Bone Room's mascot. "Just... stop."

Iphy looked miserable, his face a mixture of nausea and sadness. "Nu-uh... no way; not Theo."

Behind me, Korvid cursed softly under his breath; a faint exhalation in the still air. "How's Eddie taking it?" he asked with his gentle voice.

"Not very well," Jax admitted as we all stepped into the McCloy house for the first time. It was easily the nicest house in our neighborhood, and probably one of the nicer houses in our town. It was a house of polished hardwood floors, granite countertops, full-size freezers and guest bedrooms — but none of that mattered. We made our way up the staircase, our hands gripping and slipping on the elegant banister, our eyes taking in the paintings on the wall, and the grandiose frames that held them still. The rooms upstairs were all dark, like ominous eyes that watched us and shunned us. Only one room was lighted, and even then it was a small crack of light that poured out of a half-closed door; from behind it we could hear crying, and that was all that concerned us.

Eraliss was the first through the door, all but shoving Iphy and Jax aside in her quest to enter. Eddie was sitting on the floor, his back to his bed, curled around himself and still sobbing. With tears of her own beginning to fall, Eraliss sat next to him, put her arm around him and cried with him. Korvid sat on Eddie's other side, leaning against the younger boy; Jax settled down on the floor across from Eddie, while Iphy sat on the bed, his legs idly kicking near Korvid's side. I joined in next to Eraliss and we sat there in silence, all of us mourning the loss of Eddie's first real friend.

We stayed for a long time; hours, maybe. When our stomachs began rumbling and complaining loud enough for everyone to hear, Korvid went downstairs and made some soup with Jax's help. They brought it up to us, bowls balancing precariously on their arms. It was delicious. And though Eddie had stopped his crying, he hadn't yet uncurled from around his knees. He hardly had any of the soup: I imagine it only tasted like ashes at that moment.

According to the notes jotted on the calendar in the kitchen, Mr. and Mrs. McCloy were out watching Dan (one of Eddie's older brothers) star in the latest high school musical; Korvid assumed that they had brought Eddie's younger siblings with them. Eddie told us later that when he had told them, red-eyed and trembling, that he didn't want to go, they had been angry with him, but had told him to do as he wished.

As it got dark, Eraliss and I left (only one at a time) to tell our parents that we'd be spending the night with our friend. My mother hardly minded; she was busy pretending to ignore my father, who was flipping through the newspaper, engrossed in the news of far off places that he'd never heard of or been to.

Sometime during the ten or fifteen minutes that I had been gone, Eddie had moved from the floor to the relative safety underneath his bed covers and had started to cry again. I sat down next to Eraliss, who was still red-eyed and weepy herself. Korvid had lain down in front of Eddie's window, Jax near Eddie's bed and Iphy over by the shelf of bones. The light went out and with the darkness, silence left us. Jax and Iphy murmured to each other, Korvid adding his own two cents into the conversation where he could. Off in the darkness, Eddie continued to cry, and soon Eraliss was joining him again: not the deep, hiccupping sobs like before, but merely the faint trickle of tears and the occasional sniffle of a runny nose. We heard the McCloys come home and there was great exuberance in the world beyond Eddie's door; the happiness from downstairs made its way to the darkness of Eddie's room, but it couldn't enter. We could hear the cheers and congratulations, and the celebratory sound of champagne being opened (or fancy apple cider). It just served to remind us that though we mourned a loss, the world outside of our little family did not, and it never could. We were somehow separate from the world around us; there was only our precious six, and everything else.

The world didn't care that Eddie McCloy had lost someone so very dear to his heart, but we did.

As the celebration downstairs ended and the house became still and silent, we were all still awake. None of us had uttered a sound, but I knew just as surely as I lived and breathed, we were all still awake. Eddie had stopped his crying, but his uneven breathing attested to the fact that sleep hadn't yet come to claim him, and take him far away. We were all balanced on the edge of sleep, as though waiting for a sign that it was okay to fall away, dream and leave each other.

Beside me, Eraliss cleared her throat. "Eddie?" she whispered into the dark. "It's okay; we won't leave."

That was enough; we all slipped off to sleep.

C.S

~*~

The day that Theodore died changed everything; we went from being friends to being family. We could talk now, about everything; about all the bones and grinning skulls that had been locked away in the closets of our subconscious. Korvid told us about the time he'd just used butter while making macaroni and cheese (instead of milk, as per the instructions) and how it had tasted so nasty he had thrown the whole mess away in the backyard, where a coyote came by in broad daylight and ate the whole thing. Eddie snickered and told us about the time he'd walked in on his older brother and his girlfriend and had been able to blackmail twenty bucks off his brother for his silence. Once, Jax had been sleeping in a dark corner of the confessional booth and he'd overheard the anxious confession of Mr. Marsden, who ran the bike shop, about his lecherous affair with Ms. Lore, the widow from three neighborhoods over. Iphy claimed that in his old town he was known as something of a trouble maker, and that once he had pulled the fire alarm at his old school, and then ran around the building, pulling more and more until he was finally caught.

We laughed, and with every story that we told each other, it was like a scrapbook being filled; we each took a sampling of each others' lives, took some small memory that they had kept to themselves for all these years. I told everyone about the time I had kept a slime mold in a jam jar until my mom had tried to put some on her toast. Calm told us about the time she had made mud pies and had put them in her father's briefcase for his lunch.

They weren't always funny stories, though. Once, Korvid broke down and told us that he was afraid; afraid for his dad, who looked as though he'd never get over his wife's death; afraid for himself because he was, "a Goddamn pussy who couldn't go upstairs" for fear of his mother's ghost. But mostly he was afraid for his mother, that her spirit was still trapped in the room upstairs; could never get out and be free because she couldn't open the door, and he couldn't either. Calm cried because she'd seen suitcases in her parent's bedroom, and (temporarily forgetting her father's business trip) she was so sure that he was leaving for good. That he'd never come back and he'd find a new family and live happily ever after with them and not with her and her mother. Eddie haltingly recounted the time he had gotten a BB gun when he was younger and had went out to the pond, gathered a stack of bullfrogs and shot the whole stack; he started to cry, telling us that it was the only time he'd ever killed anything, and he was sure he was an evil person. We shared our fears now—something we had never talked about before—and through that we came to a crystal clear understanding; we weren't just friends anymore.

We had bared our souls to one another, more so than we had with parents, siblings, or anyone else in our lives.

Looking back as I write this now, years and years after that one glorious year, I wonder if it was right, the close-knit amity that we had for one another. It was wonderful back then, but our close friendship would rob us of lives in the future. No other person that we met on the bus, or in a bar, or sitting next to us on an airplane destined for far-off places, would ever get as close to us as Iphy, Jax and the others. No future person that we could meet would have Calm's searching eyes, or Eddie's cowlick, Korvid's voice, or Jax's winning smile. And no one would ever have Iphy's contagious confidence. There were other people out there in the world, but they were beneath us: they couldn't be us and they couldn't be the friends we had grown up with. As the years tore us apart (as years and hardships are bound to do) we found that we were far happier with memories than with experience. As far as we were concerned we had reached the prime moment in our lives all those years ago; now we were just waiting to be reunited again.

With Christmas came a great ice storm: it was the worst one our state had seen in fifty years. It started with a record-breaking thirteen inches of snow; school would have been cancelled if it wasn't already out for Christmas vacation. We played in the snow, the six of us, and it felt like we had an unlimited supply of the white stuff. Night fell and we parted ways with plans to meet again in the morning. But during the night it rained; a freezing, cold rain that settled on top of the snow as two straight inches of pure ice. No one was going anywhere for a good, long while. Hoarfrost, or so the weatherman claimed; two inches of ice sitting on top of thirteen inches of snow. Cars couldn't move along the road, people couldn't leave their houses. Trees sagged with the weight of the ice that bogged down their branches; some couldn't take it and snapped clear in half, littering the empty roads with their broken selves.

The first night of the ice storm it rained again, only serving to strengthen the ice and make it even worse. By the third day, I was ready to pull out my hair; cabin fever was setting in. Plus, I was getting worried: no one could leave their houses, which meant that Iphy and Jax hadn't gotten any new supplies in a few days. I tried desperately to remember how many boxes of crackers, bags of beef jerky and loaves of bread they had. Enough for a few days, a week, maybe more, maybe less. It was hard to measure time when it had become such an ephemeral concept in the last few days.

On the fourth day, I decided to try my luck; it would give me something to do, and I had to get out of the house, if only for a few hours. I waited until the snow stopped falling and bundled up as best as I could by putting on three shirts and two pairs of sweatpants underneath my jacket and my snow pants. I had a theory that if I could break through the ice to the snow, I could then make my way, step by careful step, to the New Place.

I thought if I could only stomp down hard enough, the soles of my boots would be enough to crack the ice and offer me safe passage; I was wrong. I stepped out onto our stone stoop and the instant my foot came crashing down on the slick ice, my foot was at a ninety degree angle from my hip, and my butt was introduced to the cold. I tried twice more, with embarrassingly similar results, before I realized that I would have to bring out the big guns for this endeavor. I left the front door, deciding instead to go out the back. On the way, I grabbed my mother's little hand spade from her gardener's box in the laundry room closet. The distance between the back door and the shed was a whopping fifty feet; with the ice, the journey seemed to take hours. I broke through the ice with mom's little spade, took a step, crouched, and hacked through the ice again. The going was slow, and mind-numbingly repetitive, but I hardly noticed, so glad was I to be out of the house.

When I got to the shed, I had to break away more ice around the bottom of the door, but as soon as I got a hold of the shovel in my hand, it felt like I was wielding raw power. I stuck the blade into the ice, and stomped on it with my free foot. The ice shattered into small diamonds, letting my shoes sink into the powder beneath; the going was a whole lot faster now. Still, a journey that should have taken me the better part of two minutes, took me almost an hour as I crashed my way slowly through the ice.

"Iphy? Jax?" I called into the stillness of the New Place; the snow outside acted as a muffler, and my voice fell dead instead of echoing along the walls like it normally did.

From down the hall I heard familiar voices. "Holy shit, I think it's E!" Seconds later they were there, grinning like fools.

Iphy ran a hand through his pale hair. "We didn't think anyone would be coming until the ice melted; how'd you manage?"

I gave them a grin of my own. "A shovel and some tenacity."

"Well, it's good to see you, either way." Jax smiled.

"How are your supplies doing?"

Iphy made a face. "Shitty. We'll survive another day or two, but after that we're gonna have to start eating each other."

Jax rolled his eyes, but didn't comment on Iphy's outlandish remark. "Is the ice as bad everywhere else?"

I nodded. "The whole town's covered in ice—it's like a new Ice Age."

Jax whistled. "This has to be one of the worst storms in years."

"That's totally awesome," Iphy said, leading the rest of us back into the main room. "What a story. I mean—" Before he could say what he meant, a loud gurgle erupted from his belly, echoing faintly in the still room.

"That reminds me," I said, glancing back towards the door, "I should grab some more food for you before it starts snowing again." I didn't question it back then; our uncanny ability to pilfer and steal an entire backpack's worth of food every few days, right out from under our parent's noses. Our parents didn't notice, or they didn't mind our suddenly explosive appetites. I always chalked it up to growing children needing their strength. In retrospect, I think it had more to do with our parents not caring about missing food; they all had so much more on their minds than what their children were doing, and where their food was going.

Iphy waved a hand. "Relax and stay a while: you've got plenty of time."

"Actually, she doesn't," Jax said, peering out between the cracks in the boarded up windows. "It's already snowing again."

I cursed. "Is it? Crud, I gotta get back." I quickly threw on the coat that I had discarded and made my way to front door. One glance outside confirmed that Jax hadn't been kidding. The snow was coming down again, in thick fat flakes that stuck to the ice and half-melted, half-froze. I struggled back to my house, finding the going harder than I had expected. Twice I misstepped, my holes already filling with snow.

Once inside I filled my bag with more of the usual: instant soup, crackers, a few bananas and a few apples, chunks of cheese and beef jerky, bread, canned peas and corn, candy bars and marshmallows. My mother was inside on the couch, fascinated by whatever the latest TV talk show host was saying at the time. I gave her another hasty goodbye and she told me what time to expect dinner. With that little chore taken care of, I clambered back outside, hoping that the holes wouldn't be filled yet.

Luck was one my side for the moment; I could still faintly make out the traces of cracks in the ice, rapidly vanishing in the new fallen snow. I tried hard to double-time it back to the New Place, but I fell twice; my palms landed roughly on the ice, jarring my elbows and making my bones shudder. By the time I made it back, I felt ready to collapse in the corner; Iphy and Jax had to haul me over the threshold as it was. I glanced over my shoulder, but the world beyond the door had vanished, hidden behind a curtain of snow that fell faster and thicker than ever.

"I don't think I'm going home tonight..."

Jax stuck his head out the door, as if to gauge the falling snow. "Will your mom get mad?"

"She's gonna ground me until I start retirement," I muttered, trying to rub out the pain in my elbow; it didn't help.

"Well," Iphy shrugged, "you can stay with us."

I half-snorted, half-laughed. "No duh. I couldn't find the edge of the porch in that mess, let alone my house."

He shook his head, chuckling in that way of his; he thought he was so much wiser than us. He had to hold our hands as we took the stumbling baby steps that he had already mastered long ago. "I mean *stay* with us: you know, forever."

For a full thirty seconds I took his words to heart. I thought about how it would be to live on my own, there in the abandoned house, or out in the woods at Our Place. I thought about not having to go to school, not having to listen to my mom's angry rants and her oppressive silence. I thought about doing what I wanted to, and not having to agonize over postcards from my father that were never there.

"I can't," I whispered.

"Why not?" he pressed. "It's fun, and it's easy."

I shook my head. "I'm not made out of the same stuff as you, Iphy; I wouldn't know what to do with myself if I was on my own."

"You wouldn't be on your own; you got me and Jax."

"No, I don't think it's a good idea." Jax smiled at me, an embarrassed sort of smile, as though he had forgotten my presence for a moment. "You're not made of the same stuff as Iphy, but you're made of something else that's definitely tough enough."

Iphy cleared his throat loudly, reminding us that he was still present. "So, what's the problem? If she's tough enough, why don't you think it's a good idea?"

"Because she has a roof over her head, and a family, and a life—"

"Bullshit," Iphy snorted, an almost dark ire in his eyes. "We have a roof over our heads, we have a family and last I checked we were still alive!"

Jax shook his head violently. "It's not the same!"

"The hell it isn't!"

"Hey!" I cried, stepping between the two. "It doesn't matter what the two of you want me to do, the fact of the matter is that I don't want to run away from home and quit school." There was a tremble in my voice that was hard to disguise; I was scared. It was the first time I had seen Jax and Iphy come close to a fight, and it frightened me. The thought that these two gods in the bodies of children could disagree, squabble and come to blows was too alien and terrifying to think about; a herald of a coming apocalypse. My brain tried to chalk it up to the two of them being stuck by themselves for so long because of the ice, but my heart wasn't quite convinced.

Awkwardness blossomed between the three of us, making me want to run back out into the snow. Then, Iphy threw his hands in the air, marking the end of the conversation, and Jax and I smiled and the tension evaporated. The three of us moved back into the fireplace room. We dined on chicken soup and toasted bagels, with hot, gooey marshmallows for dessert. Outside the wind pushed against the house, making the old, burned wood creak and groan in blatant protest, but inside, with the fire and the jumble of blankets, we were warm.

We talked about many things that are trivial now, but really it was just talking for talking's sake. As evening deepened into full fledged night, we paused in our ceaseless conversations about stars and space, and Molly Larson's shoes, or our collected knowledge of far-off places whose names we mispronounced. At the time, the silence wasn't awkward, but it wasn't anything special either. We didn't know at the time that the silence was proof of our friendship, because back then, and even now, it's incredibly hard to find someone who can be comfortable with our silence.

Yet, our silence passed and conversation was started up again between yawns and heavy lidded eyes. "Iphy," I started, rubbing at eyes that seemed weighted down with little balls of lead, "Why'd you run away from home anyway?"

He gave a non-committal shrug. "I felt like it."

"That's a crap answer," I murmured. "I want the truth."

"Tough cookies," was his response.

Still, I felt the need to press, as though tonight would finally reveal answers to the world's mysteries. "Did you have a fight with your parents?"

Iphy snorted. "Hardly."

"Well, what then?" He gave me no answer. "Please? You said earlier that we're family, and family doesn't keep secrets, so why don't you just tell us?"

He paused, seemed to consider the logic in my words, but he shook his head. "Maybe later."

That was the end of that conversation; Iphy's reasons for running away wouldn't be brought up again for a long while.

Instead, talk drifted about through more trivial subjects until the wind stopped howling and the world was still outside the boarded up windows. Eventually, Iphy drifted off to sleep, leaving me and Jax by our lonesome. We talked a bit about the town (a subject that we never really talked with Iphy about) and about the people that populated our small world: Mr. Smithy, the baker; the Reverend Josh Potter; Thomas Smith (no relation to Mr. Smithy) who worked at the junkyard and helped Iphy and Jax from time to time. As we talked, I noticed that Jax kept casting furtive glances at the house around us, and I remembered his initial hesitation about entering the house. I smiled at him.

"What's up? You afraid this house doesn't like you guys living in it?"

"I used to live here," he murmured his eyes attached to the blackened wallpaper.

The world outside, so silent and still, stopped completely. "You...what?"

"I used to live here," he repeated, drawing his knees up to his chest and wrapping his arms around them. "This was my parents' house."

I looked around at the blackened walls, the ash and the flowered, paisley upholstery. I wondered why I had never pieced it together: the burned house and Jax's history. "You... lived here?"

He nodded, his eyes still roving around the walls of a house that should have been familiar to him, yet he looked lost and frightened.

"Then, the fire that burned this house..." I left the words hanging. I couldn't finish my sentence, but I didn't need to; Jax finished it for me.

"...Is the same one that killed my parents."

His words brought an enormous pressure on my shoulders, like I had bags of bricks that were steadily crushing me, breaking and splintering my bones. "Jax... I'm so sorry..." I couldn't imagine staying in the very house where my parents had died. Now armed with this knowledge, I couldn't help but feel the house's loneliness and the crushing, stifling absence of life all around us. I scooted closer to Jax, leaned my head against his shoulder and shivered just as the wind decided to continue its howling outside.

We listened to the wind, which now sounded less like wind and more like the horrible wailing of people who had died and were not yet at rest. "How... did it happen?"

He didn't answer at first, and unlike with Iphy I didn't push it. A second might have passed, or an hour, but Jax did eventually answer. "How does anything like that happen? It could have been anything; the firefighters never did figure it out. Maybe it was an electrical fire, or maybe it was one of my dad's cigarettes." He paused, tightening his grip around his knees and leaning against me. "Maybe it was my fault," he murmured, his voice hitching a bit at the end.

I shook my head. "No," I said. "Never. There's no way it was your fault, Jax." I wrapped an arm around his shoulder, as though that would banish the growing darkness in his eyes.

"Yes it was." His voice cracked again, and tears made his eyes shimmer. "I think I left a candle burning. I was downstairs, it was late, and I fell asleep on the couch." His voice broke and his shoulders shook as he hiccupped and gasped for air. "I woke up, went upstairs to my room." The tears were flowing openly down his cheeks, and there was nothing I could do but hold him tighter. "I left the candle burning; I forgot all about it. I left the candle burning and it started the fire and... oh, God, Eraliss, I killed my parents. I killed them; it was my fault."

"No!" I cried, my own tears starting to stain my cheeks. "It wasn't your fault; you couldn't have known."

"I killed my parents!" His sobs were so loud, I was afraid Iphy would wake to see Jax in this vulnerable position. I didn't know what Iphy would do, but I didn't want to find out.

"Jax!" I moved to face him, grabbed his shoulders and shook them. "What happened here was terrible, but it wasn't your fault! Please, you have to believe me, Jax."

"I'm... scared. I feel like I can't move beyond this, like I can't ever go forward. I just wanna keep going in circles." He leaned forward, rested his head on my shoulder and continued to cry.

"If you keep retracing your steps, you'll never make new ones," I murmured. "Even though it's scary to let go of things that happened in the past, being able to do so is a true test of character." I didn't know where the words were coming from; some mixture of speeches I'd heard and books I'd read. "It's hard to go forward, but we have

to; if we don't, then we're done. And I'm not ready for you to be done yet."

He didn't say anything, he just cried on my shoulder. I let him. We stayed that way for an indeterminate amount of time: it could have been minutes, it could have been hours. Finally his tears slowed to a trickle and exhaustion dropped down over me in a torrent. He moved away, wiped his tears on the back of his sleeve. We didn't say anything; we just both laid down, piling the blankets on top of us.

"Good night, Eraliss," he murmured.

"Good night, Jax."

Extracted from an e-mail addressed to Eraliss Cofler from Korvid Fairington, dated ▊▊▊▊▊.

Hey, E.

Ah, yes, the ice storm. That was a real mess; I remember the tension in my house was so thick you could cut it with a knife. I don't think my dad and I had spent so much time together in probably five years.

I was surprised by your e-mail; I never knew you had hiked over to the New Place during the storm. It makes sense, though; I always wondered how those two managed without our regular contributions to their food bank. And I always wondered why your mom grounded you for a whole month. Not that it mattered; you always snuck out anyway. And I'll admit, I wondered about the abandoned house; I think a small part of me knew it was Jax's house, but the majority of me didn't want to believe it. It was too hard to think about; him living in the very house he had run away from. One of those tragic ironies. Aside from his initial hesitation (which could be chalked up to anything, including common sense) he never seemed like he had a problem staying in the house. Admittedly, I think Calm hit it on the head all those years ago, when she said she thought the house was glad to have someone occupying it again: even more so because it was someone who used to live there.

You asked me about Christmas; that Christmas was something special. The ice had all melted, but there was still a small layer of snow on the ground. A perfect snow, if you think about it: it wasn't enough to stick to the roads and make it dangerous, but it was enough to give a white dusting to the tops of the evergreen trees and picket fences. It's funny how much my thinking's changed. Back then, I wouldn't have cared about the condition of the roads; it wasn't a priority. All that mattered was that it was white and beautiful and everyone was happy.

Dad wasn't home for Christmas (he was working, like he'd done for years) so I just dropped his gift off underneath the tree. It was a sad little tree: one Iphy, Jax and I had picked out just after the ice storm. It was tiny, but that was understandable considering that the three of us had to haul it from the Christmas tree stand that Mr. Fuller had set up in the open lot next to Carver's Deli all the way back to my house on foot. Luckily, the Reverend Josh Potter drove by when we were on Main Street and offered us a ride in his pickup.

Truthfully, I was kind of worried when he pulled up; the Reverend knew practically everyone in town and Iphy was a new face. But he just smiled at us with those warm eyes of his. He was a nice man, the Reverend: he had this special quality about him, like he was everyone's old friend from long ago. Tall, solid, but not overweight, he walked with a bit of stoop, like a man carrying too many problems, but not complaining. It was his face that was most memorable, though; maybe roguishly handsome in his younger years, but as he neared the proverbial hill, it turned to a more kindly expression, framed by hair the color and consistency of straw and wheat. "Afternoon, boys; getting ready for the holidays, I see."

Jax and I nodded. "Mr. Fuller gave us this one half off, seeing as how it's kinda wimpy."

The Reverend raised a humorous eyebrow. "Is that so? How very gracious of him." He turned his attention to Jax. "I'm glad to see you running about, Jax; I'll admit I was a bit worried about you. I haven't seen you at the church in quite some time."

At this, Iphy stepped forward and gave an easy grin. "He's been staying with me and my grandparents for the winter."

"Is that so?" The Reverend smiled again. "You're a new face; I thought I knew everyone in this town." He held out a hand. "I'm the Reverend Josh Potter."

With a brazenness that was all his own, Iphy took the proffered hand. "Nice to meet you, Reverend; I'm Iphy."

After the introductions had been made, the Reverend looked at our tree, then back to me. "Don't tell me you were planning on carrying this tree all the way to your house, Korvid?"

"Actually, that was the plan," I admitted, somehow feeling sheepish for lying to him. Though, I wasn't really lying myself, I just wasn't calling Iphy on his lie. It's not quite the same thing, right?

But, the Reverend just smiled. "How about a small change of plans? I'll take you boys back to your house, Korvid, and we can put the tree in the truck bed. How's that sound?"

Iphy grinned. "That sounds like a plan and a half, Reverend."

It took us a few minutes to get the tree into the truck bed; the Reverend didn't have the biggest pickup in town, and likewise he wasn't exactly the beefiest guy around either. Still, after some hemming and hawing, he had Iphy and Jax climb into the back, and take a hold of the top of the tree, while he and I maneuvered the trunk. For being such a wimpy tree, it put up quite the fight. I don't think it liked the idea of being cut down in its prime to decorate my house as it slowly died.

(For the record, I have a fake tree now—lighted and everything. No more hassle with packing a tree from a tree farm to the house, no more dead needles everywhere, and no more spending hours untangling lights. Though I do miss the smell of pine; the fake stuff just doesn't have the same quality. Speaking of Christmas, what's your family doing this year? If you want, the offer is still on the table if you guys want to come down: we'd love to have you. If you talk to any of the others, let them know they can come, too. It'd be great to get everyone together again.)

Anyway, the Reverend drove us back to my house and helped us unload the tree and set it up in the clear spot in the living room. He asked if I needed anything, and

I told him that I was just fine, living up my vacation by running around like a chicken with its head cut off. That wasn't a lie, but I still felt wary by the Reverend's presence.

The Reverend laughed and smiled, then turned to Iphy with a kindly eye. "Where do your grandparents live, Iphy? I could drop you and Jax off, if you'd like."

"They live out on Olaha Way," Iphy replied breezily. "But they're out for the afternoon; they're planning on picking us up from here a little later."

The Reverend nodded with a smile. "Well, alright then." We showed him to the door and he waved from his truck. "You boys have a good day," he called from the driver's seat.

We all waved back, thanked him for his help, and watched as he drove off down the street. Once he was good and gone, I gave a sigh of relief.

"That was close," I muttered. I wondered briefly if helping somebody lie right to the face of the clergy was a hell-worthy sin. It certainly seemed like it, given the amount of sweat I felt.

Iphy cocked an eyebrow and gave a look that walked the border of incredulousness and temporary insanity. "How do you figure?"

"All that stuff about your grandparents living out on Olaha Way?"

"Oh, that?" he waved a hand, as though it was the most insignificant thing in the whole world. "That's all true." The way he said it, he acted like it was just one of a list of many mundane and trivial things that littered his educated world. To Jax and me, the news was like a sack of bricks dropping on top of us from a building of significant height.

"What?" I sputtered. "If you have family here in town, why the hell are you and Jax staying in a condemned building?"

"Are you kidding?" Iphy scoffed. "That place is way cooler than my grandparents' house. Their place smells like cats and old people."

That was my first real taste of the selfishness that could sometimes come over Iphy and cloud him in a shroud of only 'me, me, me'; it was the first time I was really mad at him.

"Cool or not, you could be staying there, safe and warm, eating three square meals a day, rather than waiting for all the scraps that we can *steal* for you! I mean, really, Iphy; use your brain." My voice's volume was climbing skyward with every word. "Do you know how much trouble I'll be in—and not just me, but Calm, Eddie and Eraliss too—if someone finds out we've been stealing food, and clothes, and everything else for you, just so you can play the Great Adventure Boy out in the woods?"

Iphy's face got red, a sure sign that he was just as angry as I was, and he defended himself with his own yelling voice. "Hey, I didn't ask for your charity! You want your shit back, go ahead and take it!"

Then, Jax was between the two of us, his voice calm and quiet. "Korvid, we appreciate everything you and the rest have done; you know that. And Iphy, without them, we would be in pretty bad shape."

Still sulking, Iphy gave a little snort. "Speak for yourself."

"Anyway," Jax continued, ignoring Iphy's interruption, "this is no time to be fighting: it's almost Christmas. So, let's just call it water under the bridge."

It took a few seconds, but I saw the logic in Jax's words and I nodded. "Under, and swept away."

Iphy sulked for another few seconds before he nodded. "Out in the ocean."

Satisfied, Jax gave a nod. "Good. Now, about these grandparents, Iphy; think we could go there for some Christmas dinner?"

"Nup," Iphy shook his head. "They've gone to Florida by now."

"Florida?" I asked.

"Yep. When I ran away, I was hoping to catch them before they left. They have a winter house that they live in from November to February. Apparently, they left a few weeks too early and I missed the boat. Good thing, too." He grinned.

"Why's that?" asked Jax.

"Because, if I was living it up in Florida, I'd be making friends with surfer yuppies, not upstanding pillars of society like you." And just like that, our fight was forgotten, borne away on one of his easy grins that beamed confidence and made one feel invincible. He could always do that: banish someone's darkened thoughts with a carefree grin and a dismissive wave of his hand. He could get a kind of glow around him sometimes, when the light hit his hair right, or his head was cocked just so. He was a god, playing at mortal life by disguising himself in the body of a boy. It was like Calm had said, he was not just a normal runaway child; he was special.

Christmas was scarce from my end; it was mostly hand-me-downs for Jax and Iphy; a book of bones I'd found at the local library book sale for Eddie; a journal for you, and a charm bracelet for Calm. I remember our Christmas actually started the night before, after we had snuck out from underneath the not-so-watchful eyes of our parents. Backpacks laden with food and gifts, we had snuck across the snow to meet on the porch of the New Place before we were ushered in out of the cold. We ate first, showering the two with enough cooked ham and turkey, dinner rolls and vegetable casserole to last for days.

Then, we all curled up under blankets and sleeping bags, watching Eddie's watch as we counted down the minutes until midnight, talking about our own past Christmas adventures. And once the second hand passed the twelve and Christmas was officially upon us, the gifts came out, wrapped up in newspaper and the brown recycled paper of old grocery bags. There were no 'To:' and 'From:'s on our packages; as children we just knew inexplicably what gift was what and to whom it belonged to. They were passed out in some kind of random order that wasn't entirely random; there was some kind of pattern that I couldn't place. It was mostly Iphy at first, with gifts from you and Calm, then I gave one to Jax, and Eddie gave one to you… If I thought about it long enough, and had enough blank scratch paper I could figure out some kind of mathematical formula and put my degree to some kind of good use. :)

It was a very poor Christmas, and by that I mean that the gifts that we all received were small, cheap labors of love. Even Eddie, with all his family's finances, kept the gifts humble and sincere. Iphy and Jax got everything that they didn't have but might certainly need; a frying pan bought second- or third-hand from someone's cousin so they wouldn't have to cook the eggs you gave them in the small pot anymore; a guide book to all the edible things in the surrounding woodlands of Our Place; a tiny tackle box with fishing gear for the spring and summer.

We stayed well into the early morning hours, enjoying cocoa, and even more so each other's company. We shared wishes of what the morning would hold; new books and new roller blades. We finally left after Calm had already fallen asleep, almost buried under a mass of blankets. With a moment's hesitation, we all huddled about on the porch; afraid to stay; afraid to go; afraid that we were doing too much of both already to ever really go back to the lives we'd had before. You were the first to start the trek back to your house, with promises of apple pie and popcorn balls the next night. Eddie went next, then Calm.

I stayed a few more minutes, waiting on the threshold of the New Place, Iphy and Jax watching me with curious eyes. I was thinking about what waited at home for me: sleeping in until eleven only to find a note taped the fridge wishing me a happy Christmas and warning me not to wait up. I was thinking about joining them—had been since that very first night, before Eddie and before the Wailing Woman—but I knew it couldn't happen; as angry as I was at my dad, I couldn't just leave him. It'd be too much like my mom, and I knew deep down that he couldn't go through that again. So I wished them a Merry Christmas one more time and headed off across the snow, not looking back because if I did, I'd run back to them, back to their Neverland, where I didn't have to face my empty house on the one day of the year that it shouldn't be empty.

And, true to form, the house was empty in the wee hours of the morning, and when I woke in the almost afternoon of Christmas Day, I was still alone. Taped to the refrigerator was a note from my dad, explaining (though he didn't have to) about how he had been offered the double shift and had taken it, and a warning that he'd be very late, so I needn't bother waiting up for him. Beneath the note was a twenty dollar bill and a menu for the take-out place down on Main Street. I took the money, bought a bunch of food, and went back to the New Place to be with the only family I felt I had left.

New Years was the same affair; you, Calm and Eddie all faked being sick, then we all snuck out to spend the night with Iphy and Jax. We had a bottle of sparkling cider (thanks to Eddie's substantial allowance) as well as party hats, popcorn and a small portable radio that Calm had dug out of her dad's closet. We listened to the countdown, counting along with it, eager and excited. When it finally hit midnight, we all cheered, and Iphy even threw his hat up in the air.

"Another year over, and a new one just starting!" he cried with glee.

You grinned, taking another swig of cider. "What are all your resolutions?"

"To finally talk to my dad about opening up Mom's room," I said, still debating about whether or not I was actually going to go through with it or if this resolution would just be added to a long list of 'Never Did's' that seemed to grow each year.

"You sure you're ready for that?" asked Jax.

I shrugged, "As ready as I'll ever be, I guess. I mean, it has to happen, and this has to be the year. I don't think I could stand another year of being in the basement."

"Good luck," wished Calm, not nearly as quiet as she'd been in the days following Halloween. She'd changed for the better and gotten more confidence, though she still retained her skewed perspective and her rational wisdom. "As for me, my New Year's resolution is to be more daring. Take some more risks."

"That's a good one," Iphy grinned. "Mine is… well, I don't have one."

"Why not?" you asked, throwing a piece of popcorn at him.

His grin got bigger. "I'm too perfect: I don't need one."

This got a laugh from everyone. "You're many things, Iphy, but perfect isn't one of them." Jax chuckled.

Iphy scowled a bit at the apparent lack of belief concerning his perfection. "Okay, wise guy, what's your New Year's resolution?"

Jax thought about this for a few seconds. "I want to catch a fish."

"That's a terrible resolution," scoffed Iphy, with a pinched up nose.

"No, I'm serious." Jax shook his head. "When I was younger, my dad took me fishing in the woods out there," he gestured vaguely in the direction of Our Place, "and the first fish I caught was this huge trout; it kinda jumped out of the water, and hit me square in the leg and flopped about, mouth gaping open. I screamed, dropped my pole, and all but scrambled up my dad's chest." He shook his head again, chuckling a bit at the memory. "I've been scared of catching fish ever since; I want to get over that fear."

You nodded. "Then I'd say that's a pretty good resolution; getting over your fear."

Still, Iphy snorted. "You're afraid of fish? Come on, that's weak."

"I'm afraid of spiders," you pointed out, so matter-of-factly, "and bees, and for awhile I was afraid of the dark, or that there was some kind of ankle grabbing monster that lived under my bed."

I laughed. "Hey, I was afraid of him too."

"So was I," said Calm. She pondered for a moment. "It's funny, he must really like living underneath people's beds; I bet it's all the dust and discarded dreams that don't make it to our heads at night."

Eddie cleared his throat after the moment of silence that followed Calm's musings. "Speaking of discarded dreams, I heard Thomas Smith telling Billy Sadims and my brother, Dan, that he shot a moose last fall, right before the snow hit, and that he couldn't find it. Said he searched for hours, but he lost its trail over in the ravine... you know... *her* territory." He was referring, of course, to the Wailing Woman, whom we knew haunted that stretch of wood just as surely as the aforementioned Thomas Smith worked at the junkyard for the spending cash that he loved to flaunt.

"That's my resolution: I want to find that moose's bones so I can put it together. I figure, with as bad as a winter as we've had, the body should be pretty picked clean by now. It'll take a while to find everything—I bet the coyotes have scattered the bones about by now—but it'll be awesome when it's finished."

We all nodded our approval; it was a good resolution, and Eddie was right; the moose would look amazing if he managed to find all the bones. Then, Jax looked at you with those cloudy blue eyes of his. "What's your resolution, Eraliss?"

You smiled, looking equal parts embarrassed, sheepish and defiant, as if daring any of us to laugh at what you hoped to achieve in the coming year. "I want to write a book."

Iphy whooped. "Hell, yeah! Give those boring guys in the library a run for their money!"

"No, nothing like that," you laughed. "Maybe just a short story or a kid's book. I just want to finish something for once, instead of getting a great idea and letting it fade into obscurity."

"Okay!" Iphy cried, so sure that whatever it was that he was going to say was much more important than the rest of us congratulating you on your goal. "I got my resolution."

"I thought you didn't need one," said Calm.

"Well, I don't need one—but I'll do one anyway, because I'm such a great guy." He grinned, and we all laughed. "So, here's my plan; my resolution is to help all of you with yours!" He nodded, his chest inflating with importance. "Eddie, I'm gonna help you find those moose bones; Jax, I can teach you how to fish; Calm, I'll make sure you don't wimp out on anything; Korvid, I'll help you trash talk your dad if you want, and E, if you ever need any ideas for your stories, I can give you exclusive interview rights to my wild and zany antics."

We laughed harder, knowing that not only was he serious about his resolution, but that he'd actually go through with making sure we went through with ours. (I can only imagine how some of his 'wild and zany antics' would have gone.)

With our resolutions made and the sparkling cider gone, we all packed up our things and headed back to our houses, sneaking in through second story windows or unlocked back doors. I couldn't sleep that night; I stayed buried under piles of blankets and dirty clothes, waiting for my eyes to close, but they wouldn't. I kept thinking about the coming year, and when I would finally work up the nerve to talk to dad. I only had 365 days; it wasn't enough time. I didn't get to sleep until about seven in the morning, and when I woke in the afternoon, the sun was hotter than it had been all winter—as if to herald the coming of a brand new year—and the snow had melted, revealing the patchy dead grass underneath.

I should wrap this up; there's not much more left to tell concerning Christmas and New Year's. Give me a call if you want to come down for the holidays; the kids would love to see you.

All my love,
Korvid.

~*~

The rest of winter was much of the same, with the exception of school, the Wailing Woman, and my new shoes. I got them for Christmas. They were sneakers, like I'd asked for, but there were two things wrong with them. They were white (and I mean, bright brand-new shining white that blinds in direct sunlight) and they had laces. While I thanked my mom, inwardly I groaned at the thought of having to slow down even for a second to fiddle with them. But, despite these small imperfections, I was thrilled at having shoes like Iphy's; he'd inspired me to go for the canvas sneaker look.

As for school, sometime at the tail end of January, Mr. Letham had to have some surgery preformed, so his class was going to have a sub for some two to three weeks. The sub's name was Mrs. Creager, and she never asked the nose pickers or the elbow scratchers to share their art, so everyone loved her. She was tall and willowy, with bright red hair that didn't look like it could be real, but it probably was. She talked a lot about what she called 'Art Jargon' and she brought in some of her own paintings and in the two weeks she was our sub, she took us on a field trip to an art museum two towns over.

Since the start of winter, my imagination had been trying to put a face to the Wailing Woman, trying to capture her hollowed eyes and the wispy rags she was clad in. Jotted down in my notebook were descriptions and notations: the wild scribbled words of an overactive imagination. During her stay, Mrs. Creager had an open art day; my notebook was out and I was furiously sketching out a poor excuse for a drawing.

"Your proportions are a bit off." I looked up, and Mrs. Creager was moving over a chair to join me at my desk. "But, no problem, it's a pretty easy fix." She took out a piece of paper for herself. "See, you can judge a drawing's proportions by head sizes." Her pencil flew over the paper flawlessly, sketching out a very basic person. She started talking about which body parts were how many head-lengths long and I just nodded every few seconds; my mind was elsewhere, imagining the stretch of woods that the Wailing Woman haunted, and the harrowing tale of why she haunted that particular place.

"You're not at all interested in drawing, are you?" Mrs. Creager's voice finally cut through my thoughts, and my startled look must have been enough for her, because she chuckled. "I thought so. Well, how about painting?"

I shook my head. "Not really."

"Sculpting?"

Now, admittedly, a few days before, she had brought in a bunch of actual clay for us to make whatever we wanted; I had made a snake, all coiled up like a pot because it was easy, and she helped me add the details like a checkerboard pattern on its back. She had fired the pieces and brought them back for us, and that had been really fun, but I thought that if I admitted to that, she'd make me work with Mr. Letham's bunch of modeling clay (which was nothing like the real stuff) and that was something I really didn't want to do.

Another shake of my head. "Nope."

She scrunched her lips and thought some more. "Well, this is your hour. What would you like to do?"

The answer came quickly. "I want to write about the… about this thing out in the woods."

My answer seemed to please her greatly. "Alright then; we have an art project for you."

"Writing isn't art," I pointed out; confused as to why I was telling the teacher what was what. This was before I learned that even teachers needed to learn some things from their students.

"But it is," Mrs. Creager said. "Writing is a wonderful art, and a gift not many people have. If you look at the writings of some really great writers and poets, you can tell that they were labored over just as much as any piece of art in the Louvre." She stood, tapping my notebook. "If you want to write, then by all means, write."

She left me and went to talk to Tyler Hetrick, the boy who liked to sniff glue and take little tastes of the modeling clay to see if it tasted any better this time around as opposed to the last time. I looked at my page of scribbles, and without a second thought I balled it up and tossed it into the trashcan with a perfect three-point shot. If Mrs. Creager said it was okay to write rather than draw, I certainly wasn't going to argue with her in any way, shape or form.

Instead, I opened up my notebook and I began to speculate on the origins of the Wailing Woman. First I thought murder, then scandalous murder by a jealous lover. But that got boring, so I began thinking of better things; I wondered if she'd met some kind of monster that lived in the forest, a walking skeleton with red eyes and hanging skin that had hunted her through the trees, a spirit that drove her insane in the empty woodlands.

At the end of art class, I had a large list of ideas and speculations—some wild and some that could actually be believable—but I had no answers. That's what I really wanted: answers that I would probably never get. I vowed right there and then that I would find out the answer to the Wailing Woman and her haunting cries.

That was certainly easier said than done. For weeks I searched for any piece of information that I could about the Wailing Woman. Through passed notes and conspiratorial whispers during science, I convinced Eddie and Calm to help me search for anything having to do with someone going missing or dying in the great stretch of woods behind the cul-de-sac. During our shared lunch hour we scoured the books of local history at one of the school's libraries, when by all rights we should have been running around outside, playing some kind of ball game with the other kids.

Ms. Adams—a short, plump, rosy-cheeked woman, who looked like she belonged on some kind of greeting card with a tray of still-warm, chocolate chip cookies—was the librarian who ran the Toolbox. The Toolbox was the name for the library in the basement of the school because it housed the school's collection of non-fiction, while the Loft (which was on the third story of school) contained all of the fiction books and was actually where most of the kids spent their mandated Library Time each week. Ms. Adams had been more than helpful: helping us find the books that had been misshelved; trying to find the collection of newspapers that the school was supposed to have, but had somehow gone missing; recommending titles that the school didn't have, but assured us that the public library—just a short seven blocks from school—did have in their possession. She asked us why we were so interested in local history, and Eddie made up a story about his grandfather being interested, but too old to search and hunt down the information himself. She thought this very gracious and commended our efforts.

In an uncharacteristically bold move, Calm went to Korvid's math class, stuck her head in, and told Korvid's math teacher, Mr. Lund, that she had a message for him from the office. Mr. Lund was a dreary, dismal man who looked more like a pear than a normal human being, and Korvid often complained that he was stuffy, monotonous and had a foul sense of humor (which is to say, none whatsoever). Normally Mr. Lund was the kind of teacher who would stop his lesson, get on the phone and call the office to verify, or at the very least ask Calm for some kind of note. As it was, he was feeling particularly dismal that day, and he merely waved Korvid out the door as he continued his lecture on simple algebraic equations.

Once she had gotten Korvid out of his classroom, we asked him to go back down to the Toolbox during his lunch hour and retrace our steps: see if we'd missed anything of vital importance. He agreed and promised us that he'd enlist the help of his eighth grade buddies Kyle Brigs and Will Leonard, who were the two students most renowned in our school for causing trouble.

Last year, in an attempt to stave off an important test that neither had studied for, Kyle and Will brought an almost full gallon sized jug of ammonia and had dumped the entire jug in the backs of all the toilets in the boy's restrooms on the ground floor of the school. They flushed them all and ran out, their shirts covering their noses from the harsh chemicals. Minutes later the school was evacuated for the day because of the chemical smell and the headaches it were causing.

Kyle and Will were never punished, mostly because the school had no solid proof that the boys had done it, but they bragged to everyone, and had even shown the empty jug to Korvid that afternoon. Despite all their mischief, they were pretty good guys and Korvid always swore that they would grow up to be either masterful businessmen, or international thieves.

After school that day, and for weeks afterward, the four of us would leave school and high-tail it to the public library, where Iphy and Jax were waiting. Together, the six of us would search the library's collection of old newspapers and local history books. For two and a half weeks we scanned every single local paper, looking for any kind of story about a missing person, or a dead body found in the woods. We came up with nothing of real value. There were a few false leads that we followed anywhere from a few hours to a few days: stories of missing girls and ladies, but they were always found alive, or dead somewhere far away from the woods. Once, we found a story from over 60 years ago about a child that had wandered away from home, presumably to the woods, and was never found. I ruled out that story because it was from the other end of the woods, and I couldn't imagine a child surviving long enough to cross that great stretch of wild wood only to die on our side and haunt the ravine.

Valentine's Day was the only day we didn't pore over old, cracking newspaper, instead opting to spend the afternoon running around town, getting free pieces of candy from all the shops and eating them so fast that sometimes we forgot which stores we had hit. Even still, we found nothing at all about the Wailing Woman, and the others were ready to call the search for her quits. I begged them to hang on just a little longer; I wanted to check one more place. She had somehow become an obsession in my mind; the Wailing Woman was more to me than mere shadows, dust and forgotten evils. I had to know who she really was, and what terrible fate had befallen her that she felt the need to haunt the ravine. If I couldn't find what I needed to know in the libraries, than I would go to the one place I knew she could not hide: the ravine.

It was easy to convince Iphy and Eddie to come with me; Eddie wanted to start looking for the moose, and Iphy was eager to help him. Secretly, I think half of Iphy's mind was occupied with the mysterious Wailing Woman, whom he still had yet to hear in her screeching entirety. Jax, Calm and Korvid all agreed to come after I pleaded with them. Eventually I had to promise that, after this final trip to the ravine, I would put the Wailing Woman and her mystery behind me and stop obsessing over her. Naturally, I had no intention of forgetting about her, even if I found nothing to perpetuate her existence. I knew that until I had unearthed the truth behind her, the Wailing Woman would wreak havoc in my imagination and haunt me just as surely as she haunted the ravine.

We went one Saturday near the end of February; those of us with troublesome families told our respective parents that we'd be staying at each other's houses. Thankfully, though our parents were neighbors, they were not exactly friends, and it was doubtful that there'd be any cross-chatter between them to ruin our plan. We were going to stay the night over at Our Place, unless it got completely unbearable, at which point we'd move back to the New Place to sleep. Iphy figured that two full days would be plenty of time for me to find what I was looking for or, conversely, to not find anything and be satisfied with the search.

It was a mile from Korvid's backyard to the ravine, but the forest didn't make it an easy mile. During our few months' absence from the woods, the trees seemed to have gone back to hating us, just like they did that first night on Halloween. Every few minutes one of us tripped on a hidden tree root, or some stray branch lashed out and snagged on hair or struck a face. They bunched together in places, barring our way and letting us know that we were not welcome within their borders anymore. Iphy and Jax were the only ones immune to the wrath of the woods, but I think that was more because of their status as Gods of Childhood walking among the mortal world than the woodland respecting them enough to allow them to walk unhindered.

Once we got to the ravine, all talking between us stopped and we listened. There were no birds, no chattering of squirrels or other small animals, and worse yet, there were no sounds of people. We were only a half mile — maybe three quarters of a mile — into the forest, but it felt like we were hundreds of miles from any living souls besides our own. Out there, in that expanse of quiet, with the ravine stretched out beneath us and the trees still going on as far as the eye could see in all directions, I felt the presence of the Wailing Woman all around us. She was not a lowly ghost who haunted the stretch of woods beyond the ravine, she was a living presence. She was the woods themselves: alive, breathing, flourishing. She was the last person on the earth; the last living soul as all the rest of the world fell away into nothingness. She was there, and I would find her.

While Iphy and Eddie started to climb down into the ravine, I skirted along its edge; the ravine was not really my destination, but the trees beyond it. The ravine marked the edge of the Wailing Woman's territory; for a reason unknown she would never cross that sacred ground, so I had to go find her somewhere beyond it. Iphy called out something about us all staying within shouting distance of each other, and I gave the others some kind of affirmative response. Once I had entered those woods, I was like a girl possessed; I didn't care if Jax, Korvid and Calm helped Eddie and Iphy look for the scattered bones. I had a mission to accomplish, and I could do it on my own, should it come to that.

I plunged heedlessly into the woods beyond the ravine; woods I had only trekked through that first snowfall earlier last year. These woods were so different from the woods behind the cul-de-sac. These woods had many different kinds of darkness to them — as if one weren't enough. And to make matters worse, the darkness was a rich and terrifying darkness that liked to linger with you long after you had left the woods. It was a kind of darkness that hunkered down in your mind and waited until it was late at night, and you were all alone, before it came at you full-force, like a wild animal with claws and fangs bared in a horrible grimace. And still other kinds of darkness were sticky and clung to you and made your palms sweaty, your mouth taste dirty and your skin feel clammy and you had to stop yourself from shivering, because you knew that's what gave the darkness power. The darkness of those woods wasn't gradual, either: I stepped away from the edge of the ravine, entering her territory fully, and the darkness just enveloped me, shrouded me like a funeral veil and dripped from the trees and bubbled up from hidden black springs underneath carpets of moss and long dead leaves.

Every now and then I could hear the faint shouts of my friends, calling to make sure I hadn't wandered too far. I always called back to them automatically, with no thought involved. All of my senses were focused on the ground beneath me; my eyes never left the forest floor. I don't know how it is that I never ran into a tree, or got sideswiped by a snaggly tree branch just waiting to lash out and draw blood. The wind, which had been strangely calm all week, started to rustle the dead branches and wrap its long, icy fingers around me, making me wish I'd brought a thicker coat. I moved up and down in strips, making sure to leave no bit of forest unchecked. I moved further and further away from the ravine, but I always stayed within earshot of my friends. I was so focused on my task that I didn't even notice that I wasn't alone.

"Over here!" The loud voice right behind me made me start and slip on the slick ground. I whirled around, water soaking up through the seat and cuffs of my pants, my palms dragging across stones and sticks; Jax was only a few feet behind me, looking down at me like I belonged in a padded room. "Are you alright?" he asked, reaching out a hand to help me to my feet.

"Y-yeah, just wet," I stammered, accepting his hand and scrambling up. "Why'd you yell like that?"

Jax raised an eyebrow. "The others were calling you for like three minutes; you were off in La-La Land."

I felt a burst of color enter my cheeks. "Oh."

I busied myself with brushing off leaves from my pants, flustered at Jax's appearance. I hadn't known that he'd followed me, and now that I had the information I felt awkward, like I was putting him in some kind of perilous position. It was alright for me to be checking the forest floor for some evidence of the Wailing Woman's previous life, but it somehow felt wrong to be dragging Jax along for the ride. "You know, you don't have to stay; I know it's kind of a drag, looking through the woods like this."

Jax shrugged. "That's what the others are doing: they're just looking for something else. Almost." He thought for a second. "Really, if you think about it, you're kind of looking for the same thing: you're looking for some remains of the Wailing Woman, and Eddie's looking for the remains of a moose."

Despite myself, I laughed. "At least Eddie knows that what he's looking for is actually here; I'm just guessing."

Jax laughed too. "So is Eddie; I wouldn't trust Thomas Smith's bragging with my dirty laundry." He sighed, shook his head with a smile. "For Eddie's sake, I hope Thomas wasn't lying to look cool; just Eddie's luck, he's out here for weeks looking for a skeleton that isn't here."

"I'll bet it's here." The wind was beginning to pick up a bit, making the branches rattle together like bones.

"You trust Thomas Smith?" he asked with a small, knowing smile.

"Yes, plus I have faith that Thomas doesn't care enough about someone else's opinion to make empty brags—just like I have faith that I'll find one of the Wailing Woman's secrets out here."

"You think she'd give them up so freely?"

Before I could answer the wind howled, and it rose until the Wailing Woman was screaming at us, snapping branches and throwing up great bunches of dead leaves from the ground. Her voice howled like a mad woman, more terrifying than I'd ever heard her. I shrieked and covered my ears, hunkering down as though that would help me avoid her anger and wrath. Beside me, Jax crouched, his hands covering his ears, his eyes darting about wildly, looking for the Wailing Woman herself, as though she'd step out from behind a tree—or even worse, through one — a bedraggled corpse with flesh hanging off in flimsy curtains, revealing the ivory white of her skull.

The wail died down after what seemed like a thousand years; as I straightened, I could feel my bones and muscles protesting. I looked around, goose bumps still standing straight up on my arms. "No, I guess not," I breathed, not wanting to speak too loudly and remind her of our presence on her land.

Jax looked about, an air of nervousness around him. "Maybe we should go back," he whispered.

I shook my head. "You can go back if you want to; I'm not scared."

"Then why are you whispering?"

"Out of respect," I lied; truthfully, I was terrified of these woods, and I hoped that Jax wouldn't leave me. I could already imagine what would happen after he left; as soon as the sound of his footsteps had gone, she would appear, dragging her body up out of the ground, groaning as she reached a rotting arm towards me to take my soul.

"Right." Jax saw through my fib, but he didn't call me on it; instead, he continued the search, eyes on the ground, following the path I had been taking.

We searched the rest of the day; twice more the Wailing Woman shrieked at us from some hidden place beyond the trees where we couldn't see. As we walked, we could feel her watching us, keeping tabs on our progress — or lack thereof. Finally, when the sun was beginning to sink below the level of the treetops, peering out at us as though through a mass of bony fingers that were lacing together to form a grate, I felt the first full weight of disappointment at our lack of findings. I knew my search

was a hopeless one; I could feel that the Wailing Woman would keep her secrets forever.

"It's getting late," said Jax, stating the obvious.

"Yeah, I know," I sighed, looking around me once more; I wanted to keep going, but if I wanted to get back to Our Place by dark, I had to get back to the ravine now while the sun was still fairly high in the sky.

"We'll try again tomorrow," Jax promised, putting an arm around my dropping shoulder.

I was about to tell him to just forget it — that it seemed to me that the Wailing Woman would rather die a thousand deaths before she gave up her secrets — when I noticed something sticking out of the ground. It looked like a stick, jutting out at an odd angle from a pile of leaves at the base of a tree. I dug out the leaves, revealing a small pile of stones and a small wooden cross, no taller than a foot and a half.

The cross was made of two sticks, tied together with old, rusty wire that left flakes of red on my hands. As I handled it softly, even reverently, I got a sudden urge to put the relic back, turn around and walk away. A part of me wanted nothing to do with it, but a bigger part of me wanted to have it always, keep it close and never let the small cross be forgotten. Eventually, the bigger part of me won; I picked up the cross and started back the way we had come. Beside me, Jax was speechless; we didn't say a word the entire trip back to the ravine.

I had found my proof.

"That cross could belong to anything; it could belong to some little girl's hamster." Korvid was unconvinced that my cross constituted as proof for the Wailing Woman's existence. Despite his help with the search for her origins (or maybe *because* of it), he still didn't believe that she was real.

"No way," Iphy scoffed. "Why would a little girl bury her hamster way out in the woods? Besides, it was right where Eraliss said it would be; beyond the ravine."

"That doesn't prove anything," insisted Korvid.

"Didn't you hear her?" I asked. "She yelled three times."

Now, all of them were shaking their heads. "We didn't hear anything," said Calm softly.

I was incredulous. "Nothing at all?" I hadn't thought we were *that* far away; to have heard the Wailing Woman's shrieking cries when the others didn't.

Eddie, who was now sporting a curved length of bone that he was sure was a rib, shook his head again. "Nothing at all, Eraliss."

We fell silent, each of us mulling over our separate lists of facts and speculations. Finally Korvid just shrugged. "I still say that cross marked the grave of some poor kid's pet—not the final resting place of a spirit that haunts the woods beyond the ravine."

"And you're entitled to that opinion," I said, sticking my tongue out for good measure. "It marked her grave, or at least the place where she died, but if you want to believe that it marks Harry the Hamster, then go ahead."

"Yeah," Iphy joined in with his confident grin. "But, you'd be wrong."

Korvid groaned. "Not you too, Iphy."

"Hell yes, me too," Iphy snorted. "Open your eyes, Korvid; there are magical things in these woods." The way he said it, even Korvid nodded his head in sullen agreement; it wasn't an opinion, it was a statement of fact when it came out of Iphy's mouth.

It tickled me to know that one of the Childhood Gods believed in the Wailing Woman just as much as I did, because if Iphy believed in something, then it had to be true. If Iphy believed in the lost city of Atlantis, then it was waiting somewhere at the bottom of the sea; if he believed in Santa Claus, then there was a fat man in a red suit at the top of the world; if he believed that these woods housed magical, mysterious things, then the trees lived alongside fairies, elves, and the ghost of a woman who had died and still haunted the woods. If Iphy believed in these things, then they were true. And he did believe.

And I believed in Iphy.

SPRING

From the Journal of Calm Sheldon

The first day of spring, my father left us. It was raining hard, coming down in torrents and making great wide rivers in the streets. There was no goodbye from him; I heard him come down the stairs in his usual manner, but he didn't stop inside the kitchen for his traditional breakfast of coffee and toast. I heard a small thump on the floor by the door; the door opened, and the door closed. I could faintly hear his car start up and drive away, and I wondered where it was he was going.

I thought little more of it, and finished my cereal before I ventured upstairs to where my parents slept. They hadn't fought in some time, and I was glad for that, but my heart sank as I neared their room; I could hear my mother crying. I didn't go inside: I knew if I did, she would stop crying, bottle up her sadness and try to bravely face the day. Instead, I sat down outside her door and listened to her cry, as if hearing her tears would make my own come. They didn't. I sat next to my mother's room for two whole hours, listening to her cry and scream into her pillow, and though I felt an emptiness growing in the space between my heart and my stomach, I found I couldn't cry.

If I cried, it would be too much like giving up. If I cried, it would be admitting to myself that my father was gone and he was never coming back. And I couldn't admit that; it couldn't be real. He was my father: he was one of two people who were supposed to be there for me forever. He wasn't supposed to be a man that walked out of my life without even saying goodbye. He was supposed to love me, not leave me.

When my mother had stopped her crying, I went quietly back downstairs. She didn't tell me that he had left: she merely took my hand and told me that we would spend the day cleaning the house and going shopping. I didn't argue; I felt too hollow to visit with Iphy, Jax and the others anyway. Our day was spent avoiding the issue at hand: I didn't ask about my father, she didn't tell me that he had left. That night, I heard her crying in her room; a room she used to share with a man that she loved. All I could do was listen.

The weekend went by and I didn't see my friends until Monday. I went through school, quiet like a spectator, just watching the going-ons of the day. Eraliss and Eddie tried talking with me at lunch. I only nodded at their questions. My mind was far away, thinking about what my father was doing just then. After school, on the walk home, Korvid tried his hand at getting me to talk; he wasn't successful either. Only when we were all at the New Place, joined by Iphy and Jax, did I finally talk.

"What's up with Calm?" Iphy asked. "We haven't seen her all weekend."

"Don't talk like she's not here," chided Jax.

Iphy snorted. "She might as well not be; look at her."

"She hasn't said a word all day," Eraliss murmured.

They fell silent, all of them. Iphy was giving me a funny look that walked the line between concern and the pitying look you give someone wrapped up in a straight jacket; for the first time since my father had left, I felt compelled to speak. "He's gone." My voice was squeaky and raw, and it startled me because it didn't sound like my voice should. It sounded small and afraid, and I didn't want to be either—not since Iphy had shown up.

I tried again. "My dad... he walked out... and he didn't come back."

Silence followed my statement, and in that silence I felt something big and heavy that had been hanging in the space between my heart and my stomach fall away, and the tears came hot and impossibly quickly to my cheeks. "He left, and he'll never come back."

I felt arms around me, heard Eraliss murmuring in my ear about how things would be alright—somehow, things would be alright. I wanted to believe her, but it was far too hard. It was too hard to think positive; to think that maybe, just *maybe*, my entire life hadn't been destroyed by the simple act of my father walking out our front door.

Then, Iphy sat down next to me, easy and relaxed like he was in complete control of everything around him, including this. "I know how that is," he said. "Did they say the 'D' word?"

I blinked. "The… 'D' word?"

"Divorce." He leaned back on his hands, taking the world and all the problems that it held in stride. He could do that; it was one of his godly powers that made him shine and glow enough to make the sun jealous. "My parents were talking about that before I left — screaming about it, actually." He shook his head, still so relaxed, so easy in the face of a word that held such horror for me.

"Parents are weird like that," he mused, looking so childish and so scholarly at the same time. "They scream, and they shout, and then they try to act normal when us kids are around, like we didn't hear them arguing." He shook his head, and we all leaned in closer to him, needing to be next to him as he unveiled the misty haze of unknown that still surrounded him after all this time.

"They don't get it," he sighed, and I held onto that sound, like it was the answer to all my problems. Somehow, my own problems seemed small in comparison to finally hearing Iphy speak of where he'd come from and why he'd left. Sometimes, I think he saved his own story for a time like this — when his words would make someone else's problems seem minimal. He always did like to save the best for last.

"Parents don't know how much it hurts kids to hear them argue and fight. The two people in the world who are your center, fighting and screaming even though they shouldn't. It shatters you from the inside, makes you hollow in the face of something so great and so big that you can't fully comprehend it until it's long gone, and you're left with memories tinted the wrong color."

Beside me, I could feel, rather than see, Eraliss nodding; she knew exactly what Iphy was talking about — she'd seen it herself when her own father had left for far-off places.

"And you know something went wrong," Iphy continued, but this time, his voice sounded strained — tight — like the words were trying to stay in his throat and were being forced out. I wanted to tell him to stop; it wasn't right, hearing Iphy's voice being anything but easy and carefree. This tight, unhappy voice didn't belong in Iphy's mouth, and I wanted to say so, but I couldn't. I could do nothing but listen, transfixed as the godly child continued with his story — a story that was so much more important than my own.

"Somewhere along the way, something went wrong and you don't know where, or what happened. You try to fix it; you clean your room more, you get better grades, but it's not something that you can fix. You want to scream at them, because they loved each other once, and you know that somewhere deep down they still do; they just don't want to try anymore. So, you try for them, but it's not enough: they still fight, and they still scream, and you're stuck in the middle as the two people who are supposed to be the whole world to you rip out the ground from underneath your feet. Then, you have nothing left to do but fall and bleed and break."

He fell silent and we all held our breath, silently begging him to continue. He sat silent for a few moments, and then he shrugged. With that shrug, he returned to the boy that we all recognized, as though the simple act of moving his shoulders had thrown off that horrid, tight voice, and returned his status of a carefree God of

Childhood. He grinned, his voice once again easy, "I didn't want to fall, so I left. I decided I'd head out to my grandparent's house, see if I could hang out with them for a while. Turns out they'd flown south for the winter a little too early. So, I looked for a nice place out in the woods to wait for them to come back. The rest, as they say, is history."

Then, he smiled at me. "Don't worry, Calm: if they haven't said the 'D' word, then there's nothing to worry about. He'll come back, and maybe they'll keep fighting, and maybe he'll leave again, but as long as they don't say 'divorce' then he'll always come back."

And, true to Iphy's word, my father did return. Just four days after he had left, he came back, walking through the door like nothing had happened; like it was just a business trip that he had been on. For a few hours, I convinced myself that that's what had happened: he'd been called away on a business trip and my mother had been angry at his job, not at him.

Of course, as I lay in bed, listening to them through the walls of the house, I could hear them start to fight again. They screamed, words flying back and forth so fast that I was sure neither of them heard the nasty names that they were calling each other. I listened, and I was frightened; I was straining to hear that magical word that would spell disaster for my family: divorce.

It didn't come; they continued to yell long into the night, and though I had school in the morning I stayed up as long as they did, hanging onto their every word. The hours passed and still the word didn't come up. They went to bed and fell silent, and with their silence I finally felt I could sleep. And despite their fight, I was happy. Iphy was right: my father had left, but he had come back. The word had not been uttered, and my world was alright.

C.S

~*~

The beginning of spring brought rain: lots and lots of rain. It came down in buckets, flooding the street and making the trip to and from school miserable for everyone. Waterproof jackets, umbrellas and thick soled shoes, meant for sloshing through water came out of our closets and began to decorate our persons. The rain came down hard for days, and then it would halt and the sun shone with such intensity that it felt more like summer than spring; then the rain would return a day or two later and the cycle would begin anew.

Despite the rain, it did little to ruin our good mood; we stayed dry and warm in the shelter of the New Place, and because Mr. Smithy knew that Korvid, Calm, Eddie and I were close friends with Jax, we could pick up the day olds and save Jax a rainy wet trip that could have ended in a cold, or worse. Through it all, Iphy remained confident that the rain was a good thing.

"Once the rain stops, it'll be nothing but fun in the sun."

Eddie, who had by now collected more than half of the moose's skeleton, nodded his head. "I can't wait for summer: no more school, and nothing but free time."

"Yeah," agreed Korvid. "Once summer comes, everything will be great. The days will be long, and we can have fun forever."

Despite the problems at her own house, even Calm got in on the enjoyment. "Everything looks better in the spring and summer; winter makes everything look gray and cold."

Jax stretched with a smile on his face. "It'll be great to be out in the sunshine again; I can't wait to get back to Our Place."

I nodded. "Yeah, I miss that place." I could see it already: our fire pit and the ring of boulders, the roof of woven twigs and branches that blocked out drizzle but not the brightness of the moon and the stars. I could imagine our walking through the woods, making new discoveries, finding new places to hang out and new places to call our own in a world where we all felt that we had very little.

I imagined meeting Iphy's grandparents at the beginning of summer: their smiling faces and the warm smell of fresh lemonade and home baked apple pie. They would welcome us, and they'd fall in love with Jax just like everyone always did, and they'd offer to let him stay with them. They'd take in Iphy and Jax, sparing them the cruelties that could come of facing the world alone. My dad would return and my mother would stop wallowing. Calm's dad would make up with her mother and Calm could feel like herself again. Korvid would finally talk to his dad and they'd move him up out of the basement and their house would become a home again. Eddie would complete his moose skeleton and his parents would see it all shining white like ivory; they'd finally appreciate their son just as much as they appreciated all the rest of their children.

In my imagination, we all came out of the spring and entered the summer like changed people; we all found a slice of happiness and we all got what we wanted and what we deserved. Our shattered lives were magically put back together again with super glue, sunshine and the power of Childhood Gods. The darkness of winter was over and nothing could ever go wrong again.

As it happened, the sun began to shine again as March got into full swing; with the sun came a restlessness in all of us, and often times Korvid, Calm, Eddie and I would return from school to find that Jax and Iphy had gone missing. We'd all go home, gather more odds and ends from our respective kitchens, and then we'd all head back to the New Place and wait for them to return. Sometimes the wait was only a few minutes, sometimes it was a couple of hours, but they always returned, without fail. They returned with stories of wasted afternoons searching the junkyard with Thomas Smith or of exciting adventures in which they battled stray dogs or found new places to pinch and pilfer eggs during the dead of night.

Sometimes Korvid would skip school if there were no major homework assignments due and the sun was busy shining and making the air warm. We cautioned him against it, but he paid us no mind; I never really believed that we would ever get through to him. Ever since that first night with Iphy and Jax, when we stayed out until the wee hours of the morning, Korvid had looked at them with a kind of longing. In him was a hunger for the lives that they led, though he never seriously pursued the idle dream of joining them. The more he skipped school, the more I felt like Korvid was slowly leaving the real world for a land of dreams and endless afternoons.

Other times I thought he was just trying to irritate his teachers so they would call up his dad and make him take notice of all the things that Korvid was and wasn't doing. I knew he was just vying for his dad's attention but every time that he walked over to the New Place when we gathered at the manhole cover for school, I felt like something bad was brewing.

Iphy and Jax were polar opposites when it came to the subject of Korvid skipping school to hang out with them. Iphy was all for it: as far as he was concerned he didn't need any more schooling, and if he didn't, then there was no reason that Korvid needed any more either. At first, Jax had thought it a fine idea; he always looked up to Korvid like an older brother. But, like all younger siblings, he quickly noticed that Korvid's habit of skipping school was occurring more and more frequently. He told Korvid how stupid he was being; there was plenty more for Korvid to learn. Sometimes they could get in huge fights about it and only Iphy could dispel the animosity.

Even then, Iphy's interjections only worked three-quarters of the time to pacify the two sides; sometimes, for whatever reason, Jax would be just as mad at Iphy as he was at Korvid. One afternoon, after Calm had told Korvid that he had missed a hugely important test (at least according to Kyle and Will) Jax had stormed off to sit in the ruined kitchen, fuming about Korvid and Iphy's lack of concern. I followed and eventually coaxed Jax's reasoning for his anger out of him.

"They just don't get it: they're so lucky and all they do is waste it," he sighed, leaning against my shoulder. "They have everything that I want and they just ignore it and throw it away. I never wanted to be homeless. I want a family and a house, a mother and a father. I want to go to school and take tests and have at least one meal that I don't need to worry about." He never mentioned that it wasn't fair; I'll always commend him for that. Sure, he got mad at them for squandering what he thought was a great gift, but he never brought up fairness, never questioned why him and not them if they wanted his life so badly. I knew that Jax would never wish his own misfortune on anyone else; it wasn't the way he did things.

The days went by in that fashion, with Korvid skipping school once, sometimes two times a week to spend the days roaming the town with Iphy and Jax. Some days they went out into the woods, hiking out past Our Place in hopes of finding new places to claim as our own. Other times they went out into the Wailing Woman's territory, looking for any bones they could find to bring back and give to Eddie, in case they belonged to the elusive moose skeleton.

I kept the Wailing Woman's cross on a shelf in my bedroom. When I wasn't with Iphy, Jax and the others, I was in my room, notebook open, just looking at the cross, waiting for it to speak to me and reveal its secrets. My notebook was already filled with notes and imagined facts that would go into the story about the Wailing Woman; anything that came to mind, I jotted it down. Still I chewed my pencil or pen and watched the cross, spending my time just waiting for it to speak.

Calm kept an eye on her parents, listening to them fight, waiting to hear the word that Iphy had told her would ruin her family. She stayed up late, waiting until they went to bed and the coast was clear. She certainly couldn't sleep while they were still fighting; she might miss the dreaded utterance of *that* word. In class she was bolder, speaking up when we talked about social studies and answering questions without being asked to, but back at home she returned to being quiet and meek while she listened and waited for the word to be said.

Eddie combed the woods looking for the missing bones; there were still a good number of them, according to the books he had checked out of the school's library. He had about two-thirds of the bones already, but there were still many more that he couldn't find. He wanted to ask for help from his family, but each time he asked his older brothers, they told him to wait because they were busy. They stayed busy, and Eddie never did get their help. So Eddie waited for help, from us or from his family: help that never seemed to come, but still he waited for it.

That was how the entire month of March was spent: waiting on things that never seemed to come. April brought more rain, and more afternoons and weekends holed up in the shelter of the New Place. We loathed the rain that first couple of weeks in April; we'd had so many sun breaks the month before that now we wanted nothing else. We hungered for the freedom to wander and explore; we'd already explored every nook and cranny of the New Place during the short cold days of winter.

So, when the first clear afternoon greeted us as we left the school doors, we all raced home as fast as we could. We took the many shortcuts through various yards and alleys that we had come to know during our many trips to and from school in an attempt to save precious seconds. I raced inside, expecting to see my mother on the couch with the newspaper in her lap as per usual, but she wasn't. Instead, she was in the kitchen, having a hushed conversation over the phone. Upon hearing my boisterous entrance, she hissed a quick goodbye and slammed the phone back into its cradle. I should have been concerned, or at the very least curious, but the bright sun and the adventure it promised had captured my attention.

"Mom, I'm gonna go hang out with the guys." By this time, mom had noticed me playing with the group of kids from the cul-de-sac, and she'd even met Iphy more than once; she knew him merely as 'that kid living out on Olaha Way.' She never suspected that he was really living next door to us in the abandoned house with Jax, the town orphan.

She nodded her head and told me when to expect dinner; she did this every time I told her that I'd be out, but I almost always stayed out later. Before, she would have grounded me in a heartbeat, but lately she'd been much more forgiving of that sort of thing. I took it all in stride; I noticed the change, but was too busy with my own life to care. I didn't think that it had any kind of impact on what would happen in my life; it was my mother's life that had changed, not mine.

I rushed out to the New Place; Korvid was there on the lawn with Iphy and Jax, rolling around and wrestling like boys were prone to do. If they weren't covered in grass stains and scraped elbows by nightfall, then their day had been wasted. Eddie came out of his house racing across the grass, laughing at the simple joy of running in the sunlight after weeks of rain. Their boyish exuberance rubbed off on me and I joined in the dog pile; laughing, elbowing and tumbling in the grass with the people that meant the whole world to me.

Calm came upon us like that, laughing herself as she watched us trying to untangle our limbs and get the dirt and grass out of our hair. She reached a hand out and helped Iphy to his feet. He laughed again, whooping with joy as he leaped up, reaching a hand towards the sky as if he could grasp it and climb up to greet the stars that we couldn't see.

"The woods!" he suddenly yelled, looking towards the wall of trees that stretched beyond our ring of houses. "Let's go!" And he took off.

We struggled to follow him, untangling ourselves and scrambling to our feet, all dignity lost at his command. We followed Iphy as surely as we had that first night, so captivated by his white and brown hair in the spring sunshine, by his roguish charm, his exoticness that manifested itself every now and then in the way he spoke, or the words he used. We raced after him, the five of us running to some unseen goal that Iphy was inevitably leading us to.

We ran with the freedom of childhood; we didn't care where we were going. We were unconcerned with the future. Tomorrow, the day after, five years down the line: these figures of time meant nothing to us. We ran for that very moment, right then. We ran because our friend, our *leader*, was running ahead of us, laughing, and there was nothing beyond that.

I think about that time often, when the darkness of Real Life looms over me and throws shadows over everything but that one perfect memory. Sometimes I go out jogging through the park on those perfect, crisp autumn days, and it's never the same, because this time I know what I'm running from. Back then, none of us knew; none of us had a clue why we ran so hard. We didn't realize that we ran together that day because we were all trying to escape something that's wholly inescapable. We ran to hide from Time. We ran to preserve our Innocence.

It's silly, looking back. No one can outrun Time, and no one can keep their Innocence forever, but we tried. That one beautiful afternoon; that picturesque memory that can never be dulled or broken by Real Life's sharp teeth. We ran as though we could actually achieve the impossible: defy Time and stay young forever with each other.

We needed no others, just ourselves. We could run forever and never grow old, never be hurt enough to make us grow up too fast. Iphy would always be right there in front of us, leading us, telling us what to do and where to go because he was a magical god in the body of a boy that we had come to honor, respect and yes even love with all of our hearts. He could lead us, forever, and we could run for all time, leaving behind the darkness of the world as everything passed us by in a blur of color and motion.

We caught up with him and we all ran side by side, darting through the trees and jumping over exposed roots and bushes. The wind whipped through our hair; trees that we had long surmised to hate us seemed to bend away, making room between them so that we could run. We heard each other's laughter and panting gasps, but I could never be sure which sound belonged to whom. It was as if we breathed as one, as though we were all vital pieces in some cosmic, intricate machine. We ran until the world fell away from our feet and the trees vanished in a blanket of white, and it was just the six of us — only us. There was nothing left in the world.

Then I burst through a pair of trees that I didn't register as trees, and the whiteness that had become the world suddenly exploded into color, and the terra firma that I was running on suddenly dropped away. My brain didn't register the abrupt drop and the expanse of tree tops beyond it, but my body did. My legs suddenly refused to work properly and they tried to separate: one going one way, the other going the opposite. I ended up falling backwards, my arms flailing out and catching someone else, while one of my renegade legs tripped another running body. Someone running behind me tripped over my shoulders and ended up falling on top of me, and we became a single entity of twisting limbs and curses of pain.

I tried to untangle myself from Eddie, who had fallen on top of me after tripping over my shoulders, but Calm was trapped between Korvid's elbow and Eddie's knee. Beside me, Iphy cursed as he tried to get out from underneath Jax, and Jax gave a little yelp as he tried to make room for Iphy, while untangling his leg from mine. Korvid was the first one up; he helped Iphy to his feet, then Jax. By the time the rest of us were on our feet and checking ourselves over for bruises and scrapes, Korvid had wandered over to the edge. His inhalation of breath drew the rest of us to his side like moths to a flame.

The ground opened up in front of us, dropping away into a panorama of more sky than I think I had ever seen before or since. A hundred feet below us, the trees created a carpet that stretched out in a pallet of mostly greens with random bits of blossoming colors. We all stood staring —

no, *gaping*—at the deep gouge in the earth that had nearly swallowed us in its beauty.

I'd lived most of my life at the edge of the forest, but never once had I been so far into it to have seen that cliff and the breathtaking view beyond it. From the surprised look on Iphy's face, even the boy who had lived in these woods for countless weeks had never stumbled onto this small wonder.

"Amazing," said Korvid in a hushed, revered voice; speaking too loudly would break the spell of the woods and shatter the scene before us.

"I'll say," Eddie breathed.

Calm looked over the edge and grew pale; she stepped back and had to look away. As long as I'd known her, Calm had possessed a staggering fear of heights.

We stayed quiet for a few more seconds, just drinking in a sight that we had never seen beyond the world of television nature specials and encyclopedias. Then, Iphy pointed a finger out into the valley. "Check it out: a river!"

It was true: below, in the earthly gouge, a thin line of blue worked its way through the forest, sometimes getting lost in the foliage and sometimes glaring obviously at us through patches of sparse trees.

"Let's check it out!" Iphy was already at the edge of the cliff, looking down the steep face to try and find a possible route down.

We followed the edge of the cliff for half a mile or so, until it started tilting downward: eventually we finally found an easy trail that led to the valley floor. From there, Iphy ran pell-mell into the trees; like we were destined to do, we followed him. We ran through the trees and patches of scrub, until the trees stopped and the ground sloped down into the gravel banks of a small river. We all stood in awe that almost dwarfed the panoramic view of the valley.

The water was impossibly clear; we could see the gravel pebbles turn into large river rocks about fifteen feet in, which turned into large boulders in the middle of the river. The water was cool to the touch, like liquid ice on its way from the mountain to the far-off sea. Even the sounds and smell of it enchanted us; it was quiet and pleasant, and the scent wafting up from the water wasn't fetid, or rank like the larger river that cut through the state, but refreshing and full of a kind of life that only rivers seemed to know.

In his excitement, Iphy ran straight into the water, not even stopping to remove his shirt, just ripping it off over the top of his head as he ran. He ran until the water was up to his thighs, then he dove forward, ducking under the surface and popping up seconds later, laughing and shaking his head. Jax followed after, whooping and waving his arms up above his head as he raced into the water. He stopped calf deep to tear his shirt off and toss the flag of fabric that was of no use to him right then back onto the bank, and dove into the water. For a few seconds, it was just the two of them: immortal Gods of Childhood, playing in the river, dunking each other's heads, sputtering and laughing.

Then Korvid followed them, leaving his shirt, shoes and socks on the bank. He waded in until the water was at his midsection before surging forward and swimming to where Iphy and Jax were. Eddie was next, leaving his shirt on, but taking his shoes and socks off before joining in the fun. Calm did likewise, making sure to tuck her socks into her shoes. I ran in as I was: shirt, shoes, socks and everything.

We splashed about laughing for far longer than we should have. We couldn't help it; when you grow up in the same place, over the years the familiar gets boring. You learn all of the secrets and haunts of your town, and nothing ever surprises you about it. That's what made this river magical: our town had one last surprise and Iphy had shown us the way. We timed how long we could hold our breath (Eddie won with a whopping full minute), held races to see who could cross the river the fastest (Jax beat Iphy by a landslide) and even tried to come up with our own synchronized swimming routine.

The sun dipped behind the tree line and the water grew chilly, but still we tried to linger in the river that we had only just discovered. I knew it was silly, but I felt like if we left it, we would never find it again. It would vanish into obscurity overnight and we'd only have memories of one too-short afternoon. It was only the thought of angry parents that got us moving out of the water and onto the bank. We were already chilled by the time everyone got their previously discarded articles of clothing back on, and it was almost dark by the time we had found the path back up the ridge. From there, we took one last look at the little valley that cut through what I affectionately thought of as Iphy's Forest before we turned back and picked our way through the darkened trees towards more familiar ground.

The stars were out, shining their brightest, when we emerged from the tree line behind the New Place. Korvid, Calm and I said our goodbyes to Iphy and Jax before we headed across the cul-de-sac to our respective homes, while Eddie crossed behind the abandoned house to get to his own. Iphy and Jax stayed out in the starlight, still laughing in joy about the river and the day.

I was worried that my mother would ground me until school ended, so I entered as quietly as I could. I was expecting her to turn on the light and catch me red handed, but I was lucky. She wasn't downstairs in the living room; the rest of the house was dark and quiet. Still I stepped on eggshells the entire way up the stairs, my mind amplifying every single creak and groan into rock concert proportions. When I finally managed to reach the upstairs hallway, I noticed my mom's light was on and I could hear her having a hushed conversation. I thought it was the police, but I heard her give a childish giggle—a sound I'd never heard from her before. I decided to not look a gift horse in the mouth; I darted into my room, curled up on my bed and spent the next hour straining to hear my mom and trying desperately to figure out what in the world would make her giggle like a little girl.

Korvid called me almost at the crack of dawn two days later on Saturday; Mom yelled up to me to get out of bed and answer the phone, so I wasn't particularly pleasant when I asked him why the heck he was calling so early.

"Ask your mom if you can spend the night at my house."

The early hour rendered me slow as well as irritable. "What? What are you talking about?"

"Iphy, Jax and I talked it over," The night before, as he was more and more prone to do, Korvid had stayed with Iphy and Jax way later than Calm, Eddie and I did. "If you all say you're sleeping at my place, we can go camp out at the river!"

I was instantly awake. Already, the river was acting more and more like a wondrous destination built only in godly imagination than just another piece of the landscape. "Will that work?" I asked, in a hushed tone, as though Mom was eavesdropping on the conversation and not busy singing horribly off key as she made breakfast.

"Of course it will; we've planned it all out. Everyone's gonna say they're staying at my place. That way, if anyone's parents decide to check it out with my dad, he'll just say he wasn't there. Everyone on this street knows that my dad works nights. We say we're going to help out Thomas Smith at the junkyard the next day for some spending cash, we're good until tomorrow evening."

The plan sounded ideal, but I made a face. "My mom hates Thomas."

"Everyone's parents hate Thomas: he's the kind of person parents warn their children about. All the more reason to say we're helping him; they won't bother asking *him* about it. If they do and he says we weren't, we just say he's lying. Besides, I'm sure he'll cover for us—he's cool like that."

I had to admit, the plan was more than ideal; it was simple, sweet perfection. "What do I need?"

I could hear the grin on Korvid's face in his voice. "Sleeping bag, swimsuit, flashlight and any and all food you can grab. New Place in an hour?"

Even though I knew he couldn't see it over the phone, I nodded. "See ya then."

An hour later, we were all at the New Place, readjusting backpacks and double-checking that we had everything that we needed: food; sleeping bags; swimsuits and jackets; a book of matches; Iphy's pot and pan; flashlights and Calm's dad's big floodlight.

Once at the river, we set our bags down and dove right in, glad for the cool, refreshing water on the surprisingly hot day. We laughed and splashed and Iphy even swam all the way across the river to the opposite bank, proudly declaring that land as his own with a piece of driftwood.

After we swam, we continued down the river, watching as the water changed from slow to fast the farther downriver we went. Eddie found an arrowhead made of chipped, black rock, which started an impromptu game of Cowboys and Indians. It was me, Calm and Korvid (the Cowboys) against Iphy, Jax and Eddie (the Indians.) When the sun was high in the sky our stomachs were grumbling too loudly for our liking. Iphy and Jax gathered dry branches, Korvid used the matches to make a fire, and we roasted hotdogs on sticks, not minding the bits of bark that flavored the inside.

Beyond the small rapids, we found a small, still part of the river. For a while we scoured the rocks, looking for those perfect, flat rocks that could skip a dozen times if you threw it right. Jax got to ten, Iphy to eight, and the rest of us barely managed past five; we continued on.

As we walked, the trees pressed in then pushed back, and the bank of the river got higher and higher, until soon the base of the tree trunks at the tree line were almost level with Calm's head. Then, we rounded a bend in the river, and the trees seemed to rush us, bending up and away, back into the forest, creating a tunnel with their bent trunks and sprawling foliage. We gawked at this green tunnel for a few minutes before Korvid finally figured it out.

"Aw, man... look at that! That's just gotta be the ravine!"

A second look proved his assumption to be true; we were at the tail end of the ravine. Transfixed, I started forward, spellbound by the simple magic of the forest. The tunnel pushed inward, until the sloping sides turned out of sight; I followed only until the sounds of the river grew faint in the silent forest.

"It is," I said, emerging from the trees. "That means we're in *her* territory."

"We're camping here," Iphy declared. The sky above us was bleeding into a darker blue than the sky-blue of sunny afternoons; soon it would be dark and we'd be stumbling about, tripping over rocks and making fools of ourselves.

"You really think it's safe?" asked Eddie, casting furtive glances about the trees.

"What's she gonna do? Kill us in our sleep?" Iphy snorted.

"She could," I said automatically. Everyone looked at me, and I felt my cheeks grow hot; I hadn't meant to say anything, but being here, at the edge of her territory in the coming nightfall, had spurred my voice.

Korvid grew excited. "Have you come up with anything? I mean, weren't you going to write a story about her?"

Now I was trapped; I could only nod. "I may have a solid start," I lied. I knew full well what my start was, and

I could already feel, deep in my bones, that tonight the rest of the story would come to me.

"Sweet!" Iphy cried. "You gotta tell us! Like a ghost story around the campfire."

"First things first," said Jax, eyeing the darkening sky. "We gotta set up camp before we can have a campfire story.

I volunteered to go with Korvid into the dark ravine to find some more dry firewood and kindling; just being in her woods gave me a thrill. I grabbed an armful of dry branches, trying to think about how much we'd need for the night. Korvid came up behind me, his arms also full.

"We should have enough."

"Here's hoping," I murmured, afraid to speak too loudly and warn the Wailing Woman of our presence.

"So, do you really have some thoughts on her?" he asked, giving me a curious look.

"I think so."

"How? We couldn't find anything in the libraries."

I nodded. "Mostly it's stuff I made up; but looking at that cross.... I don't know. It makes me feel connected to her somehow." His silence told me that he still didn't think the cross in my room had any correlation with her. "And whenever we're in this place—her territory—I always feel like she's trying to tell us something."

"You think? I always think she's trying to get rid of us."

Admittedly, I felt like that sometimes too; I didn't say as much. "I'd like to think that she sees something special in us; she knows she can trust us with her secrets."

He nodded again, looking up through the canopy of trees at the tiny glimmer of stars that tried to reach us through the leaves. "I'd like that. To be good enough for her, if she's really out there."

We made our way back to the others.

By the time our fire had been made and was burning brightly, the air had grown chilly and damp. The sky was a dark, solid indigo lit up by millions of tiny pricks of light that shimmered and blinked at us like eyes watching with great interest. Our sleeping bags had been spread out on a smooth part of the bank, far enough away from the river, but not quite under the cover of the trees, either. We huddled around the fire, listening to it pop and crackle as Iphy told us dozens of little horror stories that always happened to a friend of a friend of his older brother. Just as Iphy was finishing one, Jax looked at me.

"Weren't you going to tell us about the Wailing Woman?"

For a split second a look of annoyance flashed across Iphy's features, but then he grinned. "Yeah, you were gonna tell us how she ended up haunting these woods."

A blush crept up my face. "I don't know for certain," I started off lamely.

"That doesn't matter," Iphy waved his hand.

I looked around for some kind of escape, but there was none to be had. My heart fluttered in my chest; I had never told my stories to anyone before. Even though these were my closest friends, I was nervous and tense. Then, I looked back at Iphy—all grins and confidence—and I felt a confidence building up in me, as though through osmosis. Despite my initial fear, I was excited; I could practically feel the Wailing Woman at my shoulder, whispering in my ear, telling me her tale of sadness and woe. She believed that I would get her story right, and my friends were waiting. I smiled at them, their faces lit by the glow of the fire. In a hushed voice, I began to relate the tale of the Wailing Woman.

"This happened a long time ago; too long for anyone to even remember the stories properly. Time likes to take things and twist them, obscuring fact from fiction and blurring the lines between what really happened, what people think happened, and what people *wanted* to happen.

Before our town was founded, there was another town in its place: a smaller, simpler town. And in this town there was a woman. Her name's been forgotten over time, but maybe that's a good thing; she could be anyone's mother, sister or best friend. She had a husband, but not one of her choosing. It had been arranged by their parents, and while he seemed fine with his indifferent wife, she was not so happy with her partner. She had a lover, whose name has also been lost these many years, and they met every other night.

Finally, she couldn't take living with her husband another day. Her lover suggested that they run off into the night and elope in some far away little town, where no one would find them and no one knew them. She agreed, feeling hope and happiness blossom in her chest; it was decided that they should leave that very night. Her lover left her, promising to meet her in the woods outside of town, past the church and after the bells rang midnight. She left everything she had, even her baby still sleeping in his crib, and was at the church just as the bells tolled midnight. Thinking she'd be late, she raced into the woods, so eager to find her lover amongst the darkened trees.

She ran and searched, frantically looking for the man she loved and the new life he had promised her; all she found was darkness. Far away, the church bells tolled one o'clock, and she was suddenly afraid: all around her, she could feel the eyes of something in the forest, watching her in the dark. She backed up, looking about and trying to peer through the darkness. Then, she felt the hands.

For a moment, she felt safe in her lover's arms, but as the seconds passed, she realized that those hands couldn't possibly belong to her one and only lover. They were cold, clammy hands; rough and solid. She turned with a shriek, looking into the empty hollow eye sockets of the skull of some monstrous beast. She tried to shrink back in terror, her voice silent and terrified in her throat as the beast loomed over her. It was tall and bulky, its body hidden in swirls of shadow. The sockets burned with an unnatural red glow and the jaw clattered open, revealing rows of needle teeth. A single sharp horn swept backward from the brow, and from the open maw a chittering laugh rushed out in one sudden force of air that knocked her to the forest floor.

She had heard stories of this beast: a monster that haunted all the forests of the world, traveling between them all, looking for flesh to consume after the midnight tolling of the church bells. It loomed over her now, swelling in size until the trees bent aside for it, and there was nothing left but her and it.

Finally, her voice found her and a scream ripped from her throat, but it was drowned out completely by the monster's roar. Its gaping mouth filled her vision and surrounded her, knocking the life out of her body just as easily as she used to knock dandelion seeds from the white puffballs that grew in her yard.

She felt warm all over—and light—like she was made of air. She looked down and saw the beast swallowing her body, gulping it down in one long slurp. She felt that she should be angry, but she could only feel sadness; her lover would never know what happened to her. She watched as the monster finished its meal and moved on, shrinking in size until it could flit through the trees and vanish.

She felt a tugging, like something trying to pull her along. She felt torn in two: compelled to go, but needing to stay for her lover's sake. She could not imagine him suffering a similar fate; she wouldn't let it happen to him. So, she stayed, drifting through the trees, trying in vain to find the lover that was supposed to meet her after the church's midnight toll. Dawn began to break, and still her lover did not come for her. She found that the people who came to the forest would not acknowledge her, as though she did not exist in their world. She could not move beyond the boundaries of the forest to search for her lover, so she listened as the tolling of the bells rose, fell, and rose again with the coming night. All day she waited for her beloved to come to the forest to search for her; she refused to let herself believe that he, too, had fallen victim to the wandering monster of the forests.

Then, midnight rang on the church bells once again, and she saw another doe eyed maiden like herself, treading lightly through the forest's trees. She watched mutely as this maiden walked, casting furtive glances around the dark shapes of trees and brush. The maiden that reminded her so much of her own self suddenly gave a cry of happiness, and ran into her lover's arms — the very arms that the spectral woman had waited for the night before. Her lover had been seeing another, and it was she that he met in the forest when the church bells tolled midnight.

The spectral woman felt a wrenching pain in her chest; something was being tugged out through a jagged hole that had been cut out of her. Every joyful thing that she had ever felt leaked out of her through tears of grief that no one could see. As she watched as the only happiness she had ever known embraced and loved another woman, she was left hollow and empty; a bottle broken on a tavern floor.

It was the other woman's laughter that did it. The sound sparked something in the specter; something that burned fiercely inside of her, filling every empty nook and cranny with flame and fire. Jealousy and rage that couldn't be reconciled, filled her, bubbling up until there was no way that she could keep the emotion inside. It burst in a scream that ripped out of her throat and filled the forest with such anger and sorrow that even the trees quaked to hear it. She screamed until there was nothing left inside her, the sound carrying for miles and shaking the stubborn leaves off the trees. The sound was so sudden, so loud, and so terrifyingly real that both her lover and his other woman shrieked in terror, clutching at their chests as their very hearts burst from the unadulterated sound of pure rage and sadness. So great was her anger that she could not mourn their passing. She screamed again, wailing her sorrows aloud to the trees, though they were the only living beings to hear her.

From that day on, she haunted the stretch of forest where her life had been taken from her, and her happiness had collapsed. She continues to cry, to remind people that she once existed; that she continues to exist, even when she shouldn't. The town in which she once lived has long since dried up and blown away, and new ones have sprouted in its place three times since. Despite her cries, she remains forgotten, but still she tries in vain to be remembered, because to be remembered is to be loved — and that's all she's ever wanted."

Extracted from an e-mail addressed to Eraliss Cofler from Korvid Fairington, dated ▇▇▇▇▇▇▇.

Sorry it took so long to get back to you, E; just one of those weeks, you know? Hopefully this long recollection makes up for my slacking.

Of course I remember the story you told us about the Wailing Woman: that was the night we camped out on the river, before the whole business with Iphy and Calm. I was so unnerved by how she had died, that I couldn't fall asleep for the longest time. I kept looking over at the black tunnel that led up to the ravine, half expecting the monster (the one that walked through all the forests in the world) to come slinking out of the darkness to swallow us all whole. And I know I wasn't the only one: but none of us wanted to bring it up, lest our talking conjure up the nastiness that we were all trying to avoid.

Somehow we managed to stay alive though the night was fraught with bad dreams, ghosts and all manner of nighttime sounds that brought to mind monsters, demons and other things that went bump in the darkness. To this day Calm insists that she woke up in the middle of the night to see a vague, gray shape at the edge of the trees, watching us from the sheltering darkness. Maybe she did; maybe she didn't. Despite what happened later (or maybe *because* of what happened) I believe in all manner of things; especially her. The Wailing Woman will always be the boogey man hiding in the closet for me. I know for a while back then I gave you a hard time about her, and for that I apologize.

After our frightening night in the woods, we continued further upstream; I still don't know what Iphy was looking for. Maybe another place to hang out or maybe just another small adventure for us to have before school started back up the next day. We followed Iphy as he climbed over boulders and sloshed through the chilly water; he seemed to be looking for something that only he could discover.

It was only mid-morning when we came to the really rough part of the river; the bottom dropped away, leaving only a swirling dark void in the middle of a river that stretched at least half a mile to the opposite bank. Huge rocks jutted out at odd angles and rapids sprayed at us in fits of white water. We continued on for another mile and a half, and then Iphy saw the tree.

By then the bank had begun to recede, creeping closer and closer to the tree line, but this tree defied the tree line and reached out above the river, clinging doggedly to a small rise above the bank. It was old — ancient even — and despite being spring, it was bare of both leaves and blossoms. The trunk was withered and twisted, and the branches stretched so far away from the trunk, they looked like they were trying to escape. Its roots were knotted and tangled about each other; dancers who had lost their footing. The bark was rough and there were bare patches scattered throughout, including a complete bare ring at the base of the tree, where ancient words of love and lost initials were scratched into bare tree.

"This is perfect!" Iphy scrambled up onto the first branch he could reach. "This should be our new hang out spot," he declared with a definite nod. "In fact, Jax, we should move out here—it'd be so awesome!"

Jax shook his head. "It'd be way too cold next to the river; besides, it'd take us all day to hike back to town to get any kind of supplies. What if something happened to us? There's no way we could get help."

The logic wasn't lost on Iphy, but he seemed displeased nonetheless. "You're no fun," he muttered darkly. "Anyway, what could happen to us out here? We don't need anyone or anything back in town."

You made an indignant little noise. "What about us? We could never hang out with you, except on weekends. There's no way we could hike out here after school."

"Fine, fine, fine." Iphy stuck out his tongue. "You all suck; no sense of adventure, the lot of you."

"Well, so long as we're here, let's enjoy it." That was Eddie, all good sense. We took his advice to heart, and Iphy started climbing through the tree, going from branch to branch with his confident, contagious grin. It didn't take him long to find the rope.

It was an old rope with tatters at the end, but thick and strong, like something you'd find discarded in a dockyard. It was coiled around a branch, tied to one of the thicker, stouter branches further up the trunk. Weather-worn and frayed with age, it had probably been up in that tree before our parents were even born. That didn't stop Iphy from hefting it with his familiar grin.

"Check this out! It's awesome!"

"Wow, how cool!" You climbed up after him, admiring the rope with adventurous eyes. "I wonder if it would still hold anything."

"Of course it would," snorted Iphy. Just to prove it, he dropped the rope end, climbed down the tree, and took a flying leap off the bank, rope in hand, swinging like some kind of child who had been raised in the jungle. We all held our breaths as the rope swung wide, out over the river; the rope and branch seemed to groan together, straining to hold the weight of our friend. Then, Iphy was swinging back towards us, his face bright, a whooping holler leaving his lips as he dipped low towards the water before his feet found solid ground next to the tree. "See," he said with a smile, and an almost jittery voice. "Easy peasy."

Eddie grinned, Iphy's confidence becoming contagious. "Can I try, Iphy?"

"Just a sec." Iphy backed up, rope in hand, "Watch this!" He ran pell-mell towards the edge, swinging out as far as he could with a holler, before letting go of the rope and sailing in a neat little arc into the rough, raging part of the river.

For a second none of us could breathe, we just kept staring as Iphy sailed through the air, as if guided by Icarus' wings, straight into the heart of the river. Then, we were all at the edge of the bank, shouting for Iphy, trying to find some meager scrap of his presence in the rushing, angry river. For one chilling minute, I really thought we had lost him—that whatever deity had seen fit to bring him into our lives had yanked him away again. Then, his head burst out of the river, sporting a grin even as he sputtered and spat up water. With a powerful kick, he started back towards us, swimming expertly through the water like he'd done it a million times.

He climbed up the bank to join us, his pale hair plastered to the top of his head and his neck. He grinned as he approached, shaking his head like a dog to rid his hair of water. "Wasn't that awesome?"

You weren't so impressed; your fingertips crashed into his chest, though he took the abuse with his same grin. "You idiot! You could have been hurt; what were you thinking?"

"Pfft." He waved a hand, then went back to wringing out his shirt. "It was no problem; I'm an excellent swimmer. My old house had a pool; I was practically aquatic before moving out here." I thought it was an interesting choice of words: 'moving' here.

"Whatever; it was still stupid," you glowered.

"Can I have a swing, Iphy?" Eddie asked again, as if Iphy's latest stunt had inspired him even more than the previous one.

"Of course," he said with a grin. "In fact, you should all have a go on it." His words stung a bit, like he was somehow looking down on us because he had discovered the rope and was the first one who dared to trust the ancient fibers and swing. His grin didn't help mollify my mental accusation; he almost seemed to be daring us to follow in his footsteps. You looked ready to argue, your hands on your hips and your lower lip set in a half scowl, half pout, but he cut you off before you could get a word in edgewise. "You guys don't have to jump in, like I did, but you all have to swing at least once."

"I'll go first," Eddie volunteered. He took the rope, but once he had it in his hands, he seemed to hesitate. He gave the rope a few sharp tugs, testing it before Iphy rolled his eyes.

"Come on; the rope's fine. It held me, didn't it?"

Eddie needed no further convincing; he backed up a few more steps, his hands grimly gripping the length of rope. When he was about twenty feet from the bank, he shot forward, his short legs pumping, and then he dropped out into space, a blur of ginger hair swinging away from us. A cry of delighted terror ripped from his throat as the rope creaked and the branch strained, and then he was back on solid ground, laughing and trembling all at once.

You went next, swinging out even farther than Iphy (a little payback, I imagine) and I went after you. Jax was the second to last to go. He didn't hesitate like the rest of us: he just took the offered rope, backed up a few paces, and ran full force. As he swung, the tree made a horrible noise; it creaked and groaned, and cried out with a loud pop and snap. Jax seemed unfazed by this as he made his way back to solid ground, but as soon as his feet touched terra firma, he shook his head.

"I think we should stop." Jax looked up at the tree warily. "I don't think it'll hold."

"Seconded," you said, giving a nervous glance first at the tree, then at the rope in Jax's hand.

Iphy snorted. "Vetoed," he said. "Come on, the tree's fine; and even if it's ready to go, it can surely wait a few more seconds while Calm goes."

"I don't want to," said Calm, ignoring the rope and the tree all together, and instead looking out at the river rushing below us.

Our intrepid leader was incredulous. "What? Why? The rope will hold ya: you're a scrawny little thing."

She shook her head. "That's not the point, Iphy; the point is that I'm afraid of heights."

Still, Iphy was unyielding. "Even better! Wasn't your resolution to get over your fear?"

Here Calm hesitated. "No, I said I wanted to take more risks—"

"Then this is perfect!" Iphy snatched the rope from Jax's hands and held it out Calm. "Come on, Calm—we all did it and now it's your turn."

Jax came to her rescue. "If she doesn't want to, she doesn't have to."

"Yeah," you said. "Besides, you heard that crack: it's not safe anymore."

"Oh, come on!" Iphy gave the rope another fierce tug; despite the tree's earlier groans, the rope held firm. "See? It's fine." He turned his attention to Calm. "Come on, Calm, we all did it. It's an initiation, or a rite of passage; something like that. You don't want to be the scaredy-cat of the group, do you?"

That was enough for me to step in. "Iphy, if she doesn't want to, she doesn't have to!"

He scowled at me. "You all sound like a broken record! What's the big deal? We all did it, and now it's her turn."

Jax glowered at Iphy. "Iphy, you're being a real ass."

The older boy sneered at us before turning back to Calm; he held out the rope. "Come on, Calm, just do it."

You came up next to her, trying to take the rope from Iphy, but he wouldn't let it go. "Calm, you don't have to. Don't listen to Iphy; he's being a complete jerk."

She looked ready to cry; her head was lowered so her dark hair obscured her eyes, but she was so hunkered down, like she was trying to fold in on herself that she looked far smaller then she should have. When you tried to take the rope a second time, she straightened, and jerked the rope from Iphy's hands.

"Alright! I'll do it!" She tried to sound strong, but her voice wavered, and her hands were shaking so badly that she almost dropped the rope. "Just... just stop fighting."

Iphy took no notice of her condition, or, if he did, he didn't act like it. He just grinned and stepped aside, giving her ample space to run and swing. "Just take a big running leap; it'll be fun."

Calm backed up a few paces; you tried to get her to stop, but Iphy insisted that you let her try it. Calm gripped the rope so tightly, I was afraid her grip alone would snap the old thing in two; then, she took off running. Her eyes were closed the entire time; she didn't leap so much as run out of solid ground to run on. She gave a cry that sounded more like a squeak, and then she swinging out over the rushing water.

The only warning was the tree giving one last groan before a sudden, terrifyingly loud snap echoed around us. Calm was no longer swinging out; she was falling. Despite Iphy's previous claim, it wasn't fun; it had stopped being fun as soon as the tree had groaned in protest to Jax's swinging, but now it was downright scary. She hit the river and we lost her, just like we had lost Iphy, under the rushing water. We barely had a chance to cry out; then we were all at the edge, looking so hard for a glimpse of her dark hair. Seconds passed in terrifying silence before Eddie pointed.

"There she is!"

That was all Iphy needed: he dove in after her. He took a running leap off the ledge and disappeared under the water. Half of us watched Calm's flailing progress and the rest of us watched as Iphy swam doggedly towards her. I don't think Iphy's eyes ever left the flash of dark hair in front of him. He was a strong swimmer, and a smart one too; he went with the current, kicking against some of the larger rocks when he could. Calm was so busy trying to keep her heard above the water, she didn't even notice her rescuer until Iphy came up behind her.

By now we were all running along with them on the bank, yelling ourselves hoarse with encouragements. From my vantage point on the bank, I saw Iphy loop his arm around her waist, then he began kicking against the current, trying to get back to shore. Calm tried to help, but the current was just too strong. They continued to get dragged downstream, and we fought to keep up; I figured it was about a mile before the water got placid again, and I didn't know if Iphy and Calm could last that long.

Eddie was the first to get winded. We had long lost sight of them, but we all kept running ahead, following the river with dogged determination. He began to slow; I glanced back at him, but he waved the rest of us on. You were next: you stumbled and fell, swore like a sailor, then yelled at us to keep going. Neither Jax nor I hesitated; we kept running as fast as we could. We found Iphy and Calm a few hundred yards further; both of them were sitting on the bank, thoroughly soaked.

Iphy gave us a lazy wave. "Hey, what took ya so long?"

Jax went straight for Iphy, looking the older boy over, concern clouding his eyes. "Iphy, are you okay?"

"Of course I am," snorted Iphy, moving aside a few wet locks of pale hair that were clinging to his cheek.

"Good." Jax sat down next to our friend with a sigh, still trying to catch his breath. "I hope you're happy."

"Of course I am," he repeated, leaning back on his hands. "I saved the damsel in distress."

"She wouldn't have been in distress if it weren't for you," I snapped. I sat next to Calm and put a reassuring arm around her still shaking shoulders. "You okay?"

She looked at me for only a second before she looked back at the swirling water. "Yeah, I'm okay." I wanted to believe her, but it was hard.

You and Eddie came a few minutes later: him huffing and puffing, and you limping slightly. Jax looked around and made an executive decision. "Let's get back home; this is enough adventure for one day."

Iphy was the only one to protest. I was already leading Calm away; she was shivering and tripping over her own two feet every few steps. A few days later she told me that, for the longest time she wanted nothing more than to be worthy of some kind of respect in Iphy's eyes. After the incident at the river, she said that she wasn't so sure that Iphy was the right kind of person to be leading us. I was saddened by that; she had lost her faith in Iphy and his status of Childhood God. I didn't tell her then (and it still doesn't feel right) but little by little I was starting to agree with her.

We didn't get back to town until late that night. Calm was coughing and shivering badly, and you were hobbling so much that you needed to lean against Jax for support. Staying the night at the New Place and waiting the last few hours until morning wasn't an option. We went straight to Calm's house, knocking on her door in the wee hours of the morning. At first, her parents didn't show up; Iphy got impatient and began ringing the bell to some kind of tune. Her parents came down a few minutes later, furious as heck, but their fury quickly turned to shock and concern when they saw their daughter. Jax and Eddie decided to take you over to your place and try and help explain things to your mother; Iphy and I stayed with Calm and her parents.

They let us in, wrapped Calm up in blankets and called a doctor. While Calm's mother chatted away with an endless list of what was wrong with her daughter, Calm's father sat down in front of us and softly demanded to know what had happened. I let Iphy field the question; this was his brainchild from the start. To Iphy's credit, he started right in by saying it was his fault; that he had convinced us all to go into the woods to hike and camp when we were supposed to just be hanging out at each other's houses. He told Calm's father all about the river, and the tree, and the rope. He failed to mention that it was his idea to push Calm into doing something she didn't want to; it was on the tip of my tongue to say it, but I didn't. As angry as I was at Iphy right then, I couldn't say anything: it felt like I'd be betraying him somehow.

Calm's dad watched us as Iphy continued his tale; I couldn't tell if he believed us or not. I felt something hard and bitter twist in my chest when Iphy didn't go into great detail about the rescue: he acted like it was no big deal, and for some reason that infuriated me. Maybe it was because of Calm's dad's reaction. He leaned forward and hugged Iphy with such intensity, thanking him for saving his little girl. Somehow I knew that Iphy had known that all along; if he just played it off like it was nothing, everyone would fawn over him for it.

And they did. Overnight Iphy became the stuff of suburban legend. I'm still not sure how it happened. You and Calm both were out sick and Eddie told me later that he had been telling everyone about what had happened. Calm's parents told the doctor, who in turn told his own kids; they backed up Eddie's claims, and soon the school was abuzz with the story of how Iphy had saved Calm. And from the school it spread like wildfire to the rest of our town.

As if that wasn't enough, a couple days after the incident at the river, Iphy, Jax and I were walking down to Smithy's Bakery when a reporter stopped us. She asked us if we knew where to find a child named Iphy; our intrepid leader was instantly all smiles and charm. She told us she was from the local paper, doing a story on the town's very own hero. The questions came like waves, one rolling after the other, but Iphy managed to answer them all with the charm and wit that had first captured our attention. He told her about living with his grandparents out on Olaha Way, he gave her a last name (something like Daniels; it sounded fake to me) and a brief personal history. He seemed to soak up the attention; it exuded from his very pores in the guise of sunlight. He literally sparkled as he talked, and the reporter ate every word of it. And she wasn't the only reporter: there were at least three others, one of them from out in the big city just north of us.

Once he was in the newspaper, that was it: Iphy became the star of our town. Everyone knew him, even more so than they knew Jax. And once it got around that we were friends with him, it was like I was in some kind of exclusive club. People badgered me at school in the following weeks, asking about him. What did he do? What was he like? I always felt put on the spot; I had real trouble answering that particular question. Mostly because I didn't know what to say. He was like... everyone. Anyone. He was human; our experience at the river convinced me of that (though I'm not sure I believe it now—not after everything that happened). As outrageous as he was, he was still human, even if he acted like a Childhood God of Freedom. People always smiled when I told them his good qualities: he was brave and daring; he lived by his own rules; he was charming and magnificent in ways that no other mortals could be. But they always frowned when I mentioned his bad qualities: he was bullheaded and oblivious to other people's feelings; he would never accept help from anyone; he couldn't stand to be anything other than center stage. It was as if they wanted me to keep those things to myself, like they weren't really Iphy: he couldn't be anything but stellar and amazing and some kind of folk hero.

Even the Reverend Josh Potter believed what Iphy spun for him. He found us one afternoon and he asked Iphy about his grandparents. He claimed that he'd been out to Olaha Way and had seen Iphy's grandparent's house empty. Iphy just grinned and waved a hand. "S'okay, Reverend," he said, all smiles and charm, "they went on vacation; anniversary honeymoon or something. So I'm staying with Korvid until they get back next week."

For a second I hoped—even *prayed*—that the Reverend would somehow see through Iphy's ruse. I thought that maybe, just maybe, if Iphy got caught just *once* in his lies, something miraculous would happen and everything else would work out, as though the Reverend Josh Potter had the power of prophecy and he could look ahead to the future and see what was to come, and somehow be able to put a stop to it by just raising an eyebrow and telling Iphy that he knew our fearless leader was lying. Of course, the Reverend had no such power, and more importantly he had no reason to disbelieve Iphy, so he merely nodded and wished us a good day. We watched him leave, and I was momentarily gripped with a powerful urge to call after him, to tell him everything. But, as angry as I was at Iphy and as much as I wanted the Reverend—if no one else—to know the truth, I couldn't call out. It went against some internal sense of honor that I had for Iphy; I couldn't betray him, even as much as I wanted to speak.

It made me mad in a way: everyone just seemed to blindly accept that Iphy was something to look up to and worship with their praise and attention. I know that's so hypocritical of me that you could write a novel on that alone, but it burned me up a bit for a couple weeks. Of course, it could have been jealousy too; before, Iphy had been something that we had kept secret from everyone else. Like Our Place and the New Place, Iphy was something just for us, because we had been the ones to find him out in the woods that dark night last year. In a way, I think he was always supposed to remain ours; it would have made things much easier.

This is… hard, E. I didn't think it would be this hard to remember that year. I thought it would be easy and simple, like our lives used to be back then. Shows what I know, huh?

All my love,
Korvid.

~*~

After the incident at the river, Iphy became a local celebrity. Our whole school was ablaze with talk about what had happened, and everyone wanted to know more. Suddenly kids we hardly knew were sitting with us, asking us questions, trying to discern myth from reality and find out what had really happened out there on the river. We were all questioned at least twenty times a day apiece by children whom we didn't even really know. And even when they knew all that we did, they still vied for our attention. Just by knowing Iphy, we were special in some way we never had known before; his charm and charisma had somehow rubbed off on us. It was magical in a way, going from being a small, close group of friends to the most popular kids in school. All because of Iphy.

Even our teachers got in on the action. The day after Calm returned to school Mr. Neil took the two of us off to one side, asking how we were doing in light of recent events. We told him exactly what we told everyone else: we were fine. Mr. Letham, who had surprisingly enough agreed with Mrs. Creager that writing was indeed art, asked me one day to write about the experience; he pinned it up on the wall next to his desk, where he kept all the 'Star Art' for the week.

Our parents never seemed to leave us alone, either. About a week after the news story ran on Iphy, Mom wanted to know if he would come eat dinner with us one Saturday.

I blinked at her in surprise. "What?"

"Your friend, Iphy," she said, happily moving about the kitchen. Early morning light was filtering through the window, highlighting her hair and making her seem prettier than I had seen her in a while. "I was wondering if you wanted to invite him to dinner tonight."

It was going to be a slow weekend. Calm had relatives from out of state staying at her house, and she had told us the day before that she wouldn't be able to hang out. Korvid had similar issues, in that his out-of-work actor uncle had stopped by earlier in the week to borrow their couch for a few days: he had also insisted that he and Korvid bond over the weekend while Korvid's dad worked. Eddie was gone from the cul-de-sac altogether, his parents having whisked the whole family away on a vacation to New York City: his older brother Dan wanted to attend an open house for the New York Film Academy, where he hoped to enroll in the fall.

"What about Jax?" I asked.

Mom seemed to consider this, and then shook her head. "Not this time, Eraliss. Maybe some other time."

I tilted my head to one side. "Why not?"

"We won't have the room," she said, still happily going about morning kitchen chores.

"What are you talking about? We have room enough for four." Admittedly, I was more than a little miffed. I didn't want to have to go invite my famous friend to a hot meal while my not-so-famous friend spent the evening by himself.

"No, we don't." My mom gave me a bit of a glare. "What makes you think you're the only one with friends coming for dinner tonight?"

This floored me; it had never occurred to me that while I was going around hanging out with my friends, my mother was moving on with her own life and making some new friends of her own. It strikes me now as something almost wholly unforgivable: I never knew my mother when I was a child. Only now, as an adult do I truly know the woman who raised me. As a child, she was just my mother; it meant a lot to me, but not enough. My friends meant more to me back then. And if I'm going to be completely honest, sometimes they still mean more to me now.

They say that friends are God's way of apologizing for our families. I believed that back then, and I still believe it now. But who does God give us to apologize for our friends?

I went out to the New Place, hoping to find Iphy and Jax in the abandoned house, but a quick search proved that it was as empty as it had been before Iphy had graced it with his presence. I took to the woods, moving along familiar pathways we'd etched into the ground to Our Place, but still I couldn't find them. I went even further, to the ridge, looking down at the awe-inspiring panorama, my eyes trained on the river. I couldn't be sure, but I thought I saw some splashes of bright color along the river; it was good enough for me to investigate.

As it turns out, they were at the river, enjoying the mid-day sun. Iphy was chucking rocks into the slow moving water while Jax waited patiently with his fishing pole in hand; both their eyes were trained on the water and they didn't notice me as I came upon them.

"I'm telling you, I've seen its tracks; we should look for it." Iphy was saying, tossing another small rock into the river, grinning as it made a small ker-plunk sound.

"You're scaring all the fish," Jax said. "And besides, it's not a good idea to go looking for trouble, and that thing would be trouble with a capital T."

"Trouble's my middle name." Iphy puffed his chest out as far as he could. "I bet we could take it on; it'd be fun."

"Take what on?" I asked, stepping carefully around the bigger rocks that littered the river bank.

Iphy turned his infectious grin to me. "I saw animal tracks—big ones! I'm not sure what kind, but I was thinking we should hunt it down, go all <u>Lord of the Flies</u> on it."

Despite myself, I snickered. "That wasn't an animal they killed in <u>Lord of the Flies</u>: it was a person."

He waved his hand dismissively. "That other shipwrecked guy then. Whatever. So long as we can track it down and kill it and stuff."

I frowned at him; his reason didn't seem like the best. "You don't even know what it is. What makes you think you can kill it?"

"Korvid says his dad has a pistol. We could use that."

"How big of an animal are we talking about?" When Iphy shrugged, I rolled my eyes; boys being boys and all that. "How big of a track was it?"

He held out his hands a half a foot apart, making a large box in the air. "About like that."

Even with his habit for exaggerating the truth, I guessed the real track would have to be at least a few inches across, which made for a very large animal. "That thing would be huge! There's no way a pistol could kill it!"

Iphy only smiled. "How do you know? Maybe it could."

I was about to argue further, when Jax gasped, "I've got a bite!" We both turned to watch as the line went taut and Jax began to pull on the pole.

"Don't pull!" Iphy barked. "You've got to reel it in first!"

Jax fumbled with the pole, still staring at the spot in the river where the fishing line was zipping about. What happened next is something I'll always remember. When the question was brought up amongst us about when things became different—when things went *bad*—I always came back to this moment. Others would claim it started earlier, others later, but for me, this moment stood out.

Jax continued to struggle with the pole, and Iphy watched with ever-increasing impatience. Finally, after a few seconds, he jumped forward, taking a hold of the pole. There was a look of animalistic need on his face as he tried to take the pole from Jax. "Here, let me do it!"

At first Jax wouldn't relinquish the pole; he just gaped at Iphy's sudden interference. "Hey! I've got it!"

Iphy shook his head, his pale hair waving about in a frenzied halo. "No! You're gonna fuck it up!"

I'd never heard that word come from Iphy's mouth before. Though he had sworn many times in the months we'd known him, he'd never uttered that word. Before I could try to intervene there was a horrible snapping sound and then they were both on the ground: the line had broken.

I moved to help Iphy, hoisting him to his feet with an outstretched hand. He stood, dusted off his tattered jeans and reached down. I thought Iphy was going to help Jax, but instead he grabbed the pole, inspecting the tattered end of the line and making it a point not to look at Jax.

"Damn. That would have been a big 'ol fish, yeah?" He looked back at us as I helped Jax to his feet, still giving us his sunny smile as though nothing was wrong.

I couldn't say anything, rendered mute by the travesty that had just occurred in front of me. Jax wasn't speechless; he spoke with a quiet dignity and an almost heart wrenching sadness. "Yeah. It's a shame the line broke."

"What are you two doing out here, anyway?" I asked, finally finding my voice and just wanting to forget what had happened. "I went looking everywhere for you."

"And you found us here." Iphy kept his grin and waved a hand, as though getting rid of bothersome insects. "I was getting tired of everyone trying to talk to us in town, so we came out here. Jax wanted to see if he could catch a fish and stop being all scared of them. You know, one resolution down."

I nodded my understanding, keeping back the words that wanted to claw their way out of my mouth. I didn't tell Iphy that if he'd succeeded in taking the pole, then it wouldn't have been Jax who caught the fish; it would have been him. Instead, I smiled. "Think you can stand one more person talking to you? My mom wants you over for dinner, probably to ask you more about what happened out there."

"Or just to have a local celebrity at her table, right?" Somehow his smile got even bigger and he nodded his head. "Sure, so long as food's involved I think we can find the time to join you. Right, Jax?"

Jax looked first at Iphy, then over at me. "Am I invited?" He sounded neutral, like he didn't dare to sound hopeful, but it broke my heart just the same. I couldn't look at him; instead, I studied my shoes, still not seeing what Calm always saw when she looked down.

"Mom's got company too, so there's only room for one..." The excuse tasted like bile in my mouth, and I could have died the second it left my lips; Jax deserved better.

Iphy thought so too. "That's bullshit." He folded his arms over his chest, giving me a glare that painted me with disgrace. "If he doesn't come, I don't come."

Before I could argue (or agree... I'm still not sure what I would have done, given the chance) Jax shook his head. "Go ahead, Iphy: if E's mom wants to talk to you, you shouldn't shun the invitation." He gave a wan smile and tried to make it look legitimate. "All I ask is that you bring me back something."

We were still unsure; Iphy raised an eyebrow and gave Jax a look that came as close to pure pity as I'd ever seen on our fearless leader's face. "You sure, Jax?"

Jax nodded again, mimicking Iphy's usual sunny smile. "It's fine." He even had the strength to laugh. "Who knows? Maybe I'll catch a fish while you're gone and have a feast of my own."

Iphy nodded, the pity vanishing from his face, replaced by confidence and charm once again. "Yeah, maybe you'll even break the world record! Or get some kind of rare exotic fish that someone dumped in here years ago! You'll be famous."

When Jax laughed and waved us away, I fell into step next to Iphy. "Wouldn't that be something: you and Jax, famous celebrities from our town?"

Iphy snickered. "Yeah, that'd show them."

"Who?" The question was meant to be good natured, but it sent a bolt of annoyance and even anger across Iphy's face. Then, the dark emotion was gone, replaced by his wide grin. "Everyone! Anyone who ever doubted us."

I laughed, "I don't think I've ever heard someone doubt you, Iphy."

"Got that right, E." He grinned, as if he truly believed it. But, there was still something in his eyes; some flicker of hollow sadness that reminded me of other emotions I had seen in him lately. It struck me then how very little I knew about the Childhood God that I so willingly followed, but I didn't care. It almost scared me.

We went through the woods, racing through the trees in an age-old child's race of who could get through the woods the quickest. Iphy won, but that was no surprise. Besides being older and longer of limb than I was, there was no way I could beat him: it was incredulous. He was the one I followed, and I would always follow him because, while he had his faults, Iphy could never do any *real* wrong. They say to err is human, and despite his looks, Iphy was not human; he was something much grander. Maybe not divine, but certainly more than a mere

212

mortal; and therefore he could not err. I stayed behind him the whole way.

It was afternoon, almost bleeding into evening when we came upon my house, and there was a strange car in the driveway. It didn't mean that much to me, but it did drive home that my mom had a life outside of me that I had been largely ignorant of. It was when the front door opened that everything stopped.

The person who opened the door wasn't Mom, but someone else both instantly recognizable and wholly unknown. He had aged some, if the lines etching out from his eyes were any indication, but he was still the same. He smiled at me, like he had just come home from the market and hadn't been gone for three years. "Hey, kiddo. Wow, look at you. Your mom said you'd grown, but dang." He stepped to one side, holding the door open for us and sweeping his arm back. "Come on in: dinner's almost ready."

At first I couldn't move; there was no way that my dad could be standing here, holding open the door like some old fashioned gentleman. It took Iphy giving me a small push to get my feet in working order before I could cross the threshold.

My dad looked at Iphy, giving him the once over before smiling and holding out his hand. "So, you're the one. What's it like to be a hero?"

To his credit, Iphy looked at the hand dubiously before sliding into the role of sweet, innocent child. He shook the offered hand, smiling up at my dad. "Gosh, Sir, I don't really consider myself a hero: I was just doing what I thought was right."

I almost lost it; I had to choke back the eruption of laughter into a small bout of coughing. My dad didn't notice Iphy's false sincerity, but even now I doubt that many adults ever see their children and their friends for who they really are.

My dad just smiled and nodded his approval (like Iphy needed *any* adult's approval) and closed the door behind us. He said something about wanting to show us some things he'd picked up along his travels, but the words didn't really register. Iphy led me into the living room, where my dad had a trunk full of photos, knickknacks and cheesy souvenir t-shirts. He went through the photos first, telling me and Iphy about the stories behind them. If it weren't for Iphy's occasional "Golly gee, mister," and his over-exaggerated exclamations of wonder, I would have drifted from the conversation altogether. As it was, these blatant displays of un-Iphyness kept me snickering and subsequently grounded

During dinner it was different; maybe it was the food, or maybe I was just following in my mom's footsteps, but I hung onto my dad's every word. He told us about the mountains he'd climbed and the beaches he'd been to. He told us funny anecdotes about the people he'd met and we laughed. Even Iphy was laughing without any traces of sarcasm and contempt. As my dad talked more and more, I felt a lightness in me.

Everything was going to be okay.

After dinner, when I saw Iphy to the door with his bag of leftovers for Jax, he turned to me and gave me a quizzical look. There was something in the air between us: a trepidation or just plain uncertainty. He cleared his throat, and then looked beyond me, making sure that we were well and truly alone. He needn't have bothered: Mom was with Dad in the living room, listening to more of his stories. I wanted to go back and join them.

"You know if you ever need a shoulder to cry on, I'm your guy." He flashed a smile that was cracked with hesitation.

I thought it sweet that he'd want to help me out, and if my dad's return had gone any other way, I might have taken him up on it. I never knew how much anger I had held in my heart for my dad until his very presence had lightened the load. I shook my head, smiling like Iphy usually did with the full power of the sun.

He glanced back over my shoulder, listening to the laughing going on in the other room. "You sure?" He seemed almost afraid of the answer, like he wanted me to need him.

I waved him off. "I'm fine, Iphy," I assured him with a smile, though he didn't smile back. I felt the need to make him understand, if only a little, how something as tangible as Happiness could be so vague and mysterious. But, I opted for the easy way out. "Everything's gonna be okay."

In the coming days, it was a phrase I would repeat in the darkness of my room, hanging onto the words with the childlike belief that if I continued to believe in them, they would inevitably become fact.

"Everything's gonna be okay."

From the Journal of Calm Sheldon

When Eraliss' father came back, several things happened. The first was that Eraliss spent less and less time with us. The few times she was with us, all she could talk about was her dad and where he had been. She seemed to forget that just a month ago he was little more than a vague, unhappy memory that still couldn't remember to call her on her birthday.

Not to say that he was spiteful or even mean: he was just like us children. His continued happiness was the forefront of his thoughts and his one major focus; everything else, including his daughter, came second. But, he was a very likable guy; he was funny and friendly, and charming in a roughish rover sort of way. He could make anyone his friend if they didn't know him. And as much as Eraliss had disliked him in the years before his second coming, she hadn't ever really *known* him; she became his friend.

Even the rest of us, so tainted by Eraliss' many angry, tearful rants about how much her father had hurt with his silence and his absence on the most important days of her young life, were swept up in the easy way her dad talked. We would never be his friend (how could we, when he'd hurt Eraliss so?) but we could each see ourselves, in another place and another time, liking Eraliss' father a great deal. And we all could see why Eraliss would essentially abandon us for the glamour of being reunited with her father. All of us, except for Iphy.

Iphy took Eraliss' lack of interest in the rest of us in the most personal way: he was moody and snappish to the rest of us, and livid with Eraliss and her father.

"Doesn't she remember how much of an asshole he was?" he ranted one day. The day was gorgeous as they usually were after winter, but the brilliance seemed lost on him.

"You should be happy for her," Eddie admonished softly. "I'd give anything to hang out with my dad."

Korvid nodded, a wistful sigh escaping his lips, "Yeah, same here."

"Why?" Iphy raved, going so far as to throw his arms up in exasperation. "What's the point? They're all assholes! Every last one of them!" He ran his fingers through his bleached hair, getting the long strands out of his face. "No dad's ever done anything all that special."

"My dad used to take me out to the pond when it froze over in the winter," I said quietly. I was looking out into the woods surrounding Our Place, as if I could peer through the maze of trees and see Eraliss being happy with her dad. "He taught me how to ice skate, and he'd always hold my hand so I wouldn't fall down."

Jax nodded his approval, even as Iphy snorted, "And now he's fighting with your mom, trying to tear everything apart."

Iphy's words were like a fist slamming into my chest. I stared at him, absolutely horrified. His words might have just been the hurt ramblings of a shunned child, but they hurt just as surely as sticks and stones. Whoever came up with that old schoolyard rhyme must never have had any dealings with a child's angry words.

Korvid shot to his feet, his hands balled into fists of frustrations, "Iphy! What the hell's your problem?"

For a second, Iphy's face twisted into a mask of surprise and ire, but then he glanced down at me, and his emotions warped into something like shame and regret. I'd never seen those emotions on his face, and their brief, fleeting existence on his countenance surprised me more than words can really express. I hadn't thought him capable of feeling those kinds of emotions: they just weren't the way that Iphy usually was. I can't say for certain (because really, not even we few who knew him best could ever say anything with real certainty when it came to Iphy) but I think his remark to me that day was what he believed to be the second worst thing he'd ever done in our company.

As he usually did, Iphy waved it off. "Forget it; I'm just pissed off."

"Why, because E's finally having a good time with her dad?" Jax pressed, getting involved in the argument.

Iphy's face contorted into a glare full of anger and spite; it wasn't a look befitting a Childhood God of Freedom, but one of a small, normal boy who wasn't getting his way. "Do you think anything good will come of it?" he snapped. "Do you really think it'll make a difference? Her dad's an ass — he's always been one — what makes you think this time will be any different? Do you really think everything will be hunky-fucking-dory now that he's back? They're all the goddamn same!"

"No they aren't!" Jax gave Iphy a shove — just a small one. Just hard enough to make Iphy step back, but that was hard enough. "They aren't the same because we don't know them. Maybe Eraliss' dad is going to make amends and stick around; who are we to say he won't? Don't you dare take this away from her before she's even really had a chance at it!"

We were all quiet for one long moment. Iphy's face was, for once, without any kind of emotion and Jax's was one of disappointment and resentment. When I finally thought that they would never speak again—that somehow the words had been stolen from their lips, never to return—Iphy turned his head, glaring down at the ground even as a humorless smile stretched across his face.

"Fine," he said, still not looking up at any of us. "We'll just see."

The bitterness in his voice was just another reminder that he wasn't a god of any kind. He was just a boy; a child, like the rest of us.

As the end of the school year came closer, my parents finally stopped fighting. I don't remember exactly when I noticed it, but one night I realized that I couldn't hear them arguing. I checked the clock, but it was still early enough for them to be yelling. Panic seized me and I thought that my dad had finally walked out, and that's why there were no more angry sounds coming from their bedroom. I jumped out of bed and made my way downstairs, but his shoes were still by the door and his car was still in the driveway. He hadn't left: they just weren't fighting.

The next night I waited for the anger and the hurt to take a verbal form and start flying about, but again there was nothing. Not a peep. So it went for several days before I realized that my wish had come true: they had stopped fighting for good.

The very moment I realized this, my soul was split in two. I was ecstatic and so tremendously happy that, were I able, I could have flown around the room; I was terrified, gripped by a nervous fear that immobilized me and kept me grounded. Had they really made up, or was this the calm before the raging storm? I couldn't tell.

I wanted to ask Eraliss, but my best friend was still distant, off with her father, enjoying his company. I had the others, but after Iphy's outburst I was afraid to bring it up again. Korvid was busy with his friends, Kyle and Will, planning something for the end of school year, and I didn't think it appropriate to bring up family problems with the town's orphan. So one weekday afternoon, when Korvid had stayed after with Kyle and Will, Iphy had told us that he and Jax were going to the junkyard to root for useful things and Eraliss left to be with her father, I stood with Eddie McCloy in the middle of our cul-de-sac.

He looked shyly at me, and then glanced around as though expecting our friends to rush out and join us. "So, you wanna do something?"

I nodded, if only because I couldn't stand the foreboding silence back home. "What did you have in mind?"

"I was going to look for the last few bones I need; I'm just missing a couple of ribs, a handful of vertebrae and the right scapula."

I didn't pretend to know what a scapula was, but I nodded just the same and we headed off into the woods. On our way to the ravine, Eddie told me about how he had found almost half the moose skeleton in one visit with the rest of the scattered bones not more than a mile radius out from the rest. As he'd imagined, they'd been picked clean by the various bugs and scavengers of the forest during the long winter, so he figured cleaning would be a snap. I always felt privileged to hear Eddie talk about bones: he was so fascinated by them that he lit up just so, and not even being with Iphy could make him shine brighter.

He'd marked the spot of the majority of the moose skeleton with a tattered kite in a tree. I asked him where he had found the kite, but he couldn't remember; like so many other things, it had been forgotten. While he continued on, I looked up at the little scrap of bright nylon hanging by itself. It made me sad in a way I couldn't fathom. I still can't.

We went southeast from there, spreading out and rooting through the fallen leaves and the undergrowth, pulling at roots and overturning rocks, looking for any sign of the last elusive bones. I pulled a stick free and was surprised to find it smooth and curved; Eddie confirmed it was one of the ribs that he sought. Sometime later he found a clump of dirt that when brushed off and chipped away, revealed the prongs and concave surface of a vertebra.

We searched until the woods around us began first to dim, then darken as night seemed to rush out from beneath every tree and shrub. Soon, darkness had overtaken the woods and all at once we felt like we were intruding again; the forest had forgotten us in the onslaught of night and we were once again strangers to be feared and distrusted. Every tree seemed to glare at us and shun us as we started moving back to the familiar area around Our Place. But even there the trees leered at us and shuttled us along until we were out and into the empty spaces of yard behind our houses. We glanced at each other, both of us silently questioning the other as to the nature of our old hangout spot.

Eddie broke the silence. "That was... weird."

I nodded. "I guess if Iphy isn't with us, the trees don't like us."

He gave me a funny little look, and then glanced down at the grass overtaking his sneakers. "Maybe. I wish Iphy would..." he trailed off, shaking his head a bit before looking up at the stars that dotted the skies. "Things are different."

I nodded again. I had felt it, ever since the start of spring. "It's like we're... growing apart."

"But not quite. It's like we're growing apart, only to get smashed back together again a few weeks later."

"My parents stopped fighting." The words just escaped. It wasn't something I had been meaning to tell Eddie, but they had wriggled out of my mouth, unwilling to keep to themselves any longer.

"That's good, right?"

"Maybe." It was my turn to look up to the stars. "I want it to be good. But, I just can't help thinking that it's the calm before the storm. That something bad is about to happen."

Eddie looked at me curiously. "How bad?"

"Really bad."

We stood in silence for a moment, bathed by the light of a million stars above our heads. Somewhere in the woods, night animals made their noises, and the Wailing Woman watched us. There was a hesitation between us, like we wanted to move forward, but somehow we were scared; lost, without any kind of guidance. We couldn't go to our parents and we couldn't go to our friends. It was like we were the only two people still in the land of the living. Then, just as quickly as the moment started, it ended. Eddie smiled at me, and I smiled at him. We gave each other our goodnight's and see-you-tomorrows and we crossed the cul-de-sac to our respective homes. We would sleep and await the next day, hoping the dawn would push away the oppressive thunder clouds that seemed to have suddenly descended on our town.

As the final days of school loomed, many of the teachers decided to showcase their brilliant students, and Eraliss' art teacher Mr. Letham was no different. In the last couple weeks of school, he held what he called an Art Slam, to display the final projects that his students had completed. The artwork was going to stay up until the end of the year, but that first day he had all his students there, putting up their art and giving the cafeteria an explanation. Proud parents lined the walls of the open cafeteria, cheering their children's art. Korvid, Eddie, Iphy, Jax and I watched and listened with feigned interest: all we really wanted to see was Eraliss' work.

She came up onto the small stage, where other students had presented paintings, weird sculptures and even a painted t-shirt. It was strange: she wasn't acting like her usual self.

While normally she was loud and confident, today she was more like me, timid and quiet. In her hand she held a piece of paper and a small stand. Upon the stand was the cross she had found. It looked both plain and grand sitting on the small stand: both brand new and incredibly old. She looked out at the sea of faces, first latching onto our group. She smiled then, still shy and hesitant, and held our gaze for only a few seconds before searching the gathered onlookers again.

Mr. Letham seemed to sense her hesitation just like the rest of us, for he placed a comforting hand on her shoulder to calm her nerves. "Eraliss, here," he started, his voice confident and loud, "has a piece of found art and a poem she has written to go along with it."

His voice had the desired effect: it emboldened her. "Thank you, Mr. Letham." She looked back at the crowd, her shoulders suddenly straight, and her smile suddenly beaming. She looked like Iphy, all confidence and bravado.

"I found this out in the woods behind my house," she started, looking confident and sure of herself in front of the gathered students and parents. She had somehow managed to take Iphy's spunk and look more like a professional speaker than a young girl being put in the spotlight for the first time. "It was old and almost buried in the dirt at the roots of a great tree. I was searching for something, but not this. Instead of finding what I was so doggedly looking for, I came across this small token of old love, and it struck me as being incredibly sad."

Again she scanned the room, focusing not on her peers in their circular groups around round cafeteria tables, but at the adults lining the edges. Parents watched her look and sift through their faces, so full of pride for their own children's accomplishments. I didn't need to ask who she was looking for: I knew. And I didn't need to glance behind and join in her silent search to know that he wasn't there. He never had been, and he never would be, despite Jax's hope.

"I... I found it incredibly sad," she faltered a bit, still looking, still hoping for someone who wasn't there, praying that she had passed his face and overlooked him in the crowd. "Something that was once so loved and cherished to be forgotten for so long." I could see it in her eyes, the flame of hope fizzle and die. She gave up, her shoulders sagging as her eyes, too heavy with the weight of disappointment, dropped down to her battered sneakers. For a moment, I didn't think she'd continue; that she'd just vanish, fold into herself and be gone; not only from here, but from everywhere. Then, Iphy saved her.

"Go, E!" He shouted into the stillness, pumping his fist into the air.

Next to him, Jax took up the call, whooping his own encouragement. "C'mon, E!"

Korvid cupped his hands around his mouth, amplifying his voice. "Let's hear the rest!"

"Don't keep us in suspense!" I called out, surprised by my own boldness, and unexplainably happy when Iphy shot me his famous grin.

Even quiet little Eddie joined in. "What happened next?"

Other students began joining the cry, Korvid's friends Kyle and Will among them; those two were always eager to make a lot of noise at school. Eraliss just smiled at all of us, grinning from ear to ear like her usual happy self, a hint of shine in her eyes.

"But," she continued, all smiles now, "lost things are always found again—even years later. Nothing stays alone for too long, because everything is connected. For the longest time I sat in my room, trying to uncover the story behind this little cross, but some mysteries are better left unsolved. It keeps some magic in the world. I'm just glad that I was able to find this small token of love; it proves we're not alone out there in the big scheme of things. I wrote a poem about that."

She read her poem in a clear, confident voice: one that sounded much more like herself. I won't relate all of it. It was both too long and far too beautiful for my humble little journal. But there was one stanza of her poem that has stayed with me all these long years.

"I don't know where you've been
Or where you're going
I don't think we'll ever know each other
Strangers passing
On a windy road at night
Who dim their bright lights for one another
In that brief second
We prove we're all the same
Helping each other along in the dark"

We all cheered for her, louder than all the rest of the cafeteria combined. Iphy even went so far as to jump up on the table where he whooped and hollered like a monkey. Kyle and Will, never ones to be upstaged, followed suit and climbed up onto their tables, cheering until Mr. Day, the security guard, told them all to get off the tables before detentions were handed out. Eraliss laughed and beamed at the applause, giving a little bow, her face painted with joy. I was glad she was happy, that she had something to smile about. Whenever I think about our summer, and the memories threaten to bury me in sorrow, I always try to remember that day, when Eraliss smiled so warmly.

C.S.

Extracted from an e-mail addressed to Eraliss Cofler from Korvid Fairington, dated ▆▆▆▆▆▆▆.

The final two weeks of school. Of course I remember them. I don't think I'll ever forget those days. I know it's dumb—not even possible, really—but a small part of me still thinks that somehow everything that happened started there: that it was my fault.

The wedge that tore everything apart.

The straw that broke the camel's back.

Maybe it was the river, maybe it was the tree climbing contest, and maybe it was me.

It started simply enough: Kyle and Will were angry at me. Well, not angry exactly, but miffed, which was rare for them. They were never upset with anyone, so long as I knew them—it wasn't in their nature. They were happy and clever, always smiling; Kyle, with his thin, lanky frame, shaggy brown hair and brown eyes to match, was a lot like a scarecrow, and Will was like a tin man, solid and stocky, with scruffy black hair and light blue eyes. And just like L. Frank Baum's beloved characters, they completed each other, and had what the other lacked: Kyle had the heart and Will had the brains. Between them, there was nothing they couldn't do, and they never saw any reason to be at odds with anyone. So, when they cornered me outside of fifth period, I was surprised.

"You keep blowing us off," Kyle said, giving me a dark look that actually came off more like a pout.

"I am not," I protested. "I joined your group in Study Hall."

"And spent the entire time looking out the window," Will snorted.

"Can you blame me?" I asked. "It's the Monday of our second to last week of school. We have ten days left until summer."

Will rolled his eyes and ignored me. "You didn't even hear what we were working on."

My mind raced. "Neon: tenth element in the periodic table. We've got to write individual reports and put together a presentation for the class."

They looked at me like I had grown another head and started chewing on it. Kyle was the first to speak.

"Wow."

"Yeah, wow," Will followed. "You haven't been paying a lick of attention."

"Yeah. Why would we talk about anything related to school? How lame." Kyle shook his head, looking thoroughly disgusted by the very idea of it. "We were talking about the end of the year prank."

Instantly I was interested. In the few years of school that I had known them, Kyle and Will had never failed to pull off an amazing end of the year prank. Even more monumental was the fact that this was our last year in this school; at the end of summer, High School loomed dark and foreboding. So naturally this year's prank was going to be bigger and better than any they had done before.

"What's your plan for this year?" I asked.

Will frowned at me. "If you had been paying attention, you'd already know this."

I sighed. "Look guys, I'm sorry. I've just got a lot on my mind right now. Give me a break."

I could tell that they were trying to be angry at me, but their excitement was getting the best of them; they were practically fidgeting.

"One word," said Will.

"Firecrackers," finished Kyle.

It was my turn to frown. "You can't get firecrackers until July; late June at the earliest."

They began talking in a blur.

"That's the whole point."

"No one will suspect it."

"We got a bunch last year on the Fourth when they were half-off."

I couldn't help but crack a smile. "And you guys have managed to not blow something up in all that time? You must have something spectacular planned."

They grinned at me and said in unison, "We're going to blow up the boy's locker room."

I blanched. "Wait, what? You'll never manage that: Coach Jenkins stays in there until the whole school's locked up."

"Not on Monday," Will insisted. "That's when he helps Mr. Letham watch the kids in detention."

"We know because we've seen it three times now; that's no coincidence," Kyle smiled.

"He locks up the gymnasium," I pointed out.

"But," Will smirked, "there's the emergency exit by the stairs. That's open until the school closes down—it has to be. Since it's in the locked part of the gym, no one in the after-school programs get blamed, and since it's clear on the other side of the school, we're out Scott-Free before anyone comes. The perfect crime."

"All we need now," Kyle grinned, "is the perfect alibi."

I raised a skeptical eyebrow. "How you gonna pull that one off?"

"Simple," Will smirked. "You're gonna help us."

I could hardly believe my ears. "Come again?"

"Yeah. If just two of the showers explode, then everyone will know it was us. Even if we don't leave a scrap of evidence, they'll make something up."

"But," Will continued, "if you help us and three showers explode for maximum damage, they've got nothing on us. Everyone knows we're strictly a duo."

"So it's win-freaking-win!" Kyle could hardly contain himself, he was so excited. "You get to help us with the biggest and best prank this school has ever seen, and we get the secure knowledge that they can't pin it on us. C'mon, Korvid, what do ya say?"

They looked up at me, so hopeful and eager for my participation, but the plan had an ominous feel to it in my mind.

"What if Mr. Day catches us?" I never really liked our school security guard; mostly I remember his lack of hair and his lack of mercy for tardy kids.

Kyle and Will shook their heads.

"No chance."

"That King kid and Tyler Hetrick are in on this, too — they're gonna start a fight at 3:45 and get Day's attention. Their excuse is gonna be practicing for a summer camp play. Day'll be on the other side of the school for at least ten minutes."

I still had my doubts about the idea, and I knew my dad would be furious if we got caught, but it was a pretty big if. These two hadn't really been caught on anything big before, and it did seem like they had it all planned out to be fairly risk free. Then I heard it, clear as a bell in my head, as though he were standing right next to me.

"Hell yeah! Sounds like a freaking blast! Don't you dare chicken out on this, you baby: I'd do it in a heartbeat."

Iphy's voice goaded me into nodding. I couldn't let Iphy down; the very thought turned my stomach sour.

"Sound's great." I grinned at them, knowing that somewhere Iphy was proud of me.

"Yes!" Kyle sprang into the air, pumping his fist up in the tribal childhood victory dance.

Will mirrored my grin. "Okay, now you can't tell anyone about this: it's our secret. We're planning this for next Monday; I'll give you the fireworks in the morning."

We agreed to speak no more about the plan until the day of (Will was worried someone would overhear us in the hall, or maybe tap our phones) so we went off to lunch like a bunch of kids who weren't planning to blow up the boy's locker room in a week's time. All that was left was the waiting.

Monday came way too quickly; I had butterflies in my stomach as Will passed me a handful of bottle rockets to keep in my bag. This wasn't going to be okay—I could already tell. I had gone over the plan in my head a thousand times in the week leading up to this day, but I still felt like it wasn't a good idea at all. I wanted to back out, but Iphy's voice in my head wouldn't let me. We split the firecrackers behind the school, out of sight of everyone else. Kyle and Will couldn't keep themselves still in their excitement about divvying up the firecrackers.

Will grinned. "Just keep them in your locker and meet us after school sharp."

"This is gonna be great!" Kyle hissed, shouldering his backpack and glancing around. "I can't wait!"

I felt like I could wait a lifetime.

You asked me what happened that afternoon; I know about as much as you do. There was a small explosion in the hall somewhere around fourth period. I don't know how it happened, but the firecrackers in my bag exploded, destroying my locker and the ones around it. After the fire department came and the small fire was put out, it was easy for them to pinpoint the source of the blast: my locker.

After that it was a whirlwind: meetings with the principal and the superintendent. They even managed to drag my father away from his job to talk to him about all this. Through it all, I never gave up Kyle or Will. Iphy's voice in my head wouldn't let me. When they asked me why I had done it, I gave them the simplest answer: I thought it would be fun.

They suspended me for the rest of the school year (which was all of three days) with further consequences pending. They were taking into account that this was the first time I'd ever caused any trouble, but there was the magnitude of the act to consider as well. I remember I got a letter sometime in the end of July about what all my punishment was, but God, Eraliss, for the life of me I can't remember what it was. It was nothing compared to what we were going through already.

Dad drove me home, silent and fuming. I could tell he was furious, just like I knew he was going to be. But, I couldn't tell if he was more mad at my stunt, or at the fact that he'd been called away from work to face the looming threat of our empty house. That made me mad.

He slammed the door behind us as we entered; the sound echoed through the walls and empty rooms, and probably bounced off the locked door at the end of the hall.

"You are in so much trouble." His voice was practically shaking, he was so angry. "I'll deal with you when I get back from work."

I whirled on him, incredulous. "You're going back to work? When are you coming home?"

"I'm pulling another double; I'll see you sometime tomorrow."

I felt my anger rising even more. "What if I'm not here tomorrow?" I challenged. "What if I'm gone? You'd never know!"

My dad's face twisted. "For starters, you're grounded, so you're not going anywhere. There's going to be some changes around here: no more of this running off whenever you'd like. It's time for you to grow up and start taking care of things like a man."

I exploded, just like the firecrackers in my locker. "I've been taking care of this house for years! And taking care of you and making sure we don't fall apart and that's not my job! It's yours! You're the one who needs to grow up and start being my Father again!"

Anger split my father's face open, and his mouth seemed to stretch as he shouted, "Go to your room, Korvid!"

"I can't!" I couldn't stop myself, even if I wanted to; the words poured out of my mouth like water through a broken dam. I think that's what happened: something broke inside of me and I couldn't stop the jagged pieces of glass that were coming out of my mouth to cut and cause pain.

"You're in there! You've been in there for years! You won't come out and face what happened, and that means Mom *can't* come out of your room! It's not right—it's not fair! You can't leave me alone with what happened!"

The slap didn't hurt, it was more the shock that my dad had actually struck me. He hadn't done it hard; I think he just wanted me to stop. I don't think he could take the truths that I had to tell. He stared at me, both horrified by what he'd done, and what I'd said. I waited for an apology, but there was none.

"Go to your room."

I shook my head. "I can't stay here," I said, my voice quiet, but frighteningly loud in the empty house. "If I stay here, I'll disappear, just like Mom did. I can't—I *won't*—let that happen."

"Go to your room, Korvid!" His shout seemed loud enough to shake the very foundation of our house; maybe it did.

I went. I sat at the top of the stairs leading down into the basement and I listened, holding a bag of clothes. Sure enough, I heard him leave just minutes later.

I left, too.

I found Iphy and Jax at Our Place; they were talking about which superhero could beat up the other. Jax noticed me first and, ignoring Iphy's latest question about super powers, sprang up in a flash. "Korvid!" His eyes were wide as saucers. "Are you okay?"

I brought the back of my hand to my face and scrubbed away the surprising bits of dampness I found there. "I'm done."

Iphy scrambled to his feet, almost tripping over himself in his rush to rise. "With what? With school? I thought you had a few more days left."

Shaking my head, I dropped my bag; a new tenant to their outdoor apartment. "I'm leaving. I can't stand that house anymore."

Jax frowned. "You're running away from home? Have you thought this through yet, Korvid? Don't go rushing into something stupid just because—"

"He's not being stupid, he's finally being smart." Iphy clapped a hand on my shoulder; ignorant of (or just ignoring) the tears that kept coming forward no matter how much it displeased me. "Now we just need to convince the others; we'll be our own little gang with no ties to anyone but us."

"That's ridiculous. We'd never make it on our own." The hands at Jax's sides had slowly curled themselves into tight little balls of frustration.

Iphy snorted. "Bullshit. We do just fine with the six of us right now—we don't need anyone else."

"*That's* bullshit." Jax cried. "Everything we have that allows us to keep living comes from other people."

"It comes from E, and Calm, and Eddie; just like I said."

"And just where do you think they get it from, Iphy? Their parents or Thomas at the junkyard, or the Reverend or Mr. Smithy!" Jax shook his head firmly, despite the scowl on Iphy's face. "No matter what you wish was true, the fact of the matter is that we *need* help—"

"Speak for yourself!" Iphy spat, venom in his voice and ice in his gaze. "I don't need anyone's help, and neither does Korvid!"

"Enough!" I couldn't stand to see them fight; they weren't supposed to. They were above such petty bickering because they were gods and the rest of us weren't. But, right now, they were acting like simple, regular children: like the rest of us.

"Look, it doesn't matter if you think it's stupid or if you think it's awesome because that's your opinion and this is my decision." I took a deep breath. "And I've decided that I can't stay in that house anymore. I can't—I *won't*—be trapped in there like my mom is."

Jax put a comforting hand on my other shoulder. "Korvid… Your mom… she's not trapped in that house. There's no such thing as ghosts."

I thought about that day, hiding under the couch while the paramedics trampled through the house. I thought about waiting there for hours, terrified to move, even to the point of wetting myself. I thought about Dad, and the room he'd locked up for all time, and the silence that followed, echoing in the still halls. I shook my head. "You're wrong, Jax."

I told them about the firecrackers, and Kyle and Will's great prank; how it couldn't happen now that mine had gone off and I'd been pulled from school. It's funny: I think that's what troubled me most about that whole incident. Not that I'd been suspended from school, not that Dad and I had a falling out, but that I'd let Kyle and Will down, and taken from them the opportunity to have their final big hurrah. I felt inferior in a way, like if it had been Iphy that they'd confided in and asked to help them, the plan would have gone off without a hitch. Because Iphy was just like that.

Speaking of, Iphy thought the prank was a fine idea. In fact, he wished he'd thought of something like this for his last day at his old school. It was strange: now that I'd officially shed my life as a humble child and joined the ranks of free woodland dwellers, Iphy didn't stop talking. I often wonder if it was like this with Jax, if Iphy kept nothing from him and that was why Jax seemed to know so much more about our idol.

Iphy told me about his school and his town: how it was different and how it was similar. I felt bad for him; it didn't seem like he had all that much wilderness about him in his old town. I couldn't imagine growing up without all our trees; without being able to escape into the silence of the forest during the hard times. When we had run out of other things to talk about, Iphy told me about his family.

"I think my parents had only one thing in common: they liked to drink. Mom did it at home, and Dad stayed out late at the bar." He waved a hand, like it was no big thing. I thought it was incredible. Never in our time over the last year had he said much of anything about his family. I felt honored and terrified; to hear about his family would hear about how he really was just a normal child like us. "They fought all the time, especially after my brother left."

"You had a brother?" I couldn't help asking.

Iphy nodded with a smile bigger than any I'd ever seen on his face. "Haven't I mentioned him?"

"A time or two," Jax said. "You've mentioned him to me a lot, but I don't think the others have heard too much about him."

Iphy's grin got bigger. "My brother was the coolest guy around. Everyone loved him. He could float around to any group of kids, rich or poor, and they'd love him. He was smart too; he could figure out any puzzle and solve any riddle. He was everything I ever wanted to be."

I noticed he was using the past tense, and that there was a tremulous undertone of sadness that couldn't quite be masked by his gushing eagerness. It wasn't anything like I'd heard him sound; I think it was the most sincere that I'd ever heard him be.

"My brother taught me everything I know: he showed me how to fish and how to tie all these cool knots. He showed me the constellations and taught me how to always find the North Star." He gave a wistful sigh, turning his eyes to look at the sky overhead, as though he longed to see the stars in the daylight. "He'd hold me when our parents were fighting; he told me that no matter what, we'd make it out okay. He was the greatest."

I felt a twist in my chest. "What happened to him?"

With a shrug, Iphy grinned at me, throwing on his godly mask. "No clue. He made the smart move and ran away from home a year ago. Well, almost two years ago now."

"Is that why you ran away?" Jax asked.

Iphy shook his head, his pale hair swinging out. "Nah. I got tired of my parents fighting about him, so I scooted. I was hoping that I could find him; a great game of hide and seek."

"Do you have any idea where he's at?" I glanced around Our Place, suddenly wondering about the size of our abode compared to our town, or to the woods around us.

"No, but I'll find him."

"It's an awfully big world," Jax murmured. "Bigger than you can imagine."

Iphy insisted again that he could find his brother, but I was thinking about what Jax had said: it *was* an awfully big world. Our town was big to me, and the woods around it larger still. I knew the city was bigger than both, but that even the city was small compared to the state. It just kept getting bigger and bigger: the country, the continent, the world. I couldn't imagine Iphy's confidence in himself; I still can't decide if it was admirable or foolish.

"Why were your parents fighting about him?" I heard myself asking.

Iphy glowered. "They said he was getting into a bad crowd. Fuck them. They didn't even know him." He shook his head, anger bubbling forth. "That's all they ever did — fight about him. Mom said it was Dad's drinking that drove him away; he said it was her fault, letting him hang out with his friends. They kept acting like he was gone for good, like they couldn't find him. They didn't even *try*. I don't think they wanted him back; they just wanted someone to blame." He was angrier than he should have been. It felt heavy around him, like there was something that he was trying to say but he didn't know how.

"Have you heard from your brother since?" Jax's voice was quiet in the warm afternoon.

With the small shake of his head, I could see Iphy's façade start to crumble around the edges. "They kept talking about some kind of accident, but that's bullshit. That's what they were screaming about the night I snuck out: they were trying to place blame again. They were talking about getting a divorce because one of them fucked up, but they couldn't even agree on who." He sniffed, then tried to chuckle. "What idiots. They actually think he's gone; he played them good. He's out there somewhere, and I'm going to find him." His smile appeared at the corners of his lips, and it began to spread. "And when I do, everything will be awesome again." He nodded his head, trying to convince us; maybe himself. "He'll wait for me; I know he will. And besides, I've got a new family now; you guys."

His smile was fully on his face again, and he looked like the Childhood God that we'd all come to know and love. Iphy smiled—a real, warming smile—and everything seemed right with the world. Admittedly, I was a bit frightened to hear about his brother. I wanted to ask him more; I wanted to understand everything about him. But, like so much else, Iphy kept any more details to himself.

I glanced over at Jax, but he was looking at Iphy. I couldn't read the expression on his face, but it seemed haunted in a way, and that made me want to curl up and hide. There might have been pity there, or even a bit of anger or indignation. I couldn't tell. We were quiet for a time, and I thought that I really hadn't left my silent, oppressing house: that it had followed me, clinging to my back and never letting go. Then, Iphy waved his hand, saying that we should check out the junkyard to look for anything we could use.

Two days later, it was summer. And stretching before us were months of endless days and total freedom. I couldn't wait.

Gotta go,
Korvid

Extracted from an e-mail addressed to Eraliss Cofler from Korvid Fairington, dated ▮▮▮▮▮▮▮.

Eraliss, I'm sorry about the brush off at the end of my last e-mail. I had more written, but before I could hit the 'send' button, I deleted it all. It was hard, going back through all of that again. There was so much I saw that... if I had just done something different, then maybe everything would have been okay.

I'm not gonna re-type everything: it's a bunch of me whining about how I should have changed things. You've heard it all before and I don't think it'll really add that much to the story. Not too much more now, huh? All that's left is summer, and that was cut short.

I can't wait to read this when it's finished: your thoughts, Calm's, and my recollections—maybe we can finally make sense of everything.

All my love (and my apologies),
Korvid

SUMMER

Summer came to us one glorious Thursday morning; it was the start of something wonderful. I scrambled out of bed earlier than I ever did on a school day. I didn't bother telling my mom where I was going: she was still asleep and I was still miffed. She and Dad had been out, and had lost track of the time: that's why they had missed my reading. They had offered to make it up to me, but I assured them that there wasn't really much that they could do; I was mad, upset and hurt beyond belief. Dad took me aside and promised me chocolate chip pancakes for breakfast the first day of summer. Even after telling him five times that I had moved away from pancakes to French toast, he still didn't get it. That was one of the many reasons I was leaving so early.

When I stepped outside in my not-so-new-anymore shoes, the day was bright, birds were singing, and the trees around our cul-de-sac were green and flowering and wonderful. It felt like this day was just a prelude to the magic that was going to happen this summer. We had it all planned out: slumber parties under the blackened roof of the New Place, camping trips out past the Wailing Woman's territory and even a trip down the river if we could find a boat.

That was another reason I was leaving so early: Thomas Smith. Many things have been said about Thomas Smith (some of them pretty colorful, depending on which adult was talking) but the one thing that is usually never said about him is that he actually had a good heart. He smoked, cussed, openly drank illegally, got into fights all around town, was loud, crass, crude, cranky and sometimes just downright mean, but beneath all that (and I mean pretty deep, like a well, or the Marianas Trench) was a kid who liked life enough to make sure that it was alright for those who sometimes couldn't help themselves. Thomas let the homeless of our town—Iphy and Jax included—root through the junkyard where he worked and take whatever they needed.

Thomas Smith worked at the junkyard only part time because legally at seventeen he was still a minor, but he practically ran the place when the stuffy old owner wasn't there. He was tall, with a battered face of someone who worked hard for a living; as such, he looked much older than he should have. I was rattling the chain-links together to try and get his attention when he came up the gate. His jaw was scruffy with several days' worth of facial hair. A crumpled cigarette hung from his lips, his hands were black with oil and grease and his usually dishwater-blonde hair was streaked with residue from his fingers.

He frowned at me. "What do you want? Scram." He almost had his own dialect because of the cigarette in the corner of his mouth, but I'd been around him long enough to decipher it.

"I wanna know if you have something."

"What? I ain't got time for babies."

I kept at it. "A boat of some kind: a canoe or a raft?" I was thinking of getting it as a surprise for everyone else, which was another reason I had gotten up so early. I didn't want anyone coming with me.

He snorted. "Shit. I don't know. You think I know every piece of junk here? Now get the hell out of here."

"Can I look?"

"What the hell you need a boat for anyway?" He raised a bushy eyebrow at me, still frowning, and not looking at all like he was going to unlock the gate.

I rolled my eyes. "We found a big river in the woods; we're gonna head downstream for a bit."

"Stupidest idea I ever heard. Your parents know about this?"

"No, and you're not gonna tell 'em."

At that, he snickered. "No, probably not. Ain't my place to go talking to your folks." He glanced around, but it was just him and me. "Fine," he relented, digging the keys out of his pocket. "Two things: first, if you guys end up crashing and drowning, you didn't get nothing here; second, let me know if there's any good fishing—I'm looking for a new steelhead spot."

"Deal."

Thomas opened the gate and stepped to one side. "Be quick. I want you out of here before we actually open and real people start filing in."

It was my turn to snicker. "You don't think I'm real?"

"You hang out with the Iphy kid, right? Shit, I don't know what to think about any of your crazy ass lot except that he ain't as real as he seems. Besides, I'm talking about actual paying customers."

I nodded and continued my search, looking as quickly as I could through the entire junkyard. The junkyard was a massive lot at the far edge of town; almost out of the city limits. There were enormous piles of stuff from years and years gone by; sometimes it was fun just to dig around and see what we could find, but this time I was on a mission. I moved further and further into the junk piles, focusing on the task of looking for some sort of boat. I had started my search with high hopes, but as I kept going deeper and deeper, I started to feel the prickling of doubt. I kept searching until I came across something I'd never seen before: a battered, rusty chain link fence. It was similar to the one in the front of the junkyard, but this one looked older and more abused; there were holes and even a whole section that had been cut away.

"I told you to be quick." Thomas' sudden and unexpected voice behind me made me jump a mile high.

A quick glance down at my watch made my stomach flop: I'd been in the junkyard almost two and half hours. I had known the place was big, but never could I have imagined that it was as big as it really was.

"Your fence is all busted back here," was all I could think to say. I was still embarrassed about jumping and taking as much time as I did.

"It's been like that forever."

I frowned. "I thought the owner hated trespassers." More than once he'd hollered at Iphy and Jax to get lost, even going so far as to threaten them with his shotgun and NRA membership.

"He does; we ain't had any trespassers through the back fence."

"Really? Why?"

A sudden roar exploded in my ear and the wind whipped at me, threatening to knock me off my feet. Thunder boomed around me, echoing off the towering piles of junk, and the world felt like it was turning in on itself. Fear at the sudden force of sound and movement dropped me to my knees as my hair whipped around me, freed from its ponytail by the power of the wind. I squeezed my eyes shut against the whirlwind of dust and I think I screamed; if I did, the noise around me swallowed my voice. It felt like it went on forever, then it passed; the wind stopped, and the sound moved on, leaving my ears ringing.

I shakily raised my head, parting my hair and looking up at the behemoth that had thundered by. It was a train. I hadn't even noticed the tracks beyond the junkyard's fence: there were two pairs of them that ran alongside the battered fence for a few hundred yards before disappearing back into the woods.

Thomas snickered and held out a hand to help me. "Train keeps them out."

"Y-yeah, I guess," I murmured, taking the offered hand. "I didn't even know we had a train in this town."

"That's because we don't." He jerked a thumb at the tracks. "That fence is the city limit; technically, we ain't got any trains in town."

"Still, you think I would have heard it; trains are loud."

He snorted. "When you're close to them. Out in town, with all the shit you're doing, it's easy to miss them."

I looked at the pairs of tracks. "Them? You mean there's more than one?"

Thomas nodded. "Got four of them that come through every day: one in the morning, two in the afternoon and one at exactly midnight." He looked at me for a second, appraisal in his eyes. "Where do you live?"

I told him and he nodded. "That's the street with the abandoned house, yeah?"

Inside, I snickered; only six people knew that the New Place hadn't been completely abandoned. "Yeah, that's the one."

"That's a good spot; you got the ravine and the valley down that way — sound carries well out there." He smiled a bit; it was an actual warm smile, not a snarky one like he liked to flaunt. "Open your window come midnight tonight. You should just be able to hear it."

"Really? All the way out there?"

He nodded again. "Like I said, sound carries well out there." He glanced around, looking with his appraising eyes at the junk around us. "You find anything yet?"

I shook my head. "No. I don't think you've got anything."

Thomas shrugged. "Next time then; it's not like you ain't got time. You kids have the whole summer ahead of you."

When he put it that way, I didn't feel so bad coming back empty handed. I thanked Thomas and he promised to keep an eye out for anything that could ferry us down the river. By the time I had hiked back to our street, it was well into the afternoon, and by the time I had found the others (way back in the woods, playing at the edge of the river) the low sun was creating long shadows.

We stayed there for a few more hours before starting back to Our Place; we splashed and ran around and tried to skip stones in the stiller parts of the water. Down in the valley, I noticed that Thomas was right: the sound was different here. It carried better, and our echoes sounded strange and otherworldly. I tried to listen for the trains that came by in the afternoon, but I knew they were too far away from our river to hear them properly, especially with Iphy making such a loud ruckus. He was hooting and hollering with joy now that we all officially belonged to him. And that's exactly how he put it.

"School's out! You got nothing there for you; you're all mine now!"

His enthusiasm was contagious, like everything else about him. We were all whooping for joy that afternoon. Summer stretched before us like a road that never ended; we couldn't even fathom the start of school, just two and half short months away. Time didn't work the same way in the summer as it did the rest of the year. It went by slower and quicker all at once. Minutes, even hours, could stretch by, taking all the time in the world, and you could just sit and listen to your friends or watch the world drift by for ages, but then you blink and a week has passed, then two, and suddenly, while the individual minutes and hours laze on, the days slip by quicker and quicker.

That afternoon the minutes lazed by but darkness crept in all at once: the shadows lengthened as the sun began to sink. Even with the longer days, the sun still died every night and darkness still claimed the world for a time. We took the shadows as our cue to head home; we still had a couple hours' trek through the woods to get back to the safety of our yards. Iphy was still talking about all the fantastic things we were gonna do that summer: catching fish, rafting down the river, finding buried treasure, trekking through the woods until we came across something that no one had ever seen before.

"And we'll do it together." He grinned, standing at the edge of the woods, on the border of his world and ours. With a flip of his hand and a casual goodnight, he turned and began to vanish back into his world. Already he had converted two of us to follow him and live the wondrous, exciting life of a Childhood God. Jax had long since joined Iphy (way, way back in Autumn) but it still felt strange, watching Korvid as he went with Iphy and Jax back into the woods after our parting. I didn't know what to make of the change; I couldn't tell if I should be happy, angry, or even sad that he'd left home to join our friends. But I decided to try and just let things be. It was his decision, and I couldn't entirely say I blamed him. More than once I had thought about leaving my blasé mother behind to join in Iphy's frolicking. He made everything so grand and my life just felt so dull.

As Eddie and Calm began making their way down to the street, I found myself lingering at the edge, wanting more than anything to go back into the woods and have Iphy induct me into the life he lived so carelessly. I was reminded of our first meeting, when Korvid had stayed behind. Maybe it meant that I was to be the next in line to join their happy band.

But, not that night. Maybe not even that summer. I couldn't tell what I wanted. I started through my yard, heading to the back door; I would wait it out and see. I promised myself that I wouldn't rush into leaving my life behind, as fun and exciting as it sounded.

Up in my room, I stayed awake, watching the clock tick through the seconds, thinking about everything that had happened. When midnight neared, I opened my window and stuck my head out, listening to the silence. The stars were amazing, even dulled by the lights of our town. Then, I heard it; the faint faraway sound of a train's horn. It was beyond me, away in the world outside our town. And I suddenly realized how much bigger everything was. The train tracks only briefly glanced by my world before setting out into the endless space beyond it. Iphy would see that space—all of it—I was sure.

I didn't want to be left behind.

When I was young, I had the dream that my dad would come back into my life and everything would be all right. He sent me postcards from the places that he visited and I marked them on a large map in my room. I dreamed about traveling with him, seeing all the wonderful places that he saw.

That summer, my dream died.

Despite my continued insistence that I didn't like pancakes, Dad was determined to make them for me. I finally relented, especially when he told me that I wasn't leaving until I tasted his special banana pancakes—a recipe that he got from his many years of travel. He talked nonstop while he worked and I listened as he talked, trying to throw in my own two cents, but I found it difficult.

"It's hard, you know? Well, you don't know—you're just a kid—kids don't know what hard is."

"Actually—"

"Anyway, it's hard traveling around; not knowing which hotel you'll get the best discount from. Sometimes I have to sleep in my car—when I have one. That's rough: roughest place you can sleep, let me tell you."

"You know, my friend Iphy—"

"Speaking for friends, I can't tell you how many of those I've lost. You know, you try to be a nice guy and all they do is walk all over you. You have any friends, Eraliss?"

"A bunch; we hang out—"

"Cause I've got friends. Can't get through life without friends. And family. Sometimes I stay with my cousin— he's a good guy."

"Do I know him?"

"Doubtful; your mom was never keen on you getting out of this place. I couldn't wait to get out of here, you know? Well, you don't know—you're just a kid—but boy, I was excited: finally getting out on the open road, nothing holding me back."

Like a rock thrown at my chest, those words hurt. "Mom and I were holding you back?"

Dad looked over his shoulder at me, an obvious 'busted' look crossing his face for a second. "Nah, I didn't say that. But it was hard for me, you know? Wanting more out of life than what I had."

"Mom said you had a great job."

"A desk job." He shook his head incredulously. "Can you believe that that's what she wanted me to do? Work behind a desk? For what? For money? Money's nothing— you're just a kid now, but you'll learn that eventually."

There was a squirming little eel in the space between my heart and my stomach. "You have a job now though, right?"

"I did. But I had to get out of that one too."

"Why?"

"Because, kiddo, it just wasn't working for me."

"What was it?"

"Trekking around in the woods. Can you believe that? They actually wanted me to go stomping around, getting all sorts of dirty, for what? For minimum wage. I couldn't do it. So of course my girlfriend kicks me out—" He stopped suddenly, guilt painting his face as he looked over his shoulder at me. "Heh. Never mind me, kiddo. I'm just running my mouth off—"

"You had another girlfriend?" My mouth was slack; I couldn't believe what he had just said.

He shrugged, still sheepish. "Not anymore."

"Because she booted you out after you quit your job!"

With a sigh, Dad stopped mixing pancake batter and turned to me, a pained look on his face. "Eraliss, I didn't quit: I got fired. This isn't my fault."

"Then whose fault is it, Dad?"

"My employers changed my schedule; I had to get up two hours early to catch the bus and I missed it a few times."

"I thought you had a car? That brand new, bright red one that you bought last year. Remember, you sent me a photo of it."

Again, he gave a sheepish laugh. "Did I say that one was mine? I just saw it and thought it looked cool. I sold my car three years ago to buy a guitar."

This was the first I'd ever heard of him wanting to be a musician. "When did you learn how to play? Did someone teach you while you were out seeing the world?"

"No, I'm still learning."

I couldn't even begin to believe my ears. "So, you just decided to be a musician? Have you ever played that thing at all?"

Dad shrugged. "I found this kid who had a garage band; I played with him and his friends a few times."

Everything around me seemed to be shifting about; my feet felt like they were about to collapse out from underneath me. My father wasn't the man I thought he was. This didn't feel right; this didn't feel like my real father. The father I had was a heroic traveler, who thought of his family often, but had to go to feed the wanderlust that burned in his belly.

"Why do you want to be a musician?" I heard the question being asked, but it didn't feel like I had asked it: it sounded hollow and foreign.

"Kiddo, being a musician is one hundred percent party time. No troubles at all and no responsibilities to speak of; it would be one smooth ride."

I couldn't stay. The legs of my chair made a scraping sound as I scooted away from the table. Upstairs I could still faintly hear the sound of the shower going. "Excuse me," I murmured, more to myself than to my dad.

"Where you going kiddo? We're having pancakes, remember."

"I'm going out; I don't want pancakes."

"Oh, come on — you love pancakes."

"No, I don't!" I glared at him, feeling my cheeks turn warm and wet. "You never listen! I don't want pancakes and I don't want to stay here!" I wiped at my eyes, hating myself for crying and hating him for making me.

He frowned at me, lines working their way into his forehead. "Eraliss, what's wrong with you?"

"What's wrong with you?" I countered, feeling all my bottled emotions about him rising to the surface. For too long he'd been gone from my life, leaving me and my mother alone. For all that time I'd imagined that he'd been gone for better reasons—that he still loved us and wanted to come back. Every child imagines their parents to be some kind of superhero, and when that innocence is lost, sometimes it can shatter someone completely.

"You left us so you could party and not give a shit!" Underneath my flurry of emotions for my father, there was a bit of surprise at my own boldness. "You never wanted me and you never wanted Mom! You just wanted a meal ticket and a place to crash. And don't tell me I don't know what hard is! Do you know how hard it is to have one of your parents walk out of your life and not bother to remember you? Because that's what you're doing to me, Dad! The last three years, you've never called me on my birthday! It's always a week late, or a few days early, and this year I didn't get a call at all!" I sniffled, embarrassed by the tears still running down my face. "What's wrong with you? I'm sorry we're not good enough, but that doesn't mean that we don't have feelings, and it doesn't mean that we exist only when it's convenient for you!"

Upstairs I heard my mother calling down to us, asking what all the yelling was about. I couldn't stand to let her see me like I was, and I couldn't stand to be in the same room as my father. I bolted out the back door.

I ran, not towards the woods and the safety of Our Place, but down the street and past our familiar houses. I kept running, not paying attention to my surroundings; there was a tunnel of white was around me. I kept going until my legs threatened to stop working, my lungs wheezed and my throat was dry, scratchy and tasted of blood. I looked about, taking in the green around me. The smell of fruit and the faraway sounds of children playing let me know; I was on Mr. Wiesner's farm. More specifically, I was in the grove of trees where we had first discovered Iphy and Jax's divinity. I tried for hours to find the exact tree that they had climbed so long ago, but I couldn't; all the trees looked alike.

I reached out and touched the nearest tree; it didn't feel special or magical. It didn't feel like it could bestow any kind of special gift. Gritting my teeth, I pulled myself up into the tree and I kept climbing until I was among the top branches. Sunshine sprinkled down on me, warming the top of my head, but I felt nothing else. No godly powers surging through my veins.

It wasn't the tree: it was them. I'd always thought that they were the ones who were special, but I still held onto the hope that maybe it was something given to them by some higher power. If that were true, than whatever higher power had bequeathed upon them their grand prowess didn't see fit to bless me the same way. Whatever the case, I didn't find the godly powers that I was looking for. I stayed up in the tree and cried until the sun began to sink.

I made my way slowly home, taking the familiar roads rather than risking the woods' wrath in the coming twilight. When I climbed the steps, I felt every ounce of spirit that I had left in me get sucked out with each step. My hand was shaking on the doorknob; I couldn't face what was inside, or rather, what wasn't there anymore. Even before I opened the door and heard her crying; I knew my mom would be alone.

I was too weary to try and hide my appearance; she saw me from the kitchen, her eyes red and puffy with the many tears. "He left again."

All I wanted was to go upstairs and flop on my bed, but I felt compelled to tell her the truth. "He probably went back to his girlfriend's."

She didn't seem surprised. "I was hoping he'd stay for you."

Emotion — the one thing I didn't think I had any more of — flared up in me. "I don't want him. You shouldn't either."

"I tried to keep him here; he's your father."

"No! He's my sperm donor! A father is someone who raises you, who loves you. That's not what he did."

She didn't try and defend him; she remained silent, which confirmed my worst fears.

"You knew! You knew he didn't love us; that he had others. You still let him stay here! How could you do that?"

"I did it for you! You needed him —"

I shook my head violently, tears making their way down my cheeks. "I never needed him! You didn't either. I hope I never see him again."

Mom got to her feet, slamming her hands down on the table with a loud crack of noise. "Don't you dare say that!"

"It's true! He never wanted us, so I don't want him! You don't want him either!"

Her face flushed bright red. "How dare you!"

"How dare you!" I screamed back. "How could you take him back if you knew he'd do this? That he's done this before! He's nothing but… but poison! You want him because you think you need him to play the father role — the protector — but he never will! You can't…" I tried to bite back the sob, but it forced its way out. "You can't make him love us! He won't!"

She started to say something else, but I couldn't stand to be there anymore; I ran upstairs, slamming my door behind me. I looked around my room — my sanctuary — and I couldn't stomach looking at it. All around me were pictures of my father, of the places he'd been rather than with us. There was the bulletin board of postcards, and worst of all, the map. It stood pinned up against the wall; a silent shrine to my father and all the places that he'd decided he'd rather be. If he'd even been to them. I couldn't tell what was real anymore and I didn't want to wade through the lies for fear of them sticking to me like black tar.

I grabbed the map, not even bothering to take out the dozens of pins. I ripped it from the wall, scattering pins all over my floor. I tore it to pieces, shredding the cities, the roads, the rivers and all of my excited notations. Bits of the country rained down to carpet my floor, joining the scattered pins. Next were the post cards: I ripped them from their thumbtacks and flung them about. Some I shredded, some I just crumpled. Last to be attacked were the photos. I tore them from the walls, but found that I couldn't bear to tear them into pieces; instead, they were thrown to the ground, to join the rest of the trash.

The only photo left was the only one I had ever framed; it was a photo of my dad, standing next to a bright red, brand new car. He was smiling, flashing a 'thumbs up', and even though I couldn't see it, on the back were the scribbled words, 'Ain't it nice? I'll have to stop by and take you for a spin. Love, Dad.' I glared at the picture, my hands shaking. I had put so much stock into this photo: I had believed that my dad was out there doing great things, achieving and getting rewarded for his efforts. I had believed that he wanted to come back to us, maybe even for good. I had believed that he loved me. And maybe, deep down, he did; he just loved his freedom more, and I couldn't stand that.

I hurled the frame out the window, aiming for the woods. I screamed as I threw it, hoping the Wailing Woman would hear and come to take away what I was offering. It was dark and I couldn't see where the photo landed, but I didn't care.

I never went looking for it.

Extracted from an e-mail addressed to Eraliss Cofler from Korvid Fairington, dated ▉▉▉▉▉▉▉.

Living with Iphy and Jax was probably one of the most terrifying things I have ever done in my whole life. The woods hated me; I could tell. I felt them always watching me and I couldn't stand it. They knew that I didn't belong with Iphy and Jax, and they always seemed to crowd around me, trying to physically push me out of their realm. Then there was the insecurity: I never knew what was going to happen next. You think living in the woods wouldn't be too much of a change from living in your own house (except that there aren't any parents or chores or anything like that) but there's also no security. You never expect something dangerous when you're sleeping in your own bed, but out in the woods it's hard to go to sleep. Out there, there's no walls to keep the bad stuff out, no blanket to hide under and no light next to you that you can flip on to scare away the night.

My first night with them, reveling in my freedom, I heard the Wailing Woman. She screamed from down in the valley, where the river was. She was probably at the mouth of the ravine, but sound carried strangely down there; for all I knew, she could have been closer, watching me and studying me because I was a stranger.

There's a kind of primal fear being out there in the woods, away from any real help. There are no parents out there, no police or teachers—you can't imagine how terrifying it was, those first few nights. You have no idea where you'll find your next meal; you have to rely on your friends, hoping they'll bring enough of the good stuff. If I wasn't so furious with my dad, so terrified of the house and my mother's restless spirit, I would have gone back. I don't know how Iphy and Jax managed it for so long; especially when they didn't have to.

Your suspicions were right, E: Iphy's grandparents were back from their vacation long before summer. I saw them once, from far away. Iphy, Jax and I were trekking through the woods, like we were prone to do in those few glorious days of summer. Iphy was leading us to a spot where he'd pinched some of the better tasting veggies for us; he wanted to get some potatoes to mash up that night. He stopped just inside the tree line, swearing and glaring out into the yard of some large plot of land

It was a nice yard, in the back of a nice house. An elderly couple was working in the yard, tending the small vegetable patch that Iphy must have been intent on robbing. I couldn't see them all that clearly through the trees, but the house and the secluded yard looked nice enough.

Jax elbowed Iphy. "You've been stealing from elderly people?"

Our leader scoffed. "It's no big deal; they'd give us whatever we needed anyway."

At that, Jax shook his head. "You don't know that, Iphy. What if this garden is all they have?"

"As if." Iphy rolled his eyes. "These guys are rich; they have plenty of food, or at least plenty of money to buy plenty of food."

Jax frowned. "How do you know?"

Before Iphy could answer, the reason came to me. "This is Olaha Way," I said quietly. Jax looked confused, but Iphy grinned. "These are your grandparents."

"That's right: good ol' Gran and Gram."

Jax still seemed confused. "I thought they were in Florida or somewhere."

Iphy snickered. "Yeah, for the winter; it's summer now. They've been home for weeks, maybe even months."

That wasn't the answer Jax wanted to hear. "They've been here all this time? Why haven't you talked to them? You could be staying with them, warm in their house, not out in the woods."

"It's plenty warm these nights," our leader snorted, looking rather put off at Jax's tone of voice. "Besides, if I talk to them, they'll want me to call my Mom and Dad, and that's not something that I want to do."

"But you don't have to be homeless!"

"Maybe I want to be! Maybe I don't want to go back to my parents and their fighting!"

I tried to quiet them with a hand on each of their shoulders. "Guys, quiet; you get any louder and they'll hear you, whether you want them to or not."

We stood at the tree line, probably invisible to the pair in the yard, for about twenty minutes, watching to see if they'd leave. When they showed no signs of leaving for some time, Iphy snorted and turned back into the woods. Jax and I followed, because that's what we were supposed to do: Iphy led us, and we followed him. He headed into the woods, taking paths that by now had to be familiar to him and his stomping, a storm cloud swirling around him. I don't think he was angry that his grandparents weren't leaving their yard and giving him opportunity to get some potatoes; I think he was mad that Jax seemed intent on fighting his decision.

Iphy took us into the valley, down along where the river raced beside us. He was still fuming and he didn't see Jax sneak closer to the river. He didn't notice Jax scoop some of the cold water into cupped hands and dump it all over his head. I laughed so hard that I thought I was going to wet my pants. To his credit, Iphy laughed too, and in true Iphy fashion, he had to one-up his self-proclaimed little brother. He jumped forward, wrestling with Jax until they both ended up falling into the cold water. I kept laughing, now on my knees, holding my sides as though my insides were going to burst out. They both splashed me, spraying up water in a fine wave, and soon I was joining them, laughing and splashing and just being three free kids in a river, far away from any responsibilities at all.

Then she shrieked: the Wailing Woman sent up her terrible cry and it seemed to echo all around us. I couldn't tell where it was coming from, just that it was suddenly there, filling my ears and sending chills down my spine. We stopped our playing, all of us frozen in place by the sound. There was something slightly off about the sound; there was no question that it was the Wailing Woman, but there was something missing. There weren't enough echoes or enough of a drag to the last notes of her scream, but it was definitely her.

She shrieked again, and a third time, and all we could do was stand frozen, up to our calves in the frigid water. None of us dared to move. What if she saw us? What if she had heard our laughter and was jealous enough to try and harm us? It would have been just like her to try and take from us what she no longer had: happiness, life and laughter. But, she didn't—not *then*, anyway—but I wouldn't be surprised if she was the reason that everything went bad.

When we were sure that she wasn't going to come out of her ravine to take our souls, we breathed a sigh of relief. I looked around at the other two, still frightened by her sound. It hadn't sounded quite right, but there was no doubt in my mind. "We should get out of here; she obviously doesn't like us here."

Iphy glanced upriver, towards the ravine. "We should try to find her."

I was aghast. "Are you nuts? That's the stupidest idea to ever come out of your mouth."

He snorted. "How do you figure? I've never heard her while we've been down here; this'll be awesome. Haven't you ever wanted to see her?" When neither of us stirred, he pouted. "Eraliss would have come; she'd be all over this. You know how obsessed she is with her. We should at least look for her sake."

That's right, E; Iphy conned us into going with him by dropping your name.

So we followed him, like we always did. Not even then—so close to the end—could we really *not* follow him. We could question him (and we did, a lot) but we couldn't ever really say 'No' to him. It didn't take us long to find the ravine; the entrance to her territory. At first, even Iphy was afraid to enter; he would never admit it, but there was a hesitation and an obvious fear on his face as he looked up at the green tunnel in the trees, before him. He must have felt our eyes on him, thinking we were judging him when we weren't, because he gritted his teeth together and stepped into the tunnel, squeezing his eyes shut as he entered. The Wailing Woman didn't swoop down upon him to suck the life from his soul: all that happened was the loud snapping of the twig that he stepped on. He took another step, and another, and soon the three of us were traveling as one, packed and pressed together, moving through her world.

We must have spent a few hours in her territory, but we never found her. Then, as the night was creeping out from under the shadows of the trees, we heard her call again, but this time from farther down in the valley. Her cry sounded better in the trees, more like herself; it must have been all the echoing through the trunks that gave it its punch. As soon as he heard it, Iphy bolted back down the ravine; he went crashing through the trees until he burst out into the valley. Jax and I raced behind him, yelling at him to be careful: he could slip, or trip, or get his soul sucked out by a terrible, terrible apparition that we had never actually seen.

Iphy sprinted down along the river, the two of us still trying to keep up with him. The light was really starting to fade by the time that he slowed to a stop, hands on his knees, gulping in air and wheezing a bit as he did. "Couldn't see her," he gasped.

"What would you have done if you had?" Jax panted, falling to his butt, and leaning back on his palms.

Iphy shrugged, and despite my aching sides and legs, I chuckled. "That's you, Iphy: always planning things out in advance." I joined Jax on the ground, and that's when I noticed it in the sandy dirt near the river. I got up and leaned over, looking at the print in the ground. It was almost three inches across, with four little finger impressions and a big heel pad; it was a cat's track. A big one.

"What'cha looking at?" Iphy looked down at it and whistled. "It's huge! It's the same track I've been seeing all spring!"

I gulped. "That's a mountain lion track."

"No way! You serious?" Iphy grinned, looking around us, as though hoping to see the beast in the failing light.

"We should get out of here; those things can be nasty."

Iphy snorted. "We could take it on."

Jax shook his head. "With what? We don't have anything but the clothes on our backs."

"We've got river rocks; we could throw them at it."

I had to put my foot down and stand up. "Nu-uh. No way. All that would do is piss the thing off."

Iphy looked ready to argue, but the Wailing Woman shrieked again, closer than ever this time. We all jumped a mile high and before we knew it, we were running back towards our familiar woods, back to the safety of Our Place. Behind us, the Wailing Woman shrieked her indignation again, warning us away from her territory. None of us mentioned the track; I think it was forgotten in our flight, and then lost in our minds when things went bad.

To tell you the truth, E, I'm surprised I remembered it. And, just so you know, I don't agree with the Reverend or the police on that account; there's no way that it was just a mountain lion that we heard. I know their cries are eerie and otherworldly, but the Wailing Woman's shriek is something that will always haunt my darkest nightmares. I know she had something to do with what happened. She took them away; robbed the world of a shining piece of light and happiness. There's no way that she was just some echoing mountain lion, no matter what anyone else says.

You were right: she was something beyond all of us.

She wasn't part of our world anymore; she was only part of her own.

I wish… well, it doesn't matter anymore.

Lots of love,

Korvid.

From the Journal of Calm Sheldon

Iphy had told me not to fear for my parents until they dropped the 'D' word: divorce. They fought, they yelled, but they never said that magical deciding word. Then, the first weekend in July it was said. Yelled, actually. My father screamed across the house at my mother; if this was how things were going to work, then they might as well call a spade a spade and get a divorce. I was sitting on the stairs, trying to block out their yelling, but that one word slithered through my fingers.

I looked down, watching as my father stormed out, slamming the door behind him. I was terrified, frightened, but also venomously angry. I couldn't stand my father and his selfishness; if nothing else, he should have at least waited until I was gone so I couldn't hear him. So I wouldn't have to hear him say that he didn't want to be part of our family anymore. I was also scared that this was the final emotion that I would feel for him, that I would only hold anger in my heart for him. I couldn't stand that thought.

I left; I couldn't bear to hear my mother crying and throwing things against the kitchen wall. I raced upstairs, slamming my own door in a poor imitation of my father. I climbed through my window and scrambled up onto the roof, suddenly terrified by the massive expanse of sky around me. I screamed at it until my voice cracked, but still the sky hung above me. I cried, hot tears rolling down my cheeks. I sobbed; feeling like something was trying to escape from my chest through my throat. My shoulders shook and I felt like curling up in a ball and dying.

Cold had slithered into my heart and into the base of my spine with terrifying quickness. I couldn't stand the feeling, the tearing at my heart; the 'D' word had been said.

"Calm?"

I looked up, seeing Jax leaning over me; tears were still fresh on my face, and the sky was dazzling beyond us. I couldn't for the life of me figure out what Jax was doing on my roof. He was kneeling next to me, concern in his eyes.

"She okay?" Iphy's voice floated up from my yard.

"I think so." Jax looked over his shoulder, then back down at me. "Are you okay, Calm?"

I blinked up at him. "You're on my roof."

He smiled a bit, the concern not leaving. "I am. We heard you crying up here; everything okay?"

I shook my head. "I can't stay here tonight."

"Why not?" Iphy called, scrambling up on to the roof. He almost fell, just barely managing to catch himself. He inched his way along the roof, not nearly as graceful as Jax was. "What happened?"

Seeing Iphy made it all come flying back to me; it made it real all over again. I picked myself up and threw my arms around his shoulders, sobbing anew. "They said it! Divorce! He's leaving, and this time he won't come back."

Iphy tried to comfort me while Jax yelled for Korvid. Soon, the four of us were on my roof, all of them telling me that it would be okay, that I was strong enough to get through this mess. I shook my head, unable to speak, unable to tell them that I wasn't strong; I couldn't look ahead and still see myself as I was. All I could see was a dark void and nothing seemed to fit quite right. I couldn't fathom why my parents couldn't work anything out, why they had to stop loving each other.

"Let's go somewhere," Jax murmured. He looked towards the woods, where he and Iphy, and maybe even Korvid, were welcome. "Tonight. Let's all go camping or something; I know the perfect spot."

Jax stayed with me up on the roof while Iphy and Korvid went and fetched the others. It seemed like forever since I had seen Eraliss' freckles, or Eddie's round face; could it have been only the day before? Too much had happened: time had both stopped altogether and rushed on ahead without me.

The preparation for camping blurred by me in Time's rush; at some point Jax coaxed me down from the roof and Eraliss had grabbed my sleeping bag from my downstairs closet without alerting my mother. We were moving through the woods next, taking trails that were at one time familiar to me, but right then looked like strange, even dangerous paths through the trees. Then, Iphy was sitting with me on soft grass on a broad hillside. He was talking casually about everything, about nothing. It was just white noise that I tried to focus on, but like radio static it was hard to keep interest.

Then, Jax's voice burst through my isolation and my head instinctively looked up. He was pointing out a brilliant, shining star that was streaking across the sky. "Take a look at that! A shooting star!"

Finally broken from my stupor, I looked around. The sky was starting to darken, the sun already behind the mass of trees beyond the small valley's borders. I recognized this place; it was the same little valley that Korvid, Eraliss and I had first stumbled upon when we were looking for Iphy, back when I thought he was just a shadowy egg robber. I looked around the rapidly darkening sky and, sure enough, there was Venus, still shining down on us, laughing in the way that stars, planets and other lights in the sky will.

"There's another!" Eraliss pointed a finger as another star whizzed by on its way to its secret destination.

Another and another streaked by, inciting peals of laughter and delight from the others. I tried to join in their joy, but the 'D' word still loomed, like a black, shadowy boogeyman. When we had pointed out about a dozen of the shooting stars, Jax sat down on my other side.

"We should count them," he murmured.

I looked over at him, unsure of his meaning, but Iphy knew. He stretched out and looked to the sky. "You've heard of that too, Jax?"

"Yeah, my parents told me about it. Did your brother tell you?"

While Iphy slowly nodded, Eddie looked between the two of them. "What are you guys talking about?"

"Counting shooting stars," Iphy grinned.

Jax nodded. "If you get to ninety-nine, then you make a wish. If you see the one-hundredth star, then your wish will come true."

"Is that true?" Eraliss asked looking up as another star went traveling across the sky. She held her breath as another appeared. "We should! We'll count them all!"

"How many do we have already?" Iphy asked, scanning the inky sky.

As another and another went by, Korvid smiled. "I think that's eighteen."

"Nineteen!" Eddie yelled, pointing out one that we almost missed as it came in low, near the tree line.

"Twenty!"

"Twenty-one!"

We all sat on that hill, each of us looking in a different direction, counting the stars as they fell all around us. I couldn't believe it; it was like the stars were weeping for my plight, passing close to earth to show their sympathy. Some of them seemed to spin as they fell, like when you're trying to catch your breath after running or crying. They dazzled us, awed us and inspired us. As each star came close, I felt like maybe, just maybe, I could convince my parents that their love was still there. It had to be.

As the night wore on, the stars became fewer and fewer. They stayed in place, blinking and watching us from their fixtures in the night sky. One more blinked and dropped, smudging the sky a bit with light.

"That's ninety-nine." Iphy smiled as his elbow jostled me a bit. "Make your wish, Calm."

I looked up at the stars, ready to beg from them the gift of my parent's continued love. "I wish my parents wouldn't get a divorce; I don't want my father to leave."

I don't know if the stars heard me or not. I don't know if they thought it was a frivolous wish or if something as vast and complicated as Love was just too far out of their reach and they couldn't do anything for me. Maybe stars are just like us; maybe they can't grasp so abstract of a concept any easier than we can. In any case, it wasn't to pass. We saw no more falling stars that night. We stayed up as late as we could; watching the sky with such fervent hope, such expectation, but nothing sparkled and fell for us to see. The sky was silent to my pleas.

Still, the night helped; I felt like I could be myself again. I didn't have to hide from the whole world because my small one was falling apart. And it felt like my small world shattering brought everyone else's together again. This night showed us the enchantment of the world around us, as though we had somehow forgotten the simplistic joy of all of us just being together. Maybe it was their shared knowledge of counting stars, but for that night, and the time after, Iphy and Jax seemed even closer than they had ever been. They were in perfect sync again, like they had been all those long days ago when we had first sat around the warm fire of Our Place. It was as though being told the same information by people whom they had both lost so suddenly and so tragically made them brothers in more than just words and feelings; it united them in their divinity.

Maybe that's why everything seemed to go so bad so quickly: because just minutes before, they were the shining example of all that was good in life. Korvid has said that he thinks it's his fault; Eraliss thought maybe it was hers. I've tried to tell them that it's no one's fault, but deep down, I think it's mine. And if I could count the stars again, I'd make a new wish: that they hadn't found me on my roof, that they hadn't tried so hard to cheer me up, that the stars had never fallen, and that we hadn't gone to the river the next day.

C.S

Extracted from an e-mail addressed to Eraliss Cofler from Edward McCloy, dated ███████.

I don't know how you found my e-mail address, Eraliss, but don't contact me again. These are wounds that I don't want to reopen. I will always cherish your friendship, and that year was one of the best of my life, but I've put it behind me. You may want to wade through the memories, but I don't.

I'm sorry, but don't contact me again.

E. McCloy

~*~

The entries are getting smaller; Korvid and Calm have less and less to say. I can't blame them — there's not much left to say. I had hoped that writing this all down, putting events in order and going through it again would help make things clear, but while the memories are still clear and rose-tinged, the answers to the questions that we and everyone else asked are still murky and dark.

The day after we counted stars, a bright July Monday, we all headed out from our camping spot on the hill early, just as the sun was setting the top tree branches alight with color. Iphy, spurred on by some tracks he had seen (and still more evidence of the Wailing Woman) was determined to follow the river as far as we could and finally catch a glimpse of the specter that haunted his woods. We made it down into the valley and managed to pass her ravine before we stopped for a break; the sun was shining down on us, lighting our way and warming our bones. Even after the events of the day before, nothing could seem bad in this light, where we were, in that moment. Even Calm was giving small smiles, watching the sun sparkle off the river beside us, laughing as Eddie and Jax splashed about in the water.

We continued moving, singing loudly in the sunshine and following the river past even the gnarled tree with its broken rope swing. We made good time, mostly because Iphy didn't stop or slow down; he kept urging us on, telling us that just ahead, around the next corner or past the next bend, we'd find her special, secret realm. We raced with him, climbing, jogging, and running to keep up with his enthusiasm. We probably would have kept going forever if it weren't for the tree.

The tree was grand. It was nothing like the old gnarled tree that had seemed so captivating some months before; this was the kind of tree that all the master storytellers wrote about: tall, wide, with thick sprawling branches, a canopy of bright green leaves and large, twisted roots that tore through the ground. It put all other trees to shame, and maybe that's why it stayed out away from the others, like some regal king of the arbor folk. We all stared up at it in awe, taking in the details, tracing the lines in the branches with our eyes. It was bigger than any tree I've ever seen, and it seemed to suck in the light around it; it was a tree for gods.

"It's perfect," Iphy whispered his voice soft and even reverent.

"You say something, Iph?" Jax asked, his eyes never leaving the great tree.

"This place is perfect!" Iphy dropped to his butt, quickly tugging off his shoes. They had hardly changed.

There were some more marks of color from pilfered markers, doodled during the rare occasion when something wasn't happening. Along with the color there was the stink of stepped-upon rotting fruit; dried, caked-on mud from trekking through creeks and dirt; even another quickly sewn-up rip courtesy of Calm's old sewing kit. His laces—brown way back in the Fall—were almost black now, stained by grime and dirty water and the exhilaration of just living.

We finally tore our eyes away from the great tree to watch Iphy with varying degrees of curiosity.

"Iphy," Korvid finally asked, as our leader was tying his black laces together, "what the heck are you doing?"

"What's it look like?" Iphy held his tied together shoes in one hand, before flinging them with all his might at the tree. The battered shoes spun through the air until they caught on a high branch and dangled from the tree.

"Nice going," I rolled my eyes. "Now what are you going to do? Climb up and get them?"

He shook his head. "No way; I'm gonna leave them there."

"Why?" Calm asked, looking down at Iphy's bare feet. "You can't walk around the woods like that."

"Why not?" He stuffed his socks into his pockets and wiggled his toes. "It's just sand and dirt—sometimes sticks."

"And sometimes rocks. And what if there's broken glass?" Korvid shook his head. "You're gonna cut your feet to ribbons."

Obviously irritated by our lack of faith, Iphy stuck his tongue out at us. "You guys are no fun." He dropped the knapsack that he had and reached inside, producing a pair of worn-looking sandals. He dropped them on the ground and slipped his feet into them like it was no big deal.

Jax looked inside Iphy's bag; there were more sandals. "Where'd you get those?"

"Thomas gave them to me."

"What for?" Eddie looked once more back up at Iphy's dangling shoes. "I mean, you had a perfectly good pair."

"Yeah, but its summer: we should be wearing sandals; not hot, sweaty sneakers." Iphy grinned. "Come on, guys — let's make this the official start of summer. We'll get rid of our old shoes — our old lives! — and start again, fresh."

"Haven't we done that already?" Calm smiled a bit as Iphy pouted at our lack of enthusiasm.

"Don't you guys know? You always have to start again. No matter what. Hell, even a new day is a new start. New seasons, new years." He grinned. "New exploring. Come on guys; this is our time."

Eddie needed no further convincing; he kicked his shoes off with gusto, quick to follow Iphy's example. He tied his together but quick, and watched as Iphy mimicked his throwing motion. Eddie followed suit, hurling his shoes into the tree and practically jumping for joy when they caught. I was surprised and amused at his disregard for his old hand-me-down shoes. Before, he had always been careful with them, but now he followed Iphy's example because it was the sacred gospel of Childhood Gods. I was glad that Eddie had found faith in Iphy again.

He reached to take a pair of sandals, but then paused. He grinned at Iphy. "It's too hot for shoes; of any kind." He walked the few feet down to the sandy river shore.

"I'm with Iphy: let's go barefoot." In a surprisingly un-Eddie like move, he kicked water at us, sending up a large splash.

I laughed, throwing up my hands, trying in vain to protect myself from Eddie's assault. And just as suddenly as the water hit, I was dragged into the idea as well. I dropped to the ground, tugging my own shoes off. I smiled; my shoes were looking more like me now. They were rugged and worn, stained by grass, gravel and trips into town. They were no longer stiff and pristine, or that brilliant, blinding white. They were comfortable, lived in, and loved. I was glad now to have laces as I tied my shoes together and threw them into the tree to join Iphy and Eddie's; I couldn't have done it with my old shoes. I smiled for a moment, basking in the summer sun and the flow of Time around me. "Come on guys, you heard Iphy: shoes off."

Calm's shoes were next to be added to the tree. They weren't black anymore; there were other colors as well. Brown in the form of dirt, gray in the form of scuffs in the shiny polish, yellow and red from stepped-on flower petals that were still holding on for the ride, and green—brilliant green—from a leaf she'd woven through her laces. I grinned at her and she smiled back at me, confident and wise. No longer could she say that her shoes were black and lifeless.

We threw her shoes into the tree as one, laughing with delight as they snagged the same branch as mine had and came to rest next to mine, together always. Calm looked at Jax and Korvid, the first real smile on her face since the 'D' word had been dropped. "Please, guys, it'll be fun. It'll be our very own shoe tree."

"A shoe tree?" Iphy grinned. "What's that? Sounds cool."

Calm shrugged. "I saw one once, when my father took me along on one of his trips last year. There was a tree right outside of town; there must have been twenty pairs of shoes on that tree, of all shapes and sizes."

"That's great!" Iphy turned his eyes to the great tree: they glimmered with some hidden emotion. "A place to keep everything that we've done together: our adventures, our losses, and even our friendship. It's the epitome of Our Place, and better than the New Place or the river; it's ours. It's everything we are, and maybe everything we'll ever be." He smiled back at us, and it was a smile that I hadn't ever seen before on his face; it was a smile tinged with longing. "You guys think a tree could ever really do that for us?"

"Only one way to find out." Jax smiled up at the tree before kicking his mismatched shoes off. His high-tops had long since lost many of the red patches that had been attached; now there was just one lone scrap of red barely hanging on to the faded brown canvas underneath.

"Why don't you just rip that last scrap off? Looks tacky," Iphy asked as Jax tied his mismatched shoes together.

"It's the last piece of my old shoes; the ones my parents got for me before the fire."

Iphy scoffed. "All the more reason to leave it behind."

Jax looked hurt by the crass statement. "You might be ready to give up everything, but I'll just wait until it falls off on its own." With a sad little smile, he threw his shoes into the tree, to hang with the rest.

"So you can throw it in a tree, but not get rid of it?" Iphy started to chuckle, but the sound died on his lips as he saw Jax's hurt frown. "I'm only saying that you can't hang on to stuff like that, Jax. Sometimes you've just gotta let stuff go." He threw his arm around Jax's shoulder. "You've got us, and you'll always have us. And even if these guys ever leave, I won't. You're like my little brother now."

A smile began creeping across Jax's face. "Aren't you already looking for one brother?"

"Lost one, found another; same difference." Iphy grinned, tussling Jax's hair.

Korvid was the last to join in; I think he was reluctant to travel the river barefoot. Now everyone turned towards him. "Come on, Korvid," I pleaded. "Think how awesome it'll be; a shoe tree!"

He sighed, but he sat down as well, tugging his shoes off. I noticed right away that his shoes weren't clean anymore. And I don't mean that they'd been dirtied by our latest excursion to the river; it looked like he'd stopped caring about cleaning them since living with Iphy and Jax. I was sad to see that he'd changed in that regard, but I noticed that his laces were still double knotted: he was still afraid that they would come undone if he didn't hold on tight.

He tied the laces together, and with a smile spreading across his face, he flung them as hard as he could. They landed high in the tree, near Iphy's. "There! You guys finally satisfied?" He huffed, still trying to contain his smile.

Iphy whooped, laughing in the sun. "Awesome!" He grinned at all of us, and I swear I could see the energy rippling off him in waves. "Let's go!" He tore into the water, kicking and splashing us with pure liquid sunlight. He raced ahead of us, turned around and raced back, until we were all running through the river after him, whooping and laughing, following his lead. I don't know what he was running from, or where he was running to, but we were all content to follow him and help him. For all I know, he's still running.

We stopped for lunch somewhere after the shoe tree, sitting on the bank of the river, letting our feet dangle in the water: relishing the feeling of being barefoot in the middle of the woods in the middle of summer. Just like in our first official meeting with Iphy, we dug through our backpacks, pulling out pilfered goodies ranging from sandwiches and beef jerky to candy and soda. We ate quickly, laughing and sharing, biting off each other's offered food, not bothering with thoughts of germs. Iphy was the first to finish, and while he waited for the rest of us, he waded out into the water.

This part of the river was slow and I wasn't worried about Iphy wading out to his thighs. I watched him as I munched on my sandwich, alternating between a bite and a swig of cream soda. I almost laughed when he teetered to one side, his arms shooting out and waving about, helping him keep his balance. Then, he swore and pointed upriver. "Jax! Take a look at this monster!"

Jax set his bag of chips down and waded out to where Iphy was still waving and pointing. "What are you talking about?"

"Look!"

When Jax did a double take, it got me and Eddie interested. I stuffed the last bite of bologna and cheese into my mouth and rose to my feet. Eddie waded into the water after his heroes, but I didn't go as deep. Eddie gave a little shout and I tried to follow the path of his eye to see what was making such a fuss. It was a fish; a large, beautiful, dapple-backed fish that was lazing about in the slow moving water.

"We've got to catch that thing," Iphy decided, clapping Jax on the back. "For your resolution. Time to get over your fear."

"We don't have anything we can use to catch it," Jax murmured, never taking his eyes off the glorious fish.

"Speak for yourself." Iphy sloshed through the water back to the shore, where he dug through his backpack full of sandals. "Thomas threw in this little travel fishing kit; we've got line, hooks, even lures!"

Korvid got to his feet, trying to see the fish from the shore. "You don't have a pole."

"Don't need one; we'll do this old-fashioned style." Iphy went about readying the line, tying on hook, lures, and weights. "Calm, find me a nice, heavy branch. Make sure it doesn't bend too much." He glanced up from his work, his eyes masked by the curtain his long bangs made. "Make sure you guys don't lose sight of it!"

"We won't," I called back, still transfixed by the large fish. Jax left Eddie and me in the water, moving slow enough not to spook the fish, and joined Iphy on the shore. He helped Iphy tie the line to the branch Calm had found, while Korvid moved up to the tree line; he must have been looking for bait of some kind because he came back with a massive black beetle.

While Eddie waded a bit closer to the fish, I stayed put, keeping one eye on it, and one eye on the goings-on at the shoreline. Jax hefted the branch and Iphy held up the weighted line. "Where is it?" he called out, his grin infectious.

I grinned myself, pointing upriver. "About fifty feet up from us!"

To his credit, Iphy didn't go charging into the water like I was expecting; he and Jax crept quietly up the shore until they saw the shadow on the surface of the river. His face nearly split in half by his smile, Iphy threw the hook into the water, and began to tug the line a bit, always watching the water. I stood frozen, as did Eddie; on shore, Calm and Korvid leaned forward on the tips of their toes.

The fish must have been hungry; it didn't take long for it to bite. I saw the line zipping about as Iphy suddenly dropped his hold of it. "Yes!" He jumped, a fist in the air. "We rock!" He scrambled back to where Jax was holding the makeshift pole. "Come on, back up; drag it out of the water!"

Jax did as instructed, keeping his grip on the branch as he backed up, dragging the struggling fish along with him. Korvid and Calm came rushing to his aid, congratulations and cries of excitement on their lips. Eddie started heading for shore, but I took a tip from Iphy's book and charged ahead, getting behind the fish and urging it closer and closer to the shore. By the time it was in the shallows, Iphy had grabbed the line again, this time dragging the fish completely out of the water, laughing with excitement.

I couldn't believe that we had actually caught the darn thing; I'd never have believed it if I hadn't been there myself. Jax came forward, hesitating only for a second before he crouched next to the flopping fish. He reached out a trembling hand and brushed his fingertips along its side. "Wow. It's... so pretty."

It was true, the fish was a dazzling display of colors: a shiny, orange-ish olive green on the top and a stripe of pearly pink and steely gray before fading to a creamy belly. Then there were the spots: there was a healthy smattering of black spots on its back and on its side and all over its fins. And the eye, it was a beautiful golden color, and it seemed to move, looking at each of us in turn, just as we were all admiring it.

Iphy smiled and nudged Jax with his elbow. "See, it's not so scary."

Jax slowly shook his head. "No... it's beautiful."

It really was.

"And now the finale."

In Iphy's hands was a large, jagged rock. Before any of us could even think about what he was doing, he brought the rock down with a sickening wet thud onto the fish's head. The fish's tail stopped waving, and the fins stopped flopping about wildly; it was deathly still on the warm sand of the shore.

For a second there was silence, then noise erupted from everywhere at once.

"Iphy!"

"No! Don't!"

"Stop!"

"Are you crazy?!"

Then, Jax's voice, loud and angry, came bubbling up as he scrambled to his feet, grabbing Iphy's shirt in his balled fists. "What the hell did you do, Iphy? What the hell did you do!?"

Surprise and anger sprouted along Iphy's face and he shoved Jax away from him, back towards the river. "What's your problem? It's dinner."

Jax furiously shook his head. "No, Iphy, it isn't! We don't have anything to keep it in, we've got nothing to clean it, and we don't... you didn't need..." He looked up at Iphy and there were tears in his eyes: hot, angry, frustrated tears. "What's the matter with you? We didn't need it!"

"No, but it would have been awesome!" Iphy glared at Jax, ignoring the other boy's tears. "You always do this! You always have some kind of problem! This is what people living in the woods do! This is what fishermen do! You catch a fish and you eat it!"

"It's called catch and release, Iphy!" Jax screamed. "You didn't have to kill it! And you're not homeless! You have a home and a family! It's time to grow up!" He wiped at his eyes and sniffled. "You didn't have to kill it..."

Iphy rolled his eyes, still indifferent to how upset Jax was. "Whatever. You're just being a baby."

Calm shook her head, tears in her own eyes. "No, Iphy, he's right. Why'd you... you didn't have to."

"Pfft." Iphy shot her a sour look. "You don't understand, Calm: it's kill or be killed. Korvid gets it; he's out with me and Jax, living in the wild. Only if you've lived it can you understand."

"Speak for yourself," Korvid spat; he had moved next to Jax and he was glaring at Iphy, mirroring our leader's ugly look.

"You think I'd speak for you?" Iphy shot back, returning Korvid's glare.

I tried to keep the peace, despite the chilling circumstances. "Guys, let's just stop fighting." I glanced at Calm; I didn't want her hearing any more fighting. "Iphy, just apologize—"

"Fuck that!" he kicked the dead fish away. It never was in Iphy's nature to be sorry for anything he ever did. "Let's... let's just forget it." He glanced at all of us and I could tell that he was angry and even hurt that none of us were siding with him. He looked hard at Jax, who returned the cold look. "Let's just forget it, Jax; brothers shouldn't fight."

Jax nodded slowly, but there was something behind his eyes: some small bit of defiance, some sadness for the innocent life that had just died. There was so much understanding and sorrow in that small, sad look; so infinitely wise and resigned to the doings of the world. He looked like a young god, still saddened by what we mortals did upon this earth, but full of the knowledge of what we did and why. I could have looked into his eyes for an eternity and never figured out all that was there, hidden in the lines of color.

Iphy didn't notice the look; he just nodded and started heading upriver. "Come on; let's go."

Slowly at first, we all started forward, following our leader, because that's what we did. Jax stayed behind us for a few seconds. I glanced over my shoulder and noticed why: he'd buried the dead fish in the sand.

It wasn't even an hour after the incident at the river before the woods opened up. A wide swatch of clearing spread out in front of us, an imitation of the river that we'd just left a mile or so ago. And in the middle of the clearing, a gleaming set of train tracks. They were clean and polished, like sparkling jewels, or shining shark teeth.

"The hell?" Iphy hopped up onto the tracks, looking up and down both directions. "I didn't know we had a train coming through town."

"We don't," you said simply, looking back in the direction of our town. "These must be the tracks that run behind the junkyard; Thomas was telling me about them."

Iphy snorted, still obviously sore about your siding with Jax. "Then they go through town, don't they?"

Jax came to your defense, shaking his head. "Not necessarily. The junkyard's just inside the city limits; these tracks must be right outside the limit."

"Whatever," Iphy spat. "You still think we would have heard them."

"We're pretty far from the town." Calm looked up at the sky, as though the great expanse of blue held all the answers. "We probably can't hear them over all of the town's noise." She looked back at you, her held tilted slightly to one side. "Did Thomas say whether they run at night?" I guess your communication with Thomas made you the de facto expert on the matter.

I laughed. "Even if they did, there's no way we'd hear them out in the woods—not with Iphy snoring the way he does."

"I hear them at night," you said, still looking like you were following the track with your mind. You reminded me of Calm just then; further proof that we were all becoming like one another. "It's really faint, but around midnight you can hear one's whistle."

Eddie nodded. "I've heard it, too: once or twice. I could never tell if I was imagining it."

That seemed to settle it; Iphy nodded. "Let's follow these tracks home; maybe we'll see a train."

It was an innocent enough request and none of us saw any kind of problem with it. Iphy strode ahead with Eddie close behind, walking along the wooden ties, always careful not to step on the gravel between; you and Calm were in the middle, holding a stick between you as you balanced on the parallel rails; Jax and I took up the rear, not walking on the rails or on the ties, but taking the easy route alongside.

We were only walking along the tracks for a little while—we couldn't have even gone a mile—before Jax's call made us all turn.

"Train!"

Sure enough, we could see the clouds of smoke reaching up over the sparse trees around the clearing. We all moved off the tracks, Eddie even going so far as to jump from the railing down to the rest of us. Only Iphy hesitated. He stood his ground, looking in the direction of the oncoming train. Already we could hear the huge behemoth moving closer, and for one horrible second I thought Iphy was going to do something incredibly stupid.

"Iphy," you shouted, "come on!"

Your voice must have snapped our fearless leader out of his thoughts, because he looked down at the rest of us, a puzzled expression on his face; when he looked back up at the tracks, he grimaced at the train bearing down on him. He quickly scrambled down, and we all stood for a few minutes until the train came around the bend, roaring past us.

It was all dust and noise and raw power shaking the ground until it seeped up through our bare feet into our very bones and rattled around in our souls. I cracked an eye open, shielding it with my hand, trying in vain to keep the dust away that was swarming around us. I saw the train racing by so close that I could have run up to it and grabbed it by the side-rail; I was in awe at its power. I don't think I've ever seen anything as powerful as that train, even to this day. Maybe that's why Iphy did what he did.

As I watched, my awe turned to horror: Iphy was moving—it felt like slow motion—running first at the train, then alongside. I screamed at him, but the train stole any and all noise that came from me; just snatched it out of the wind like it was nothing. I reached for him, *almost* managed to grab a flailing scrap of his shirt, but then he was gone: vanished from this world.

Even over the noise of the train, I could hear Iphy's whoop of joy, as loud and wild as ever it had been in life. I don't know how he managed it, except that he had special godly powers that we could never understand. I still didn't know what was happening; there was too much noise and wind and dust and confusion. Jax pushed past me, racing along with the train, and for a horrified second I thought he was going to follow Iphy right to the death. I reached for him, stumbled on feet that were still too frightened by everything going around them, and dropped to the ground, skinning my knee.

Then you were there, urging me to my feet, screaming at me in a voice I couldn't understand, dragging me along the tracks. I tried dumbly to follow, but I didn't know what was happening, couldn't grasp anything over the noise and the power and the confusion. All I knew was that Iphy had been there with us, and in one second he had vanished, and all that was left was the roaring train. And just as quickly as it had been upon us, the train was gone — the noise, dust and confusion going with it — leaving only us there on the side of the tracks, looking over ourselves, trying to figure out what happened and if we were all okay. And Iphy was there, some few hundred yards further down the tracks, lying flat on his back in the grass, laughing and hanging onto his sides.

We raced to him, looking him over, crowding him, and asking him a million questions at once. He just laughed, waved everything off, and accepted Jax's offered hand. Back on his feet, he grinned at all of us, his hair wild from his short ride.

"What… were you… thinking?" Jax asked, sucking in big gulps of air as he tried to regain his breath. He couldn't hide the smile and the admiration in his eyes. He laughed, shaking his head. "Looked like fun!"

Iphy just shook his head, all smiles. "It was incredible! What a rush!"

"That was awesome!" Eddie laughed, first doubling over, and then falling backward onto his butt. "That was so cool, Iphy!"

Now that I was beginning to piece things together, I had to admit, "That *was* incredible... You could have been killed..."

He shrugged. "Thought never crossed my mind: it was just too cool to pass up. It was like Life was daring me to do it." He grinned. "And it's not like this is the first time or anything; my brother and I did this back at our old home. He was a pro at it; grabbing the train and letting it take him for a ride."

You shook your head. "That's crazy..." Then you laughed. "That's so incredibly crazy! I can't believe you!"

Iphy grinned. "I am pretty unbelievable. Hell, I might even do it again. Ride it into town."

"If there's another train," Calm interjected, smiling herself, the same adoration in her eyes that Eddie, Jax and all the rest of us held in ours. "You weren't scared a bit?" She sounded incredulous.

Iphy shook his head. "No way. Fear is nothing to be afraid of: it's just a word. And no matter what you say, a word like that is only transitory; it doesn't last."

She nodded, awe blossoming in her eyes at our leader's poetic words. We all felt it, the godliness that he possessed, emerging from the cracks of his mortal façade. It was like the train had taken his mortality with it as it ran along, and left only his divinity in its place.

Then, we were all moving again, but not like before: now we were moving together, in sync and as one. We all laughed, jostled each other and tousled our hair. We hooted and hollered and mock-wrestled along the tracks, happy to be together. All our grievances were forgotten in those happy moments. Then we heard the other train.

It was a faint whistle, accompanied by a thin plume of smoke in the distance behind us. Iphy turned, a sly smile creeping along his face. We vacated the tracks, watching as Iphy lingered for a few seconds longer before joining us. His smile turned to a grin as the train neared us.

"You're really going to go through with this?" Jax asked, watching the spot where the train would appear.

Iphy nodded. "Of course: it's so much fun. I'll just grab it and ride it all the way into town. To the junkyard."

Calm was surprised. "That far?"

"It's not that far; I can make it."

The train whistled again, closer this time.

Then a light suddenly appeared in Iphy's eyes, and he whirled to face Jax. "You should do it!"

Everything stopped except for the sound of the oncoming train.

"M-me?" Jax stammered, a small sprig of fear in his voice.

"Yeah, there's nothing to it!" Iphy grinned his infectious grin, and I could see Jax's fear melt away. You said it best, E; you could fly when Iphy was around. "Come on, Jax—you have to!"

Jax nodded, slowly at first, but then with more resolve. "Alright; I'll do it." Iphy and Eddie cheered, and I couldn't help but laugh.

By now the train was in view, coming around the small bend some few hundred yards away. It was smaller than the last one had been, but it was no less imposing. Jax looked at Iphy, suddenly terrified again. "What do I do?"

Iphy smiled, "It's easy: just run alongside of it for a bit, until you feel the right moment. You'll know it when it hits; it's like a sudden ringing in your ears and you know it's now or never. Then just jump up, grab onto one of the side rails and hang on tight!"

They were running now, side by side as the train broke even with them for a fraction of a second before reaching ahead. "Any other bits of advice?" Jax called over the roar of the engine.

"Just when you get a hold of the rail, lean in towards the train; if you hang out you're liable to get ripped off by a tree or something! And when you let go, just remember to roll!" Iphy laughed and stopped running as Jax suddenly jumped, his bare feet pushing off the ground to give him wings. I held my breath as he soared, and let it out with relief when his hands caught the side rail, and his feet scrambled to find a hold on the rail's bottom. Then he was gone, whisked away further into the forest by the speeding train.

Iphy laughed and threw his fist up into the air, cheering. He turned around as the train disappeared into the forest, his grin lighting up his face. "Come on!" he hollered before running after the train, still laughing. "We'll meet him at the junkyard; we can't keep him waiting too long!"

We all ran after him: what else could we do? We ran after him. I think we're still running after him. Don't you, E?

All my love,
Korvid.

From the Journal of Calm Sheldon

Jax wasn't waiting for us. I don't know what we were expecting; I don't even know what *I* was expecting. Maybe to see him, sitting on a small pile of junk, talking with Thomas Smith, waiting like it was no big deal. We'd run up to him and he'd smile and wave at us as we approached, hug us all when we got to him. Iphy would clasp his hand around Jax's shoulders, laughing and mussing Jax's hedgehog hair, and he'd call him brother and their relationship would mend. Jax would talk about what he saw (maybe a hunting hawk or even a fleeing family of deer) and we'd all hang out until we had to go home. And even there we'd sit up in our beds, unable to sleep, recounting the events of Jax's trip, wishing we had all gone with him, planning to be the next ones to jump and let the trains take us home.

That didn't happen. Jax wasn't waiting for us when we got to the junkyard. Thomas asked us what we were doing there, and when Iphy excitedly told him about Jax's adventure, Thomas frowned, dark lines appearing in his forehead. He asked us what the hell we were thinking, but Iphy brushed him off, asking where Jax was. Thomas' next words still haunt me.

"He's not here."

For a second there was silence. Then, Iphy scoffed. "Yeah, right. He hiding from us? Do we have to go find him, is that it?"

Thomas' face contorted, becoming an angry demon's mask. "No, you little shit! I mean he ain't here! He didn't get off the train!"

A light seemed to dawn in Iphy's eyes: he could see this wasn't any kind of joke. He swore, and we all ran after him as he crashed through the junkyard, stopping only a second to scale the back fence. Korvid followed him, climbing up the old chain link fence in his dirty bare feet. Eddie moved for the fence, but Eraliss silently grabbed Eddie's shoulder before the other boy could follow; instead, she raced with us to a section of fence that had been cut away long ago.

Before us stretched the tracks, silent but nonetheless frightening, mocking us with the quiet. Iphy jabbed a finger at Eraliss, Eddie and I, his voice booming and godly with edges of desperation. "You three check down there; see if he let go a little too early. Korvid and I are gonna see if he missed his mark!"

We ran, all of us screaming for Jax as we combed the sparse trees on either side of the tracks. Behind us, I could hear Iphy and Korvid calling as well, and I prayed silently to all the stars in the sky that we had counted that we would find him.

We didn't.

When we'd gone about half a mile, Eraliss swore, kicking at a dirt clod that was in her way. She turned around, breezing past us as she ran back the way we had come. "Come on!" she called back at us, not even turning around to see if we were following her.

Korvid must have had the same idea, because they were already back at the junkyard by the time we'd gotten there. For a second I hoped that they had found him—a little sore, but still in good spirits about everything. But Jax wasn't with them. Instead, Thomas was with them, shaking his head and running his fingers through his messy hair. The Reverend Josh Potter was there as well.

The Reverend looked worse than I'd ever seen him: his hair was wild and his eyes frantic and wet with tears. He had Iphy by the shoulders, shaking him slightly in his fear. "What were you thinking? What could you *possibly* have been thinking!?"

The tears in the Reverend's eyes must have sparked something in Iphy, because our leader's eyes became glassy and wet themselves, before tears began running down his cheeks. "We... we were just hanging out," he murmured his voice small and meek in the face of what was before him. "Having fun."

It wasn't fun anymore; it had stopped being fun when we crested the hill in front of the junkyard and hadn't been greeted by the comforting sight of our friend. It had stopped being fun when Thomas Smith told us that Jax hadn't been there. It started getting scary when we searched the tracks and screamed for him and only silence and echoes came back to us from the trees. It started getting terrifying when we heard the sound of sirens, making our horror much more real than it had been some twenty minutes previous.

I was scared then.

I'm still scared.

Police came and asked us all questions about what had happened, when we had last seen Jax. Iphy and Korvid told them that they could tell them the exact spot, and when there were more police gathered, two of the officers took our friends with them; it was the last I saw them that day. The police took us all home, one at a time, talking to our parents and telling them what had happened. It got discovered that we hadn't been staying with each other like we had all said. Our parents found out that we had really snuck off into the woods to camp without any supervision. My mother yelled at me until her voice broke, screaming that I couldn't leave her like my father had. I couldn't stop crying enough to defend myself.

They dredged the river behind our houses; the train tracks ran over them between where Jax left us and the junkyard. Had we known—had we *thought* about it—we never would have let Jax go. The town was in an uproar; everyone wanted to help. Search parties were formed by the county sheriff and everyone (the Reverend, Mr. Smithy, Thomas, Mr. Neil and Mr. Letham) joined in to try and find our beloved friend. They searched for days—weeks—expanding the search area more and more, and soon it included all of the counties around ours, stretching even to the edge of the state.

They found nothing.

Our lives changed after the police brought us home to our parents; our freedom was gone, stolen on the same hellish wind that had carried Jax off. My mother did something that she had never done before: she forbade me to leave the house and wouldn't let anyone come over to talk to me. Eraliss' mother grounded her and took down the trellis that made it so easy for her daughter to escape the house. We tried to talk on the phone, to learn updates and stay in contact with each other in the days after the accident, but neither of our parents let us on the phone for more than a few minutes. I don't think Eddie's parents even knew that their middle son had friends until the police delivered him back home; I didn't see him outside at all in the time after the accident, so I guess his parents grounded him as well. Korvid didn't return to the woods: he stayed with his father, in his basement room, in their haunted house. I sometimes caught glimpses of him through the windows; he looked miserable and frightened and I couldn't blame him. More than anything else, I wanted all of us to be together again.

The one time I had any real contact with any of my friends was when Iphy came over. He was accompanied by his parents and I could tell that he wasn't happy about having them around. He was hunched over, dark and sulky. At first I hardly recognized him as the great grinning god I knew him to be. I looked from him to the two adults behind him, and I knew instantly that these were his parents. They looked a bit like Iphy: his dad was tall, like Iphy was going to be, but his mother had the same brilliant blue eyes that Iphy had beneath his furrowed brows. My mother came to the door, asking what the visit was about.

Our parents talked for a time, and I could tell that Iphy hadn't been lying about his parents fighting. They were curt with each other, talking mostly to my mother and never to the other. Their words were clipped and angry, a honed edge on every other syllable. You could hear it in their voices that Love didn't exist in their world—not even for their son, who pleaded silently with me with his eyes.

Iphy's eyes troubled me most: they had lost some of their clarity and were murky and gray. It was as if all life had been sapped from him. As our parents talked, he nibbled at the corner of his lip until it started to bleed.

I learned quite a bit from his parents in the short time they were on our porch: they were sorry that Iphy had been such a destructive influence on me and the other children of the cul-de-sac; Iphy was far too much like his late brother, who'd also gone down a bad road; both of them were to blame, but neither of them actually owned up to it, instead insisting that it was obviously the other's bad parenting that had led their child astray; they were hoping to get Iphy some help in the near future; they were staying with Iphy's grandparents down on Olaha Way, but only until the memorial service—then they were going home. Through it all Iphy's desperate eyes pleaded with me. I didn't know how to answer them. I still don't.

The search for Jax continued for weeks, but hope dwindled. I listened to the news and talked with Eraliss over the phone in a hushed voice, but we learned nothing new. Soon, it was decided—by Revered Josh Potter, or by the police, or maybe even by the entire town itself—that there was no more hope of finding him alive. Word spread like fire across town that there was going to be a memorial service held for Jax on the last day of July. My mother asked me if I wanted to go; I broke down into tears and cried for an hour before I could tell her that yes, I wanted to go with all my heart. That night I clutched my comforter up to my chin, trying in vain to disappear into my bed, praying with all my heart that Jax would pull some kind of move right from a Mark Twain novel and show up at his own funeral. I prayed again to the stars above, and to anyone else out there who could hear me, that our lives would be blessed with a miracle that day.

The church was packed; people stood outside, surrounding the building after the pews were filled and the standing space was taken. Luckily, the Reverend had set aside some seats up front for us and our families; I finally got to see Eraliss and Korvid and Eddie and Iphy again. We hugged each other, whispering in quiet tones about what was happening, what everyone had heard and when they were going to find Jax. When we all cast a glance up towards the beautiful flowered wreath, Iphy snorted.

"He's not dead."

Then, the ceremony started and it was... hard doesn't even begin to describe it. I didn't think I would make it through the service: the Reverend's words were beautiful and touching, but they were wrong. Jax wasn't dead; Iphy had said so, and I wanted to believe him.

I still want to believe him.

Our summer... maybe even our own lives ended that day. It was the last I saw of Iphy. It was the last time I held faith in my heart for forces I couldn't see. When the service was over, we couldn't speak to each other; we couldn't tell ourselves that things were going to be okay, that things would ever be normal again, because we knew that they weren't.

Nothing would ever be okay, because when your life is smudged, dirtied or shattered, there's no real way to properly clean it up or put the pieces back together. You just have to move on.

And that's what we did.

All of us.

C.S.

AFTER SUMMER

Extracted from an e-mail addressed to Eraliss Cofler from Korvid Fairington, dated ███████.

After everything died down... we never really talked, did we? About anything. It was like everything had been said by everyone else. Reporters, our parents, even the Reverend, they all said what was on their minds, their versions of what we kids must have been doing. But the rest of us, you and me, Calm and Eddie, even Iphy—we never spoke about what really happened.

And to tell you the truth, even now I'm not completely sure what happened. He can't have... Shit, I can't even type it out; like even the small act of acknowledging it as a possibility would somehow make it true. And it... it can't be true. I believed the Reverend about a lot of things, but I couldn't believe him when he said that. At the memorial service when he said that Jax was... I was almost as angry as Iphy. If I had the nerve and the courage that Iphy had, I would have been with him, standing on the pew, screaming at the Reverend that he had no idea what he was talking about. I still can't believe that he did that. He screamed so loud, I thought he was going to race up the aisle and attack the Reverend. I was sorry to see him dragged out like he was, and I'm sorry that that's my last memory of our leader: getting forcibly removed from the church during Jax's memorial service, screaming at the Reverend that Jax wasn't dead — that we were all just stupid and wrong and... Jesus, Eraliss, what if he was right? They never did find Jax's body. To this day, I still check the local paper, looking for any news on him. You do too, don't you?

I know we all followed Iphy, but I think Jax was really the glue that kept us all together. After the service, Iphy went missing and then Eddie's parents decided to move away. I couldn't believe it: just like that, Eddie was gone. No more Bone Room, no more happy freckled face looking up at us and up *to* us because we were the only family that really understood him. I don't even think he was all that sad to be moving; he seemed almost lifeless when Jax went missing. Then, when Iphy left, he just... shut down. The Childhood Gods that he had worshipped for so long had just up and left him; they hadn't even imparted on him their great, grand wisdom that he so coveted.

Everything changed after they left and it was all we could do to try and keep up with the changes. When your father came back, sometime in August I think, I thought you were going to lose it; I honestly thought that you were going to run off and disappear on us, too. But, you stood your ground. I remember it like it was yesterday: you on the lawn, throwing things at your deadbeat dad, screaming at him to get out, to never come back if he wanted to leave you so badly. Even Calm and I got in on the action, joining you on the yard, throwing things of our own. I don't think I've ever seen you so strong.

When your mom came home, I thought it was over and done with, but she must have changed, too. When she told him to get the hell off her property, I almost cheered. You can't imagine how happy I was for you; for the both of you. Even though Jax and Iphy had gone away somewhere, they left something behind in each of us. And I don't think it was as simple as Iphy and Jax making you strong, but rather, they made it so that you could see and believe that you were strong. I'm sorry things never worked out with your dad, but I'm glad that he can't hurt you anymore, either.

After Eddie's family moved and the new school year loomed ahead of us, I think my dad finally realized that he had to move on, too. One morning, he came downstairs, rousing me out of the cocoon of blankets that I was in. "Come on, Kor." He hadn't called me that since mom died.

We went upstairs to the room that he kept locked. "You were right, you know...the day you left." He sighed, his voice heavy and choked with some stifling emotion. "I should have told you... about everything." He reached out his shaking hand to touch the doorknob; he hesitated then and I was sure that he'd give up and return to the living room like nothing had happened. But then he gripped the knob—so tightly—and he turned it, swinging open the door in one swift movement, as if any more hesitation would end his resolve.

I don't know what I was expecting: some dark, dreary room out of a horror novel, complete with some anguishing spirit clothed in rattling chains. Instead, it was just my dad's old room. There was a layer of dust over everything, but the room was filled with light; the curtains had never been drawn and had let the sun heal the room over the years. Most of all, my mother wasn't there: I could tell as soon as Dad opened the door. She had moved on long ago and hadn't been trapped in the dust and darkness like I had feared.

We spent the whole day cleaning his room, clearing the dust and airing it out. There was a musty smell, but other than that, it was just a room: nothing evil, diabolical or frightening. As we worked, I couldn't imagine that I'd ever been afraid of this room, that I'd ever thought that Mom was trapped here. I couldn't believe that I'd ever felt fear of something so trivial. That's what Iphy and Jax taught me: that life was for living, not for fearing.

Time moved forward; not even their disappearance could stop something as monumental as the progression of life. I started high school that year, and it was so strange and different, but I remembered Iphy's confidence and Jax's sensibility. Plus, it helped knowing that it was only a year until you and Calm joined me. I tried making friends—I really did—but I couldn't ever find anyone who had the same brilliant spark as Iphy, the same hidden wisdom that hid behind Jax's eyes, or even Eddie's freckled smarts. Everyone else was sub-par to the friends that I'd had only a few short months ago, and I wasn't going to smear their memory by replacing them with people who couldn't even hold a candle to them. That's not to say that I didn't have friends that year—but they were just school friends: people you talk to during class or let copy your homework. These weren't the kind of friends that you explore the woods with, or run away with, or share your soul with. They weren't Iphy and Jax.

You at least had Calm with you when you started school again, and you two were eighth graders: the top rung of the middle school social ladder. You ruled the school and had all my old homework to work off of. And I had the two of you to look forward to when the day ended. It was almost like the old days, but we never ventured from our town; we stayed in my room, listening to music, or working on homework, or just hanging out.

I was surprised by Calm when her parents finalized their divorce: she was sad, but she didn't let it consume her. Not like that night we counted stars. She didn't try to intervene; she just accepted that they couldn't stay with one another. I know they told her time and time again that it had nothing to do with her, and everything to do with them, and maybe she believed it. But she helped her mother with the house and the grief and the dirty dishes. She cried a bit when the three of us were together, but she didn't hide or try to run from the 'D' word anymore. That's what Iphy and Jax left for her: their bravery. I don't think she ever ran from anything after we lost them—not even the bee hive we found in my shed years later.

I don't know what else there is to say about that year or the time after it. You could write a book a thousand pages long about Iphy and Jax and what we did with them, and what they did for us. You could write an equally long book theorizing about them. Were they really Childhood Gods, like we believed? Were they just ordinary kids in extraordinary circumstances? Did they leave us, or were they just called back to the childhood heavens of endless adventures? That year... it wasn't something that you can just paint black and white or say definitively what happened and why.

But I hope what I gave you will help decipher things. I don't think I have much else to add. It's funny: as the end came closer and closer, I wrote less and less. It's easy to dwell on the good times, but harder to recount when everything bad happened.

Anyway, let me know when you're finished — I can't wait to read this in its entirety.

Thank you, Eraliss, for doing this. I don't know how or when I noticed, but this whole thing... it's helped. I never thought that I'd be okay with what happened (and I'm still not) but at least I feel like I've gone over it one more time. One last check, to make sure nothing slipped through the cracks.

Thank you.

All my love, and my eternal gratitude,

Korvid.

Extracted from an e-mail addressed to Eraliss Cofler from Edward McCloy, dated ▮▮▮▮▮▮▮.

I still hear trains at night. I can never tell if they comfort me or break me.

I don't think I'll ever know.

E. McCloy

~*~

Iphy went missing a few days after the memorial service; he just vanished without a trace. He and his parents had been staying with his grandparents during the search and through the memorial service. We hadn't really gotten a chance to talk with him about anything that had happened; there just wasn't time or room to breathe. While we had been almost invisible to everyone before, now it was like everyone was watching us, never letting us out of their sight: our parents, the police, even the state-appointed therapists and counselors that we were supposed to be seeing wouldn't let us take a second, get away, and just breathe. I couldn't stand it; I don't think any of us could. I almost tore my hair out in frustration; Iphy did something much more plausible. When Iphy disappeared, news spread like wildfire; everyone was looking for him, but no one could find him.

When I finally got a chance, I went out to his grandparents' house on Olaha Way. I talked briefly with his parents, but the only clue they had was Iphy's journal. I knew exactly what it was; I had one too. All of us did. We were supposed to write our thoughts and our emotions down as a kind of therapy. I didn't imagine that Iphy took to the exercise. There was only one entry in the notebook: I think it told me everything that I ever needed to know.

At first I was so angry with him; there was no way we could lose both of them at once; It wasn't fair. I thought he was being selfish and childish, that he hadn't really learned anything after what had happened. Only later did I realize that this was exactly what was destined to happen. Gods cannot live among mortals for long.

The New Place got torn down the following autumn; I was sad to see it go. I had tried to keep the city from tearing the building down, but one lone girl with a sentimental attachment can't save a condemned building. I cried when the bulldozers came: I cried for Jax, and his family, and his guilt; I cried for Iphy, and his never-ending search for family that kept leaving him; I cried for Korvid and Calm and Eddie and myself. We were losing too much, too fast. I thought about running out there to stop them, but by the time I had gotten downstairs they had already started.

The building was so old that it didn't take them long to reduce it all to rubble. It was frightening how quickly the house crumpled and folded in on itself, as if the very spirit of the New Place had simply given up. I imagined that the New Place was glad to finally be able to rest, as if it had always known that it would lose its master yet again and it was done with all the heartache. When they left the pile of splintered wood for the night, I snuck down and saved a piece of it; it's in a box in my attic, along with the Wailing Woman's cross. I watched the mess of wood and foundation all night, as if expecting Iphy and Jax to emerge from the woods to investigate the loss of one of their homes. They didn't come to pay their respects to the New Place. No one did.

Many times through the years that I lived on that street real estate signs were placed on the lawn, proclaiming that the property had been sold and that a great grand house was going to be built. They never were. The lot remained empty: nothing could fill the spot where we once played, laughed, and lived. As long as I lived on that street, nothing was ever erected on the sacred soil. Even now, when I return to my old house, the lot is still empty, overgrown with weeds. They remind me of Iphy.

I never went back to Our Place, though the thought often crossed my mind. Every time I felt like I couldn't stand where life was taking me, I wanted to run back to the life I had known with my friends, but I couldn't stand the idea of seeing it empty. It couldn't be empty because Iphy and Jax belonged there. It was their haven, even when we couldn't find them. For a while, I even believed that it wouldn't be there, if I ever looked for it. The woods had always liked Iphy and Jax best; they merely tolerated the rest of us. I was sure that if I went looking, I would never find our once great sanctuary; the woods would hide it from me or it would have simply vanished with the departure of the deities it belonged to.

The only time I ever went back was years after, when I was a senior in high school. I had thought about taking Calm with me, but it was something that I had to do on my own. It didn't take as long as I remembered it taking, and it was smaller than it had seemed all those years ago. I crouched among the trees, resting against the very rock that Iphy had once claimed as his own. Our stuff was still there, though the woods were slowly reclaiming what they had once loaned out. The rocks were covered in moss; the woven together branches were coming undone; the shaky little lean-to had long since fallen and the metal sheets were covered in dirt and old dead leaves.

All around me the trees seemed to press in close, to lean and tower over me. They were both smaller and somehow larger than I remembered them. I felt eyes watching me, and felt a distinct feeling that I was trespassing where I shouldn't be. I only stayed a few moments; the place felt haunted, like the Wailing Woman had extended her territory to include our once safe shelter.

And Our Place wasn't the only place to feel haunted: the whole town did. Everywhere I looked, I saw ghosts of what used to be: Jax sitting on the curb in front of Mr. Smithy's bakery; Iphy running down the street, hollering at us to keep up. Nothing was the same, and it was all too different; too empty. I couldn't stand it. The only thing that seemed to anchor me to our town was the train.

I could still hear it, every night at midnight. It's one of the few things that got me through school. I knew that no matter what happened in my life, the train would whistle at midnight. Once, in high school, I listened every night for a whole year for the whistle. Even then, years after the fact, I couldn't stand the loss of the Childhood Gods I had worshiped so feverishly. I knew they were out there, waiting for us to follow and find them. It was their next big adventure. I wanted to go looking for them, and I decided that when the train didn't whistle, that was the day that I'd go. They'd send me a sign in the silence of midnight.

The train whistled every night for a year, always just a few minutes after midnight.

I never went looking.

From the Journal of Calm Sheldon

Shadows fell over our memories, darkening what was once so crystal clear, letting in little blobs of color that weren't really there, but danced in front of our eyes anyway. Soon, gaps appeared, goaded on by the shadows, blotting out what we were sure was vital information, until soon our memories and recollections were riddled with holes; we had to guess at what was there by looking at what remained around it, like countries whose names had escaped us. We tried to hold on, but life didn't slow down for us, and we were yanked along vehemently though a string of years that barely registered as they passed. High School. College. All the while, we kept looking back, glancing over our shoulders as though we expected them to come bounding up to join us, to reassure us that everything was okay. They never did, no matter how hard we strained our eyes to see the details in the distance, how often we'd glance back, check, and double-check just to make sure. So we looked to ourselves for that reassurance, but soon we stopped that as well.

Maybe we saw too much of them in our eyes, nestled safe amongst the different lines of color. It was too hard. They were everywhere that we looked, liked they had owned the town all along; they were in the holes of the bagels from Smithy's Bakery, in the gaps of the trees leading to Our Place, in the empty cars we saw parked along the deserted street. We could hear them in the laughter of the townspeople, in the roaring wind coming off the river, in the silence looking up at the moon. It was like they never left us, were with us always, hiding in the places that we couldn't see, or couldn't find. And we tried to find them—for years. We still haven't found them, haven't managed to find their last hiding place in the stack of years. We talk about it, over the phone, in our postcards and letters and e-mails; we all still see them everywhere, hear them in everything, but we cannot find them.

Maybe we will never find them.

C.S

EPILOGUE

Somewhere out in the world we left behind is a tree with our shoes still attached. I never went back to look for them because I was afraid of what I'd find. I'm still afraid. Are they still there, just as we left them? Are they different in some strange way; more tattered, more worn? Or are they gone; completely and utterly lost in the great expanse of the world, where we'll never find them? I don't know. I don't think I want to know. But I do like to imagine that whatever has happened to them — be they the same, slightly different, or changed completely — they are safe. Because after everything that they've dealt with (the woods, the river, the town and the snow) the soles of our shoes deserve to be safe and happy. And I hope they stay that way for all time.

My doctor says I should write
out all my thoughts on paper—
just scribble them down as they
come, no matter what. He says
it's theraputic. I think he's full
of shit.

I don't know what went wrong.
I keep thinking about it, going
over every last detail step by step.
I can't find it. I can't find the
one place where ~~things~~ things
stopped working. I try and I
try, but every time I think
about it, details begin to get fuzzy;
the precise dates and order of
events, the words, the colors.
All I end up with is a jumble
of memories that get fainter
and vaguer the harder I try to
keep them.

It's all my fault. I know it is.
No one's said it, but they don't
need to. I can see it in their
eyes— in the way they look at
me, or the way they don't look

at me. Everything's fallen apart.
No one has said anything. No one
speaks anymore. That's what I
can't stand: the silence. Why
can't they yell at me, hit me,
hate me? Instead, we're all
~~have been~~ quiet and the silence is
so loud I want to scream myself
hoarse just to break it.
    They know it's ~~all really~~ my fault.
They blame me, but they act ~~like~~
indifferent, like it was expected,
or even planned. I can't stand it.
    Jax, you have to know that I
didn't mean for all this to have
happened. If I thought for a
second that you believed I wasn't
sorry, or that I wanted this,
I would die. I know that we
fought sometimes, but you ~~were~~
are my best friend, my little
brother. I never wanted this,
not for the whole world.

Jax, I can't stand this: wondering what happened, where you are.
I just know you're not ~~____~~ gone — you're just out there, somewhere, waiting ~~_____~~ for me back at Our Place, or at the river, or hiding in the blankets we left at the New Place. You ~~___~~ have to be... the alternative is something I can't think about:
Oh god...Jax, I killed you. You're dead and it's all my fault.

The stars are beautiful tonight, Jax. I hope you can see them from wherever you are. There's so many, and there's so much space between them all... It's too big. You're up there somewhere... or out there watching them with me.
I want to ~~____~~ find you — go where you go. It's too soon, you can't leave me. We've got more things to do — more trees

---

to climb, woods to hike through and adventures to have. We have more days together, more seasons and years — High School, College. You can't be gone; you're out there, waiting, watching the stars with me.

Look, a shooting star. And another. And another. If I count a hundred of them, I'll come find you. Wait for me. I'll find you, wherever you're hiding.

Wait for me.

Please.

9084010R0

Made in the USA
Charleston, SC
09 August 2011